Stephen King's
THINNER

Encyclopocalypse Publications
www.encyclopocalypse.com

Stephen King's
THINNER

ADAPTED FOR THE SCREEN BY

TOM HOLLAND

EXT. NEW HAVEN, CONNECTICUT - DAY

A sooty industrial city in the Northeast.

A voice can be heard over.

                    (CREDITS ROLL)

               MRS. TARADASH'S (V.O.)
          —I saw him leaving but I
          never got a good look at his
          face.

EXT. FEDERAL COURT HOUSE - DAY

A huge courthouse of steel and glass, new and
cold.

Another voice intrudes over.

               JUDGE PHILLIPS (V.O.)
          That'll be all, Mrs.
          Taradash. Thank you.

INT. COURTROOM - DAY

The room is medium sized, its decor matching
the exterior.

There are a number of trial junkies scattered
about and a mixed jury seated in the box.

They are trying to look attentive as a middle-
aged woman, MRS. TARADASH, climbs out of the
witness stand.

JUDGE PHILLIPS, a graying, taciturn man, turns
to the defense attorney.

                    JUDGE PHILLIPS
          Mr. Halleck, was this
          your last witness for the
          defense?

BILLY HALLECK heaves himself to his feet.

He is a pleasant looking man in his late
thirties, attractive except for the fact that
at six feet and three hundred pounds.

He is perilously close to being grossly
overweight.

                    BILLY
          No, your honor. I'd like to
          call Mr. Max Duggenfield to
          the stand.

The jury perks up as the PROSECUTOR stands up
out of his chair.

                    PROSECUTOR
          I object! Mr. Duggenfield
          isn't on the Defense's
          subpoena list!

                    BILLY
          He was on our original list.
          We were unable to serve
          him because you had him in
          hiding.

                    PROSECUTOR
               (back to the judge)
          For his own safety, your
          honor. Given the fact the
          defendant is accused of
          ordering his death—

                    JUDGE PHILLIPS

                    (cutting him off, to
                      Billy)
          Mr. Halleck, are you quite
          sure you want this witness
          to testify?

                    BILLY
          Your honor, if Max
          Duggenfield feels my client
          was the only one who could
          have paid to have him
          killed, I want to hear him
          state it in open court.

The prosecutor opens his mouth to object again,
but Phillips cuts him off.

                    JUDGE PHILLIPS
          Call Max Duggenfield to the
          stand.

                    BAILIFF
               (rising and calling out)
          Mr. Max Duggenfield, please.

A short, spindly man, MAX DUGGENFIELD, stands
among the spectators and makes his way to the
front of the court as Billy sits.

His client, RICHIE GINELLI, leans across the
table, whispering to him as Duggenfield is
sworn in.

Ginelli is mid-fifties, a squat powerful man
with wavy black hair, hard glittery eyes, and
a penchant for tailor made suits.

                    GINELLI
          What the hell are you doing,
          Billy?

                    BILLY
          Trying to keep you out of
          jail, Richie. Now be quiet
          and pray.

The swearing in finished, Billy rises, walking
to Duggenfield.

                    BILLY
          Mr. Duggenfield, is there
          anyone else besides my
          client who might want to see
          you dead?

                    DUGGENFIELD
                 (reluctantly)
          Possibly, I guess. Any
          number of people.

There's a slight buzz in the courtroom. Ginelli
straightens in his chair, his attention
snagged.

Billy bores in on Duggenfield.

                    BILLY
          Let me phrase it another
          way. Would this be the first
          time someone has paid to
          have you killed?

                    DUGGENFIELD
                 (even more reluctant)
          Well, maybe there have been
          others.

                    BILLY
          Please, answer the question,
          Mr. Duggenfield.

                    DUGGENFIELD
          Alright, three years ago my
          wife tried to hire someone—

                    PROSECUTOR
             (coming out of his
                   chair)
          Objection, your honor!

But the case has already been lost. Pandemonium
has broken out in the courtroom. The jury
members are all grinning at Ginelli.

He's grinning at Billy, rising out of his seat
and pounding him happily on the back.

                     GINELLI
          From now on, Billy, anything
          you need, you just ask! You
          hear me? You just ask!

He wraps him in a big embrace and kisses him
on one big fat cheek.

Billy grins back.

                     BILLY
          Thanks, Richie.

He pulls some salted peanuts from his pocket
and dumps the entire packet into his mouth,
happily munching away. This guy likes to eat.
A lot.

                                   DISSOLVE TO:

EXT. FAIRVIEW, CONNECTICUT - DAY

A small bedroom community to New York City. It
is zoned for maximum charm and architectural

consistency and looks as upper income as it
is.

EXT. TOWN COMMONS - DAY

A brand new Jag pulls up in front of a building
with a sign, "Penschley and Halleck, Attorneys
at Law," attached to it. Billy slides his bulk
out, looking at the commons. He has a package
of Caramel Corn in his hand and is munching
away.

The vehicles of a Gypsy caravan have taken
up parking on both sides. They're all old
clunkers and campers with homemade shells on
top of them.

The Gypsies have made themselves at home,
spreading across the commons on aluminum
loungers and blankets, the women busily cooking
on Hibachis. A small group of townspeople have
gathered to watch them. A young Gypsy male,
GABE, juggles four Indian Clubs above his
head, yelling "Hay," every time he hurls one
into the air.

But Billy isn't watching any of them. His
attention is snagged by a beautiful Gypsy girl,
GINA Lempke, who has just finished setting
up an easel and attaching a paper target to
it. She whirls away, her gayly colored skirts
flapping around a body to die for, beautiful
black tresses spilling down her shoulders, her
full lips the color of fresh blood. She stops
and turns to the target, producing a slingshot
and three shiny silver ball bearings from the
folds of her skirt. In rapid order she fires
the bearings, each of them a bulls eye.

The young boys of the town gather around her,

clamoring for a shot. She starts collecting money and passing out ball bearings.

Across the street, Billy grins and shakes his head, murmuring to himself.

(CREDITS END)

                    BILLY
          Gypsies.

He finishes the Caramel Corn, drops the wrapper in a refuse container, and turns, waddling for the door to his law offices.

INT. SECOND-FLOOR RECEPTION AREA - DAY

Billy makes it to the top of the stairs, red-faced and huffing as JILLIAN, his middle-aged secretary, comes to her feet behind her desk, clapping her hands.

                    JILLIAN
          Congratulations, you made
          the noon news!

KIRK PENSCHLEY, Billy's law partner, appears from his office. He's small and compact and has greedy little eyes.

                    PENSCHLEY
          Billy, you pulled it off.
          And I didn't think you
          would.

                    BILLY
          (recovering his breath)
          Thanks, Kirk. Always glad to
          have your support.

                    PENSCHLEY
                (playfully punching
                Billy's stomach)
          Hey, have to take a little
          weight off there, kiddo.
          C'mon, I want to show you
          something.

Taking his arm, he drags Billy into his own
office.

INT. BILLY'S OFFICE - DAY

They come to a stop by a window, looking down
on the commons below. The Gypsies seem to be
doing a land office business with the locals,
reading fortunes and setting up games of
chance. Penschley nods down at Gina.

                    PENSCHLEY
          You see that Gypsy piece of
          ass down there?

Billy looks down at Gina. She's still running
her ball bearing game. She also hasn't lost an
iota of her beauty in the time she was out of
Billy's sight. He nods.

                    BILLY
          How could I miss her.

                    PENSCHLEY
                (his voice flooding with
                lust)
          I'd give a hundred bucks to
          fuck her. Hell, I'd give
          two.

EXT. COMMONS -DAY

Down below Gina suddenly stops running her ball bearing concession and turns, looking directly up at Billy and Penschley, framed in the window, staring down at her.

INT. BILLY'S OFFICE -DAY

Billy steps back from the window with an involuntary gasp. Penschley turns to him with a laugh.

                    PENSCHLEY
          Hey, don't be silly. She
          can't hear us from way down
          there.

                    BILLY
          I don't know. They say
          Gypsies can do some mighty
          strange things

He leans over with some difficulty because of his weight, squatting is actually more like it, and opens a bottom drawer in his desk.

It is filled with junk food, Ding Dongs, Hostess Twinkies, more Caramel Corn.

He snatches a package of Twinkies, about to tear into the paper when there's a call from across the room.

                    HEIDI (O.S.)
          Billy Halleck, don't you
          dare eat that!

Billy freezes, looking up to see his wife,

HEIDI, standing in the doorway. She's an attractive woman in her mid-thirties, dressed in upper middle-class Connecticut chic.

Guilt flashes across Billy's face and he lets the Twinkies drop into the waste can. She runs across the room and gives his ample bulk a big hug.

                    HEIDI
          Oh, Billy, I'm so proud of
          you. Mary Fisher told me you
          won.

                    PENSCHLEY
                  (grinning)
          Hey, Billy, it's all over
          town. We celebrate tonight
          at the club. I'm paying.

He turns and leaves the room. Heidi looks at Billy with a mischievous smile.

                    HEIDI
          You've had a hard day. Want
          to take the rest of it off?

                    BILLY
                (a twinkle in his eye)
          Depends on what you have in
          mind.

                    HEIDI
                (twinkling right back)
          You'll have to get me home
          to find out.

                    BILLY
          I knew there was a reason I
          married you.

He holds out his arm, the two of them heading
for the door, a fat husband and his wife on
the way home to disport themselves.

EXT. BILLY'S LAW OFFICE - DAY

They exit the front door to see the Gypsies
still clogging the commons. Heidi stares at
them, her nose wrinkling in distaste.

                    HEIDI
          Filthy vermin.

                    BILLY
          I wouldn't worry yourself
          too much. Looks like the
          calvary has arrived.

He nods across the commons. The local
constabulary has indeed arrived, three police
cars pulling up and twice as many cops getting
out. They are led by the local Chief of Police,
DUNCAN HOPLEY. He's a big, beefy man in his
early forties with an acne-scarred face. He
and his men cross the commons, shooing the
Gypsies before them.

As Heidi and Billy watch, an incredible old man,
TADZU LEMPKE, is helped across the commons by
his wife, SUZANNE LEMPKE, an equally ancient
crone. They come to a stop before Hopley, Lempke
yelling at him, wagging his finger in front of
the impassive police chief, obviously arguing
with him. Heidi nods in their direction.

                    HEIDI
          Yes, but the Indians aren't
          going peacefully.

Billy stares at Lempke, his eyes widening as

they zero in on the old Gypsy's nose. There
seems to be a hole in it, a great, big, open,
running wound.

                    BILLY
          What's wrong with his nose?

                    HEIDI
          Who knows and who cares.
          C'mon, let's get out of
          here.

She slides into the Jag, Billy following,
the two of them taking off as Hopley ignores
Lempke, he and his men continuing to move the
Gypsies out of town.

                                        CUT TO:

EXT. FAIRFIELD COUNTRY CLUB - NIGHT

Fancy foreign cars arrive, disgorging
attractive, well-fleshed members, the men
dressed in suits, the women in understated
designer originals. High-school students
moonlight as valet parking attendants.

INT. CLUB DINING ROOM - NIGHT

Comfortable, charming, looking out on the
greens, Olympic size swimming pool, and tennis
courts below. The Maître d' seats people at
comfortable tables covered with linen.

Billy, Heidi, Kirk Penschley, and his wife,
KAREN, sit at a plush booth near the back.
Karen looks like Heidi, a pretty woman leading
a coddled upper middle-class existence.

Billy has just finished gorging himself on
what must have been, judging by the size of
the well-cleaned bone, the biggest porterhouse
ever.

A napkin sits over his chest, catching the
grease as it dribbles down his chin, Billy
talking and chewing at the same time.

Nobody at his table seems to mind.

This is Billy, the compulsive eater, a side of
him they're all used to. Besides, they're all
a little oiled and having a good time.

                    BILLY
                 (laughing)
          You shoulda seen the
          prosecutor's face. He
          couldn't believe I knew
          about Duggenfield's wife.

                    PENSCHLEY
          Dumbarton Investigative
          Services. I keep telling
          you they're the best in New
          England.

Billy nods agreement as the waitress appears
with a flaming desert of cherries jubilee. She
sets it down in front of Billy. Billy blows
out the flames and digs in with a still hearty
appetite.

A couple suddenly loom over him, staring down
as he pile drives through the dessert.

                    CARY
          Hey Billy, I hear it went
          well today. Congratulations.

Billy looks up to see JUDGE CARY ROSSINGTON, a tall, patrician gentlemen in his fifties, and his wife, LEDA, a lady of approximately the same age and, if possible, even more patrician, stopping by on their way to a table.

Cary grins and offers his hand. Billy grins back and shakes.

                    BILLY
          Thanks, Judge. That means a
          lot coming from you.

Rossington smiles and moves on with his wife, Penschley turning back to Billy.

                    PENSCHLEY
          So what did Ginelli say when
          you won?

                    BILLY
          He said he owed me, that if
          I ever needed anything, all
          I had to do was call.

                    PENSCHLEY
          Hey, I'd take that
          seriously. You know what
          they say about him.

                    HEIDI
               (making a face)
          I certainly do. "Richie the
          Hammer," they call him.
          Supposedly controls most of
          the dope and prostitution
          in Eastern Connecticut. I
          dunno what you're doing
          representing a man like
          that.

                    PENSCHLEY
          We do his business deals,
          too, don't forget that. He
          owns shopping centers all
          over the damn state.

                    HEIDI
               (not impressed)
          I don't have to ask where
          the money comes from, do I?

She and Penschley stare at each other, coming
from different moral worlds with equally
different attitudes.

Billy steps in, breaking the tension with a
toast.

                    BILLY
          Hey, it doesn't matter
          anymore. I won the case. To
          winning, regardless of the
          client!

They clink glasses, Penschley muttering under
his breath, none too quietly.

                    PENSCHLEY
          And all his real estate
          deals.

Heidi shoots him a hard glance but lets it
pass as the warmth of the alcohol washes over
them all.

The waitress reappears to pick up Billy's
decimated dessert.

He looks at the remains longingly.

                         BILLY
          Hey, you know, I might take
          another one of those

                         HEIDI
               (stepping in)
          That does it. We're outta
          here before you explode.

She rises to her feet, trying to pull her huge
husband out of his chair.

Penschley and his wife both laugh, Penschley
raising his hand, and, true to his word,
signaling for the check.

EXT. COUNTRY CLUB - NIGHT

The Hallecks and the Penschleys stumble out of
the club, obviously feeling no pain.

They say their good-byes, the valets pulling
up their separate cars.

The Penschleys disappear into theirs, a four-
door Beamer, Billy and Heidi into the Jag.

INT. JAG - NIGHT

Heidi shoots Billy a glance as he starts the
car up, and they pull out of the club and down
the long drive toward the street.

                         HEIDI
          Billy, you've got to stop
          eating so much.

Billy nods agreeably, rubbing his huge stomach
contentedly.

He's heard this all before ad infinitum.

                    BILLY
I know, I know—

                    HEIDI
No, I'm serious. You know
what Dr. Houston told you.
For a man your age and
weight you—

                    BILLY
          (finishing for her)
-have just entered heart
attack country. Look, could
we talk about something
pleasanter.

                    HEIDI
Like what?

                    BILLY
It's our anniversary coming
up soon, you know.

                    HEIDI
I haven't forgotten.

                    BILLY
Well, I thought we might
kill two birds with one
stone. Celebrate the case
<u>and</u> our anniversary by going
to Mohonk for a few days.

                    HEIDI
          (whirling on him,
             delighted)
Mohonk!

EXT. GATE TO CLUB - CONSTREET - NIGHT

The Jag passes the club gates, and pulls into
the street, tooling toward home.

INT. JAG - NIGHT

Billy throws Heidi a look, smiling with equal
delight.

                    BILLY
          Why, you don't like the
          place?

                    HEIDI
          I've loved it ever since we
          honeymooned there. In fact,
          almost as much as I love
          you.

She leans in, giving him a good long hard
kiss. She pulls away, sobering as one hand
probes his more than ample belly.

                    HEIDI
          If only you'd lose some
          weight everything would be
          perfect.

                    BILLY
             (his face falling)
          Oh, Heidi, don't start on
          that again.

                    HEIDI
          What am I supposed to do.
          Look!

She flips open the glove compartment. A pot-

pourri of junk food falls out, Ding Dongs,
Hostess Twinkies, Caramel Corn, old hamburger
and french fry wrappers from Burgher King and
McDonald's.

Billy looks away guiltily.

                    BILLY
          I can't help it. I'm
          starving to death all the
          time—

                    HEIDI
            (smiling seductively)
          Maybe if you were fed
          something else, you wouldn't
          be so hungry for food all
          the time—

She moves even closer to him, her hand ducking
down the front of his pants and fondling him.

His eyes widen with a mixture of pleasure and
shock.

                    BILLY
          Heidi!

                    HEIDI
            (smiling secretly)
          Now you just keep your eyes
          on the road—

Her head slips below the dashboard as she does
something in Billy's lap, his eyes widening
even more with pleasure.

                                        CUT TO:

EXT. DOWNTOWN STREET - NIGHT

An old camper with a hand painted unicorn on its side pulls up across the street from an all-night drugstore. Tadzu and Suzanne Lempke, the two ancient Gypsies from the town commons, get out.

They are followed by Gabe, the young man with the Indian Clubs, and Gina, the beautiful girl with the slingshot. They cross the street toward the pharmacy.

                                        CUT BACK TO:

EXT. STREET - NIGHT

The Jag cruises slowly down the street, not doing more than thirty-five.

INT. JAG - NIGHT

Heidi goes up and down in Billy's lap, the top of her head appearing intermittently above the dashboard, slowly bringing him to orgasm.

He sits behind the wheel, grabbing it with white knuckles, his fat little eyes half-closed with pleasure.

                                        CUT BACK TO:

INT. DRUGSTORE -NIGHT

Lempke stops as he gets to the PHARMACIST, Suzanne standing nearby him, tottering on her ancient legs. Gabe and Gina drift down one of the aisles.

                    LEMPKE
               (in a heavy accent)
          I want this filled. For my
          nose.

The pharmacist stares at him. On closer look,
Lempke does have a great, big open black cancer
to one side of his left nostril.

It exposes the veins pulsing within.

                  PHARMACIST
          Yeah, right.

He finally succeeds in tearing his eyes
from the rotting hole and disappears into
the pharmacy area to fill the prescription.
Suzanne shivers, rubbing her naked arms. She
turns to Lempke.

                  SUZANNE
          I get my coat.

He nods absently, Suzanne drifting back toward
the front door as Lempke shoots a glance down
an aisle. Gabe and Gina stand there. Lempke
nods at the beautiful young girl.

She begins to fill her pockets with nostrums
from the racks as Gabe keeps a watchful eye on
the pharmacist.

                              CUT BACK TO:

INT. JAG - NIGHT

Heidi looks up from her work on Billy, her
chin moist with her own saliva. His full face
is flushed, his forehead dappled with sweat.

                    HEIDI
          You ready to promise to go
          on a diet now?

                    BILLY
                 (desperately)
          Oh, yes, anything you say,
          just don't stop—

She smiles and her head disappears beneath
the dashboard again, Billy's eyes squeezing
perilously close to shut as he continues to
drive down the street and let his wife give
him head at the same time.

                                   CUT BACK TO:

INT. DRUGSTORE - NIGHT

The pharmacist glances up from his work behind
the counter, catching sight of Gina stealing
him blind in the reflection of a round, convex
mirror set in a corner to catch things exactly
like this. He heads for the end of the counter,
yelling at her.

                    PHARMACIST
          Hey, you, what are you doing
          back there—

Gabe steps in front of her, blocking his way.

                    GABE
          She ain't doin' nothin'.

                    PHARMACIST
          She ain't, huh? Then let me
          see what's in her pockets.

Tadzu Lempke casts a glance at the threesome,

the pharmacist's back turned to him.

He begins to slip things into his voluminous pockets as Gabe continues to argue with the druggist.

EXT. DRUGSTORE, STREET - NIGHT

Suzanne Lempke comes out of the pharmacy, tottering between two parked cars, heading for the street and the camper parked on the other side.

                              CUT BACK TO:

INT. JAG - NIGHT

Billy's head is bent back, his eyes hardly on the road as Heidi's head works in his lap, up and down, up and down, his pleasure increasing with every stroke.

He begins to groan as he approaches climax.

EXT. DRUGSTORE, STREET - NIGHT

Suzanne appears between the two parked cars, tottering across the street on her ancient legs.

INT. JAG - NIGHT

Billy's head is back, his eyes at half-mast, just about to come when he suddenly sees the old Gypsy woman directly in front of him, pinned in his headlights in the middle of the street. His eyes widen in horror. He forgets his ejaculation as his foot slams down on the brake.

EXT. STREET - NIGHT

Too late. The front of the Jag plows into the old woman with a terrible thump, throwing her up and over the hood, across the roof, and over the back of the car as it fishtails to a halt.

INT. JAG - NIGHT

Heidi raises her head from Billy's lap, looking at her husband.

Billy sits there, frozen in position, staring directly ahead, his eyes wide with horror.

                    HEIDI
          Billy, what happened?

Billy doesn't answer.

She slowly turns, following his gaze, only to let out a horrified cry.

The front windshield is awash in blood, dripping down in long jagged streaks.

She starts screaming, Billy sitting there, unable to move, watching the blood run, slowly cutting off his view of the street outside.

                              DISSOLVE TO:

EXT. STREET - NIGHT

A couple of black and whites and a coroner's wagon are there.

The police patrol the area as Gina and Gabe cluster around Lempke, giving him some needed support. The paramedics bag the body and then carry it over to their meat wagon.

Heidi sits on the curb, watching numbly as Billy is questioned by Duncan Hopley, Fairview's Chief of Police. He writes down Billy's responses.

                    HOPLEY
            (caught mid-sentence)
        and you say she just ran out
        between the two cars without
        warning?

                    BILLY
        Right. I didn't have a
        chance to stop. I tried, but
        she was just too quick for
        me.
            (looking at the Gypsies)
        Where'd they all come from
        anyway? I thought you got
        them out of town.

                    HOPLEY
        I did. As far as Arncaster's
        farm. They made a deal with
        him, I guess, to stay a
        couple of days.
            (a beat, then back to
                business)
        How fast would you say you
        were going?

                    BILLY
        I don't know, twenty, thirty
        miles an hour?

                    HOPLEY
          And you weren't drinking?

Billy turns away, trying to hide his all too
obvious guilt.

                    BILLY
          No, not at all.

Hopley sees the look and ignores it, closing
his book.

                    HOPLEY
          Well, I think that'll be it—

                    BILLY
              (looking at him in
               shock)
          You're not going to give me
          a breathalizer?

                    HOPLEY
              (smiling)
          Billy, how long have I known
          you? Ten, fifteen years?
          Your word is good enough for
          me. Now why don't you and
          Heidi go home. There'll be a
          hearing in a couple of days.

He turns and walks away.

Billy helps Heidi to her feet, heading for the
Jag.

The blood has been wiped from the window
leaving ugly brown smears behind.

Heidi hesitates, staring at it. Billy looks
at her.

                    BILLY
          Well, we just can't leave it
          here. Besides, it wasn't out
          fault

They start for the car again only to have Tadzu
Lempke suddenly break away from Gina and Gabe,
tottering toward them on his ancient legs.

His face is livid with fury.

                    LEMPKE
                  (screaming)
          You kill my wife! You think
          you get away with it, but it
          no happen! You be punished,
          you understand, you be
          punished!

Hopley moves in, urging him back toward Gina
and Gabe, his cops standing silently behind
him, backing him up.

                    HOPLEY
          That's enough. You'll get
          your day in court. Now move
          along—

Hopley and his men herd the ancient Gypsy away
as Billy and Heidi climb in the Jag and take
off.

                                        CUT TO:

EXT. LANTERN STREET, BILLY'S HOUSE - NIGHT

The Jag sits in the drive. There is a light on
in the upstairs bedroom.

The house and the street scream money and

privilege.

INT. MASTER SUITE - NIGHT

Billy undresses, his wife sitting on the bed, still spaced out.

He watches her with concerned eyes.

                    BILLY
          I don't know why you feel so
          guilty. It wasn't our fault.

                    HEIDI
          But I never should have been
          doing that to you. It was
          distracting you.

                    BILLY
          Hey, I couldn't have stopped
          in time anyway. I told you
          that. She just appeared from
          nowhere.

                    HEIDI
          I know, but it was just all
          so terrible—

                    BILLY
          Well, stop dwelling on it.
          It's too late to change
          things now anyway.

He slips a robe over his huge bulk. Heidi looks up at him.

                    HEIDI
          What are you going to do
          about it?

                    BILLY
What do you mean what am I
going to do about it? Go to
the hearing, of course.

                    HEIDI
No, I mean what are you
going to tell Judge
Rossington when he asks you
why you didn't stop in time?

Billy freezes as the import of her words sink
in on him.

                    BILLY
Oh, I see what you mean. I
can't very well tell him you
were—

                    HEIDI
                 (hastily)
No, you can't. It'd be all
over town in two seconds.

                    BILLY
But I can't lie

                    HEIDI
Cary Rossington will be the
judge. He isn't going to ask
you to lie. He's a friend.

                    BILLY
Sure, just like Duncan
Hopley's a friend. He didn't
even give me a breathalizer.

                    HEIDI
And why should he? You
weren't drunk.

                    BILLY
          Heidi, that's not the point.
          The police are supposed to
          give everybody involved in
          an accident a breathalizer.

Heidi looks up at him, worried now.

                    HEIDI
          Well, you can't tell Cary
          Rossington what happened. I
          know his wife. She'll tell
          everyone.

                    BILLY
          What am I supposed to do
          then?

                    HEIDI
          I don't know. Tell them
          everything but that.

                    BILLY
          But, Heidi, that's omitting
          something. It's the same as
          lying

The door is suddenly shoved open and their
daughter, LINDA, stands there, looking in at
them sleepily.

She is fourteen-years old and on the verge of
being quite pretty, obviously speeding from
adolescence to young womanhood at warp speed.

                    LINDA
          What are you two doing up
          this late? Is something
          wrong?

                    HEIDI
              (forcing a smile)
        No, of course not, darling.
        We were just talking.

                    LINDA
              (looking at them
                doubtfully)
        You sure?

Billy smiles at her, love flooding his face.

If he has another passion in life beside food,
his daughter is it.

                    BILLY
        We're sure. You want me to
        come tuck you in?

                    LINDA
              (making a face)
        Are you kidding? I'm
        fourteen-years old.
        Fourteen-year olds don't
        need to be tucked in.

With a toss of her head, she disappears from
the doorway, closing the door behind her.

Billy smiles after her. Heidi reads his
expression.

                    HEIDI
        That's another reason you
        don't want to go public with
        what really happened in that
        car tonight.

                    BILLY
        Linda?

                    HEIDI
          Of course. I can just hear
          all her friends now. "Hey, I
          hear your parents are real
          <u>killer</u> sex maniacs. Rad,
          dude."

                    BILLY
          Heidi

                    HEIDI
          Think about it. You know how
          cruel kids are. Regardless,
          I'll support your decision
          either way. I love you.

She gives him a kiss and slips under the
covers, turning off the lights.

Billy stares at her in the darkness, muttering
to himself.

                    BILLY
          Yeah, right.

He slips out of the robe and into bed, scrunching
his bulk down under the blankets beside her,
staring up at the ceiling.

You don't know how he's going to decide, but
you know he's thinking about it hard.

                                   DISSOLVE TO:

EXT. FAIRVIEW MUNICIPAL COURTHOUSE - DAY

A nice old-fashioned courthouse facing the
commons.

INT. JUDGE ROSSINGTON'S CHAMBERS - DAY

JUDGE CARY ROSSINGTON sits behind his desk
in the smallish room. He's the silver-haired
gentleman from the country club. Billy and
Heidi sit across from him. His wife, Leda,
sits at the back, waiting for the proceedings
to end.

Duncan Hopley is on his feet, testifying in
front of the judge. You have the feeling this
is some sort of charade and they are all just
good friends, waiting for it to end so they
can go to lunch (and they are).

                    CARY
          (caught mid-sentence)
     so she just ran out in front
     of the car from nowhere?

                    HOPLEY
     As near as we could
     ascertain.

                    CARY
     What were the results of the
     breathalizer?

Billy's head comes up, his eyes piercing Duncan
Hopley. Hopley replies without even glancing
his way.

                    HOPLEY
     I didn't feel it was
     necessary. There was no
     indication Mr. Halleck was
     drinking.

Rossington's eyes dart between Billy and
Hopley.

He was at the club that night.

He saw Billy drinking and he knows what's going on, but decides to ignore it.

He turns his gaze back to Hopley.

                    CARY
          I see.
                    (to Billy)
          And there was nothing you
          could do to stop in time,
          Billy? I mean you were
          paying attention to where
          you were going?

Billy shoots a glance at Heidi.

She is looking in the other direction, studiously studying the wallpaper. He turns back to Rossington with a sigh.

                    BILLY
          Yes, Cary.

                    CARY
          Then I think we'll just rule
          the matter an accidental
          death. Case closed. Now
          shall we get some lunch.

He bangs his fist on his desk, rising with a broad smile.

He shakes Billy and Heidi's hand, Hopley and Leda congratulating them also.

Everybody seems happy about the decision except Heidi. They all move toward the door.

EXT. COURTHOUSE - DAY

They step out of the courthouse, Cary, Leda, and
Hopley remaining behind to discuss something,
Billy walking Heidi toward their car parked at
the curb.

She throws him a glum glance.

                    HEIDI
          Well, that was easy enough—

                    BILLY
                  (glumly)
          Yeah, too easy—

Tadzu Lempke suddenly darts out of nowhere,
stepping in front of a startled Billy with
that rotting nose.

He raises a finger, brushing it across Billy's
face with a whisper that only Billy can hear.

                    LEMPKE
          Thinner

Billy falls back with a startled cry. Hopley
detaches himself from the Rossingtons, hurrying
over to face Lempke.

                    HOPLEY
          Hey, what are you doing
          here?

                    LEMPKE
              (smiling thinly at
               Billy)
          I just came to see that
          justice was done.

                    HOPLEY
          Justice has been done and it
          doesn't have a damn thing to
          do with you. Now move it or
          I'll throw you in jail.

Raising a placatory hand, Lempke scuttles
across the street to where the camper with
the unicorn on its side waits. He opens the
door, stopping to cast that thin smile back
at Billy again. Billy watches, catching it. It
makes the hairs rise on the back of his neck
as the old Gypsy hops into the camper, the
camper roaring to life and disappearing down
the street in a haze of oil fumes. Rossington
comes to a stop beside Billy.

                    ROSSINGTON
          You all right, Billy?

Billy nods dumbly, a hand unconsciously going
up to his cheek where Lempke stroked him.

                    BILLY
          Yeah, fine, just fine.

                    ROSSINGTON
          Well, then let's eat. I'm
          starved.

He, Leda, and Hopley start down the street,
Billy and Heidi following.

She casts a glance at her husband.

His hand still rests on his cheek where the
Gypsy touched him.

Her face floods with worry.

                         HEIDI
              What'd he say to you anyway?

                         BILLY
                (snapping out of it; a
                      little bit)
              Nothing—

                                    DISSOLVE TO:

EXT. BILLY'S HOUSE - DAY

The house looks as upper-class and comfortable
as ever. Super up on the screen: "FOUR DAYS
LATER."

INT. SECOND-FLOOR HALLWAY - DAY

Billy saunters out of his bedroom, dressed to
leave on vacation. He heads for the bathroom
as his daughter pokes her head up the top of
the stairs, shouting after him.

                         LINDA
              Hey, dad, mom says come on.

                         BILLY
              Be right there.

INT. BATHROOM - DAY

He enters the bathroom, staring at the scale
on the floor.

He takes a deep breath, empties his pockets,
kicks off his shoes, and takes off his jacket,
making himself as light as possible before he
weighs himself.

Finished, he steps onto the scale.

He looks over his more than ample belly down at the scale below.

He can't see it.

He picks up a rounded vanity mirror, holding it upside down to read the numbers in reverse.

They read 294.

His face breaks into a smile of pleasure as he mumbles to himself.

>   BILLY
>   Two ninety-four. I've lost
>   three pounds.

Then it comes echoing down the corridors of his mind, a word only he can hear.

>   LEMPKE (V.O.)
>   Thinnnnerrrrr—-

The smile disappears from Billy's face as he stares down at the scale.

His daughter's yell from the floor below jerks him out of his reverie.

>   LINDA (O.S.)
>   Hey, dad!

>   BILLY
>   Coming!

Billy replaces the mirror, steps off the scale, and, struggling to find that happy grin again, slips his shoes back on, grabs his change and coat, and heads for the door.

INT. ENTRANCE WAY - DAY

He comes down the stairs with a jaunty whistle and turns down the hallway to the kitchen.

INT. KITCHEN - DAY

Billy walks into the room to see his wife standing by the door, ready to leave. Linda sits at the table, watching her parents. Billy looks at Heidi. Her hands are empty.

                    BILLY
          Hey, where are the
          thermoses?

                    HEIDI
          I'm not packing a bunch of
          soda so you have an excuse
          to stop at every rest area
          for a bag of potato chips.

                    BILLY
          Relax, would you, my diet's
          working. I've already lost
          three pounds.

She hurumps, not believing it for a second.

                    HEIDI
          Yeah, sure.

She turns, slipping out the doors. Linda leaps to her feet, following her mother. She gives Billy's big belly a poke as she passes. It rolls like the proverbial bowlful of jelly.

                         LINDA
               Mom's right, dad. You're not
               exactly Kevin Costner yet.

She's out the door, Billy pausing a moment to
sneak a pack of corn chips from a cabinet,
hastily stuffing them in one pocket before
following.

EXT. HOUSE - DAY

Heidi already sits inside the Jag, Linda
standing with the driver's side door open.

Billy stops, giving her a kiss.

                         BILLY
               I know you're going to be
               okay staying at Georgia's,
               but I still want you—

                         HEIDI
               (finishing for him by
                    rote)
               to call every day just so I
               can be sure.

                         BILLY
               (smiling in spite of
                    himself)
               Right.

He leans down, gives her a kiss, and slides
his considerable bulk into the car.

As Linda waves good-bye, the Jag pulls out of
the drive, and tools down the street.

INT. JAG - DAY

Billy drives. Heidi casts a suspicious glance
in his direction.

> HEIDI
> You sure you're sticking to
> your diet?

> BILLY
> (looking guiltily away)
> Of course. I said so, didn't
> I?

Heidi makes a dive for his pockets, patting
him down like a cop.

She comes up with the packet of corn chips.

> HEIDI
> Aha! What are these?

> BILLY
> Just a little snack. But
> I've been losing weight—

> HEIDI
> Well, I don't know how. You
> sure haven't changed your
> eating habits.

She lowers the window and tosses the corn chips
out, turning back to him a playful expression.
She loses it when she sees the glumness in his
face.

> HEIDI
> What is it? That old Gypsy
> still on your mind—

                         BILLY
               Of course not—

                                        FLASH CUT TO:

EXT. STREET - NIGHT (IN BILLY'S MIND)

Billy's car plows into Suzanne Lempke, throwing
her up in the air and over the hood of his car
with that sickening thud.

INT. JAG - NIGHT

Billy's face, frozen with horror, his eyes
wide with terror.

                                        CUT BACK TO:

INT. JAG - DAY

Billy snaps out of it, trying to hide the
shiver running up his spine.

He does a pretty good job of it because a
playful grin spreads across Heidi's face.

                         HEIDI
               Okay, but I'll tell you one
               thing. We get up to Mohonk,
               we are going to burn that
               fat off you one way or
               another—

She suddenly throws herself at him, tickling
him everywhere.

Billy cries out in protest, the unpleasant
memories forgotten as the two of them break
into affectionate laughter.

                                        CUT TO:

EXT. MOHONK RESORT - NIGHT

A huge four-storied resort set high atop the
Catskill mountains.

It is still early in the evening and lights
are on all over the hotel.

Super up "TWO DAYS LATER." The sound of love
making can be heard over, a couple racing
toward climax.

INT. ROOM - NIGHT

Heidi and Billy come together, Heidi rocking
back and forth atop Billy.

As their sighs of pleasure die away, she slips
off him to lay on the bed by his side, staring
happily at the ceiling.

                    HEIDI
          I must be a nymphomaniac.
          I don't think I could go a
          week without making love.
          Either that or you're just a
          terrific lover.

He looks at her with a satisfied grin of his
own.

                    BILLY
          A bit of both actually.
          Amazing, isn't it? All these
          years and it's still like
          the first time.

Heidi rolls over, grabbing a roll of fat and squeezing it.

> HEIDI
> Yeah, except for this. You
> didn't have all this extra
> baggage fifteen years ago.

> BILLY
> (making a face)
> Aw, Heidi, don't start

She rises on an elbow, looking at him with grave eyes.

> HEIDI
> I'm serious. Do you know how
> boring it gets always using
> the same position?

> BILLY
> Well, we could always find
> another way to do it—

> HEIDI
> What? You on top of me? No,
> thank you. You'd smother
> me. Billy, you have to lose
> weight.

> BILLY
> Heidi, I told you. I've lost
> some

> HEIDI
> Oh, yeah? Where? There's
> still plenty to grab on to—

She grabs another roll of fat, tickling him.

Billy breaks up laughing, trying to fend her
off between the giggles.

                    BILLY
          Heidi, stop it, I can't
          breathe

She suddenly stops, sobering up, her hands
running across his still huge stomach.

                    HEIDI
          Billy Halleck, you really
          have lost weight. You're
          <u>skinnier!</u>

Billy lays back on the bed, slapping his huge
belly.

It sets off rolls of fat moving in every
direction.

                    BILLY
          I told you I'd lost three
          pounds.

She sits up on one elbow, looking at him.

A little concern has leaked into her eyes.

                    HEIDI
          Yeah, but I haven't seen you
          slowing down your eating.
          You sure you're all right?

                    BILLY
          What is this? I can't win
          for losing? You want me to
          lose weight, so I do, and
          now you're worried about my
          health?

                    HEIDI
                (softening)
          Well, you weigh yourself
          first thing in the morning.

                    BILLY
                (happily)
          This is a civilized hotel.
          No scales in the bathroom.

                    HEIDI
          Don't worry, we'll find one.

          She leans over and kisses
          him, looking adoringly into
          his eyes.

                    HEIDI
          I love you very much, you
          know.

                    BILLY
                (smiling contentedly)
          I know—

He kisses her back, the two of them starting
to make slow, lazy love again.

                                        DISSOLVE TO:

EXT. STREET, FAIRVIEW — NIGHT (IN BILLY'S
NIGHTMARE)

Billy's Jag comes driving down the street.

INT. JAG — NIGHT

Billy sits behind the wheel, Heidi in his lap,
orally massaging his parts. Only there's no

pleasure on his face. Just stark terror.

He's staring out the window, directly ahead.

EXT. STREET - NIGHT

The old Gypsy woman steps out between the two parked cars, not running, just tottering along on her ancient legs.

INT. JAG - NIGHT

Billy's face congeals with fear as he speeds toward her. He tries to turn the wheel.

It won't budge. Feeling like he's stuck in molasses, he sweeps Heidi aside, raising his foot to bring it down on the brake.

Sweat pops out on his face. No matter how hard he tries, he's still moving like he is stuck in molasses.

EXT. STREET - NIGHT

The old Gypsy woman comes to a halt in the middle of the street, turning to face the car bearing down on her. Only it isn't Suzanne that's looking at Billy.

It's Lempke, his face on her body, and he's grinning a vicious hate-filled grin and screaming out a single word.—

                    LEMPKE
          Thinnnnnerrrrrr!!!!

The car smashes into the old Gypsy, sweeping

him up and over the hood with that sickening thud.

INT. JAG - NIGHT

Billy screams in horror as buckets of blood spray across his windshield blotting out everything else.

SMASH CUT TO:

INT. HOTEL ROOM - NIGHT (BACK INTO REALITY)

Billy sits up with a stifled scream, sweat dappling his face and running down the folds of his stomach. Heidi lies beside him, sleeping soundly, out to the world.

Billy looks down, feeling himself as though finding something reassuring in the handfuls of fat. He finally lays back, staring up at the ceiling, trying to get his breathing under control. You just know he's in for a very long night.

DISSOLVE TO:

INT. MOHONK, FIRST FLOOR PROMENADE - DAY

Well-off people move past the shops on their way to the lake and hiking trails. Billy and Heidi appear from a sports store, their purchases clutched under their arms. Heidi sees a scale standing against one wall, one of those huge old-fashioned kind that also have a little metal window that opens and tells you your fortune along with your weight. She grabs Billy, nodding at it as she digs in her purse.

                    HEIDI
          Hop on, hero. I've got a
          penny.

She drops some change into the slot, turning to
Billy with a grin. He stares back at the huge
ornate scale like it was some sort of alien
monster, suddenly, inexplicably nervous.

                    BILLY
          You know these things don't
          weight true.

                    HEIDI
          A ball park figure's all I
          want. Come on, Billy, don't
          be a poop.

Billy reluctantly steps on, the needle pegging
out at 286 pounds. Heidi stares at it with a
mixture of fear and wonder.

                    HEIDI
          Billy, you've lost over ten
          pounds!

But Billy isn't listening. His face has paled
and his eyes are glued to the little metal
window that has snapped open revealing his
fortune. It doesn't read "Financial Matters
Will Soon Improve" or "Old Friends Will Visit."

It reads: "Thinner". Billy blinks rapidly and
when he looks again it reads: "Do Not Make
Important Decisions Hastily."

Billy steps off the scale with a stifled gasp.

Heidi looks up at her husband's suddenly pasty
face. Worry clouds her own.

                    HEIDI
          Billy, are you all right?

Billy nods numbly, trying to hide his fear and
confusion.

                    BILLY
          Yeah, fine. Just a little
          surprised by the weight
          loss. I didn't know I was
          dieting that hard.—

He tries to smile and fails. More worry floods
Heidi's face.

                                        CUT TO:

EXT. TACONIC PARKWAY - DAY

The Jag moves along with the flow of traffic.
It passes an overhead sign indicating the
Connecticut turnoff. The car swings in that
direction. Heidi's voice is heard over. Super
up "THREE DAYS LATER. II

                    HEIDI'S (V.O.)
          Thank you for a wonderful
          time.

INT. JAG - DAY

Billy is behind the wheel, his mind still
stuck on the fortune he thought he saw.

Heidi cuts a worried glance at him.

                    HEIDI
          Did you hear me, Billy?

Billy snaps out of his reverie, looking at her
with a start.

                    BILLY
          Sorry, I was wool-gathering

                    HEIDI
          I just said thank you for a
          wonderful time.

                    BILLY
               (forcing a grin)
          You're welcome. You're
          always welcome.

                    HEIDI
               (a beat, then)
          You're worried about the
          weight loss, too, aren't
          you?

                    BILLY
               (with that big forced
                grin again)
          Me? Are you kidding? What's
          a little weight—

                    HEIDI
          When we get home I want you
          to jump on our bathroom
          scale.

                    BILLY
          Come on, Heidi, I lost some
          weight, no big deal.

                    HEIDI
          Billy, unexplained weight
          loss is one of the seven
          warning signs.

                    BILLY
One of the seven signs of
what?

                    HEIDI
          (not wanting to use the
                    word)
You know what.

                    BILLY
          (stubbornly)
No, I don't.

                    HEIDI
<u>Cancer</u>. All right? There,
I've said it. I want you to
make an appointment to see
Mike Houston when we get
home.

                    BILLY
Heidi, just because I've
lost a little weight—

                    HEIDI
A little weight? I don't
call over ten pounds in a
week and a half a little
weight. Especially when you
haven't been exercising
that much and you certainly
haven't been dieting. Now
I want you to make that
appointment.

                    BILLY
I'll think about it.

                    HEIDI
Billy—

                    BILLY
                  (snapping)
        I said I'd think about it.
        Now leave me alone!

She shuts up, turning away, knowing when she's
pushed him far enough.

Billy keeps his eyes on the road ahead, refusing
to look at her.

And then it comes again, that whisper inside
his head from the other side of the grave.

               LEMPKE (V.O.)
          Thinnnnerrrrr

Billy's eyes flood with fear.

                                        CUT TO:

EXT. BILLY'S HOUSE - NIGHT

The Jag pulls into the drive, Heidi and Billy
getting out, Billy going to the trunk and
starting to unload the bags.

Linda runs out of the house, greeting them
both with big kisses.

Heidi looks at her.

                    HEIDI
        Everything all right?

                    LINDA
        No, I burned down Georgia's
        house while you were gone
        and got raped by the entire

            Varsity football team.

She turns to Billy, grinning at him as she
takes a bag from his hand.

                    LINDA
          Hey, you are turning into
          Arnold Schwarzenegger.

                    BILLY
          (staring at her blankly)
          What do you mean?

Linda pokes his belly with a grin.

                    LINDA
          Your diet. It's really
          working.

She turns, lugging the bag inside the house.
Billy looks up to see Heidi staring at him,
her eyes more worried than ever. He cuts her
off before she can speak.

                    BILLY
          I don't want to hear about
          it, you understand. Not one
          word.

He walks toward the house, carrying a couple
of suitcases.

INT. ENTRANCE WAY - NIGHT

He comes through the front door, stopping at
the foot of the stairs, staring up the steps
while he catches his breath. The scale is up
there. You just know he's thinking about it.

He starts up the stairs with the bags.

EXT. SECOND-FLOOR HALL -NIGHT

He crests the stairs, comes down the hallway, and disappears into his bedroom. A moment later he reappears without the bags, staring down the hall toward the bathroom. He casts a glance back toward the stairway. He can hear Heidi and Linda laughing in the kitchen below. For the moment he's alone and undisturbed. He heads for the bathroom.

INT. BATHROOM - NIGHT

He comes through the door, stopping to stare at the scale. Has he lost more weight? Does he dare to find out? The uncertainty is too much for him. He has to know and starts to take the change from his pockets and take off his jacket. He suddenly stops. No, he doesn't need to be any lighter, not anymore. Slipping his coat back on and putting the stuff back into his pocket. He slips his bulk on the scale, staring down. He no longer needs the mirror.

By peering over his still protruding belly— only not protruding as much, oh, no, not as much at all—he can see the numbers. They read 273 lbs. Billy is shrinking and rapidly. A strangled gasp escapes his throat. He staggers off the scale with a stricken expression and slumps in a chair. A voice speaks from behind him.

                    HEIDI (O.S.)
          What was it?

Billy looks up to see his wife standing in the

doorway, staring at him more worriedly than
ever.

> BILLY
> (in a hoarse croak)
> Two seventy-three.

> HEIDI
> (really worried now)
> Oh, Billy, you've lost
> another nine pounds! Will
> you go see Dr. Houston now?

Billy nods miserably, scared to death, all
attempts at pretense gone.

> HEIDI
> Great. I'll call him right
> now.

Heidi disappears from the doorway, running for
the phone in their bedroom. Billy squeezes his
eyes shut, trying not to cry. He mumbles to
himself.

> BILLY
> Oh, dear God, please, don't
> let it be cancer. Please!

> CUT TO:

EXT. MEDICAL BUILDING - DAY

A medical building in keeping with the rest of
the town. It exudes charm. Super up "SIX DAYS
LATER."

INT. DR. HOUSTON'S OFFICE - DAY

Billy sits in a well-upholstered office, sweating bullets as DR. MICHAEL HOUSTON sits behind his desk, silently examining Billy's lab test results. Houston is in his fifties and looks like a younger Marcus Welby. Billy is noticeably thinner, his cheeks slowly disappearing to give the first hint of hollows, his clothes just beginning to bag and hang off him.

Finished, Houston looks up at Billy.

                    DR. HOUSTON
          Everything looks fine.

Billy stares at him as if he's misheard.

                    BILLY
          What?

                    DR. HOUSTON
          Everything looks fine. We
          can do some more tests
          if you want, but I don't
          see the point. Your blood
          looks better than it has at
          your last two physicals.
          Cholesterol is down—

Billy suddenly starts to laugh, loud and deeply. It sounds like what it is: hysterical relief. Houston looks at him quizzically.

                    DR. HOUSTON
          Share the funny. In this too
          sad world, we need all the
          funnies we can get, Billy-
          boy.

                    BILLY
          Nothing. It's just, just
          that I was scared, trying to
          deal with the big C or Aids—

                    DR. HOUSTON
          It isn't Aids, I can
          guarantee you that. And
          it isn't cancer either.
          cancer's got a look. At
          least when it's already
          gobbled up almost fifty
          pounds, it does.

Concern flickers back across Billy's face.

                    BILLY
          Then if it isn't cancer or
          Aids, what is it? I'm down
          to two forty-eight and I've
          been stuffing myself like a
          pig.

                    DR. HOUSTON
          What's been going on at
          home? Heidi bugging you
          about your weight all the
          time? Been under a lot of
          emotional pressure at work?

                    BILLY
          Well, of course. All that
          and I've been worried sick
          about the weight loss—

Dr. Houston smiles, spreading his hands like
that explains everything.

                    DR. HOUSTON
          Well, there it is.

                    BILLY
          You mean—it's all in my
          mind?

                    DR. HOUSTON
          Probably. Something upsets
          you, next thing you know
          you're losing weight. My
          advice to you is to stop
          worrying. In a day or two
          you won't lose as many
          pounds, a few days after
          that you won't lose any at
          all, and before you know it,
          you'll be a fatty again.

                    BILLY
                 (fervently)
          Good God, wouldn't I love
          that.
                 (rising and shaking
                  Houston's hand)
          Thanks, Michael. I can't
          tell you how much better I
          feel.

                    DR. HOUSTON
                 (with a big smile)
          I'm glad. That's what we're
          here for.

                                        CUT TO:

EXT. BILLY'S HOUSE - DAY

Billy's Jag zips down the street and screeches
to a halt in his driveway. He heaves his
quickly diminishing bulk out of his car and
runs for the house.

INT. ENTRANCE WAY - DAY

He bursts through the door, stopping in the
entrance way, calling up the stairs.

                    BILLY
          Heidi!

Her voice answers from the kitchen.

                    HEIDI (O.S.)
          Back here.

He takes off down the hall.

INT. KITCHEN - DAY

He bursts through the door, interrupting his
wife preparing dinner at the sink. He sweeps
her up in his arms, giving her a big kiss.

                    BILLY
          I'm all right.

                    HEIDI
          What?

                    BILLY
          I'm all right. Houston says
          it isn't cancer or Aids or
          anything else he can find.

                    HEIDI
          Oh, Billy, I'm so glad!

She throws her arms around him, kissing him
twice as hard. They break, a lascivious gleam
suddenly in his eyes.

                    BILLY
          Wanna go upstairs?

                    HEIDI
            (grinning ear-to-ear)
          My goodness, you are all
          right.

                              DISSOLVE TO:

EXT. FAIRVIEW - DAY (IN BILLY'S NIGHTMARE)

A huge, mangy vulture cruises high over the
skies of Fairview.

It wears the face of Tadzu Lempke as it swoops
down over the main street and town commons,
dark, cindery dust falling from under its wing
tips and floating down on the village below.

It croaks as it swoops down main street.

               LEMPKE VULTURE
          Thinnnnnerrrrrrr—

EXT. TOWN COMMONS - DAY

Billy, as fat as he was the first time we
saw him at almost three hundred pounds,
waddles down the street, peering around him in
horror. Fairview has become a town filled with
concentration camp survivors. On the sidewalk,
big headed babies with wasted bodies scream
from expensive prams.

Two desiccated women in designer dresses lurch
out of Cherries on Top, Fairview's version of
the ye old ice-cream shoppe. Their faces are
all cheekbones and bulging brows, the necklines

of their dresses slipping from their knotty collar bones in a hideous parody of seduction.

In the center of the street, Duncan Hopley directs traffic, his Police Chief's uniform hanging off his match stick frame in folds. The cars are driven by emaciated people, their passengers, young and old alike, just as terrifyingly thin. As Billy passes, Hopley turns to him with his skeletal face, screaming at him behind teeth suddenly too big for his shrunken mouth.

> HOPLEY
> Hey, Billy, I saved your ass
> and look what happened to
> me. Look!

Cary Rossington shambles out of Heads Up, the barber store, his black judge's robes flapping over his almost non-existent, spindly body. He is screeching in a horrid, crow like voice and when he turns to Billy, he's no longer Cary Rossington, but a screaming, terrified Ronald Reagan from "King's Row," nodding dumb struck at his painfully frail frame.

> ROSSINGTON/RONALD REAGAN
> Where's the rest of me?
> WHERE'S THE REST OF ME?

Billy turns away from him, breaking into a shambling run down the street, his fat shaking and rolling in great waves across his body. That's when he sees Dr. Michael Houston heading toward him, a walking, talking skeleton, bones clattering beneath the smart Saville Row suit. Billy reverses direction, trying to run, but in the way of nightmares, its a run through thick, sticky mud. He casts a glance over his shoulder. The skeletal Dr. Houston is catching up to him, sparkling eyes bulging from sockets of naked bone, the uncovered jawbone snapping and jerking, a hand of clattering knuckle joints and finger bones reaching out to touch him, his voice a dead, papery whisper.

                    DR. HOUSTON
          It was his wife you killed,
          Billy-boy, and you're
          in trouble, sooooo much
          trouble—

                              SMASH CUT TO:

INT. BILLY'S ROOM - NIGHT (BACK INTO REALITY)

Billy jerks awake, gasping for breath, a hand clasped across his mouth to stifle his involuntary scream.

He looks about his quite ordinary room, Heidi sleeping next to him, a soft breeze outside.

He whispers to himself.

                    BILLY
          It was a nightmare, just a
          nightmare—

But he doesn't look like he thinks it was just a nightmare.

He looks like a man scared out of his wits.

He slips his bulk back down in the bed, pulling the covers tight around his now double instead of triple chin, and determinedly closes his eyes, mumbling to himself.

                         BILLY
               Go back to sleep, just go
               back to sleep—

He keeps his eyes closed, but you just know
there's no way he's going back to sleep tonight.

In fact, maybe never.

                                        CUT TO:

EXT. DOWNTOWN FAIRVIEW - DAY

Billy and Penschley exit a restaurant, picking
their teeth.

They walk back toward their offices. Penschley
stares at Billy with barely concealed disbelief.

                         PENSCHLEY
               —he says you're <u>worrying</u> the
               pounds away?

                         BILLY
                       (nodding)
               Uh-huh, so I'm just going
               to stop thinking about it
               completely.

Penschley stops, picking at Billy's suit.

It hangs on him like a tent, two, possibly
three sizes too big.

                         PENSCHLEY
               Before you go that far, do
               me a favor, huh. Get some
               new clothes. I don't want
               to appear in court with you
               looking like this.

                    BILLY
                  (smiling)
          Hey, no problem. I like the
          new image. The thin Billy
          Halleck.

Grinning he turns for the nearest up scale
men's store just down the street.

Penschley follows along.

INT. UP SCALE MEN'S STORE - DAY

A CLERK as fat as Billy was just a few weeks
ago hurries over as they enter. He's obviously
been waiting on Billy for some time because an
expression of astonishment sweeps across his
face when he sees Billy.

                    CLERK
          Mr. Halleck, you look
          wonderful! I see you finally
          found a diet that works.

                    BILLY
                (his grin a little
                    forced)
          Right, and I want a whole
          new wardrobe to go with my
          new look.

                    CLERK
                (measuring his upper
                    body)
          My goodness, you're down to
          a forty-four. Maybe even a
          forty-two. You wanna weigh
          yourself? I got a scale in
          the back room.

                    BILLY
          Un-unh. I'm not weighing
          myself anymore. I'm going
          to stop thinking about it
          completely.

                  PENSCHLEY
            (with a snide grin)
          Probably gain back
          everything you lost.

Billy smiles, pleased at the thought.

                    BILLY
          That's the idea.

The clerk looks up from measuring Billy's
waist.

There is a look of envy on his fat face.

                    CLERK
          You can take a forty pant.
            (Billy smiles proudly)
          This diet you're on—do you
          have to give up liquor?

                                        DISSOLVE TO:

EXT. HARTFORD, CONNECTICUT - DAY

Establishing shot. Super up "NINE DAYS LATER."
A voice intrudes over.

                  JUDGE BOYNTON (V.O.)
          The tax charges against Mrs.
          Rae's estate should be filed
          with the Internal Revenue
          Service.

EXT. FEDERAL COURTHOUSE - DAY

Establishing shot. The voice continues.

                    JUDGE BOYNTON (V.O,)
               Probate hearing to be
               suspended until such charges
               are filed.

INT. COURTROOM - DAY

Almost nobody in here but a couple of spectators
and Billy, his law partner, Kirk Penschley,
and JUDGE BOYNTON, a stern faced man with a
non-existent sense of humor. Billy looks like
he's lost more weight, a <u>lot</u> more weight. In
fact, he's definitely beginning to look sick:
sallow, too thin, his new clothes bagging
about him. He seems oblivious as he rises
from the defense attorney's table, Penschley
seated next to him.

                    BILLY
               Your honor, I object—

Billy suddenly stops, a queer expression
coming over his face. His pants are slipping
off his buttocks and threatening to continue
down his legs and land on the floor. Billy
makes a grab, stopping them just in time. He
abruptly sits, blushing madly. Boynton looks
at him oddly.

                    JUDGE BOYNTON
               Is that an objection, Mr.
               Halleck, or a gas attack?

Several spectators in the courtroom laugh. The
court reporter is even smiling. Billy blushes
even more furiously.

Boynton glowers at him.

                    JUDGE BOYNTON
          Court recessed for ten
          minutes.

He bangs his gravel down and rises, heading
for his chambers. The few spectators rise and
drift away. Penschley looks at his partner.

                    PENSCHLEY
          You all right, Billy?

                    BILLY
          (nodding jerkily)
          Yeah. Just have to go to the
          bathroom, that's all.

Slipping his hands into his pants pockets to
hold them up, he rises and shuffles toward the
door. Penschley stares after him quizzically.

INT. COURTHOUSE BATHROOM - DAY

Billy hurries into the empty bathroom, and
stops, trying to cinch his belt tighter. It
won't go. There are no more holes left. He
looks down at it, realizing for the first time
he has it cinched as tight as possible, the
long end flapping in his hand like a dried
leathery tongue.

He suddenly turns, looking at himself in the
mirror.

His suit hangs off him in folds, much too big
for him, not just at the waist, but everywhere.
He pales, murmuring to himself.

                    BILLY
          Jesus, I look like a kid
          dressed up in his father's
          clothes—

He staggers to the mirror, looking more closely at himself. He lets his pants drop, ignoring how silly he looks with them gathered about his ankles, his shirt flap hanging down. He slowly lifts it, looking at his reflection. There is no belly left, absolutely no belly at all.

He turns his back to the mirror, lifting his shirt above his rump. He has no rear end left either, just sagging skin with skinny thigh bones poking through his jockey shorts. He turns back to the mirror, shoving his face up to it. It is a tired face, emaciated, scooped out hollows where there used to be fat, rosy cheeks, a single chin where there used to be three.

He chokes out a few terrified words as the truth hits him.

                    BILLY
          My God, it isn't slowing
          down. It's accelerating—

Tadzu Lempke's face suddenly replaces his own reflection, grinning at him with teeth like tombstones. The old man's thin, nicotine stained lips purse and whisper to him.

                    LEMPKE (V.O.)
          Thinnnnerrrrr—

Billy gasps and stumbles back, almost tripping over his pants. He leans down and pulls them

up, staring at the bathroom mirror mumbling to
himself like a madman.

                    BILLY
          No, no, it couldn't be—

He backs away from the mirror into a stall,
slamming the door shut behind him.

INT. STALL - DAY

He stands there, pressed into a corner,
trembling all over.

He hears the bathroom door open, Kirk Penschley
yelling to him.

                 PENSCHLEY (O.S.)
          Hey, Billy, you okay?

Billy nods, getting control of his voice with
almost superhuman effort.

                    BILLY
          Fine. Just got to mail a
          package, that's all.

                 PENSCHLEY (O.S.)
          Well, hurry up. Judge
          Boynton's coming back soon.

Billy stands there, crouched in the corner,
listening to the door shut behind Penschley.

Tears well up in his eyes and his teeth begin
to chatter with fear.

He starts whispering to himself like a monk
reciting a mantra.

                    BILLY
          It's all in my head, all in
          my head

                                        CUT TO:

INT. BILLY'S HOUSE, KITCHEN - NIGHT

Billy sits at the kitchen table, gobbling
down the last of a whole roasted chicken with
something approximating desperation.

The decimated carcass sits before him.

He eats with hurried bites, hardly stopping to
chew as he gorges himself.

Heidi prepares desert at the counter, Linda
seated across from him, watching her father
inhale his food with growing disquiet.

                    LINDA
          Dad, have you been eating
          like this all the time?

Billy hardly pauses to answer in his headlong
rush to devour as much food as he can, grease
running down his chin, bits of chicken, hardly
masticated, sticking out from his mouth.

                    BILLY
          Uh-huh.

                    LINDA
          Then why do you keep losing
          so much weight?

Billy looks at her, a crazy gleam seeping into
his eyes. It's nascent hysteria.

                    BILLY
          'Cause I finally found a
          diet that works. Eat all you
          want and still lose weight!
          Funny, isn't it?

He breaks into a hyena's laugh that is
definitely not funny. Linda springs from her
chair, tears flooding her eyes, and runs from
the room. Billy stares after her, the hysteria
instantly replaced by regret. He looks up at
Heidi as she removes the chicken carcass and
places a heaping bowl of apple crumble a la
mode before him.

                    BILLY
          Why'd she do that?

                    HEIDI
          Cause you upset her, that's
          why. What's wrong with you
          anyway?

He abruptly rises from his chair without
answering, the bowl of apple crumbly in his
hand.

Eating it as he moves, he heads for the kitchen
door.

INT. ENTRANCE WAY - NIGHT

He comes down the hallway, stopping, looking
up the stairs toward the bathroom and scales
above like a man who knows he is about to face
his final, ultimate moment of truth.

Still spooning the apple crumbly and ice cream
into his mouth in huge, dribbling bites, he
starts up the stairs.

INT. SECOND-FLOOR HALL - NIGHT

He crests the top of the stairs, walking down the hall to the bathroom, packing his desert away as he comes.

INT. BATHROOM - NIGHT

He stops just inside the door, facing his scale on the floor. He stares at it, trying to calm his nerves.

Putting the now empty bowl aside, and taking a deep breath, he steps onto the scale.

He waits a moment for it to settle down and than looks down at the weight counter. It reads 207. His face absolutely crumbles, and he claps a hand over his mouth in an unsuccessful attempt to stifle a scream. He staggers off the scale, and sinks into a chair before the vanity.

He stares blankly off at nothing, hardly able to move. Heidi appears in the doorway, staring in at him. He slowly looks up to meet her worried eyes. His are even more worried; in fact, they're panicked. He answers her question without her having to ask it.

                    BILLY
          Yeah, I'm still losing
          weight. The scale says I'm
          down to two-o-seven.

Heidi staggers back like she's been hit with a sledge hammer.

                    HEIDI
          Oh, Christ—

Billy whirls on her accusingly, almost screaming at her.

> BILLY
> Why didn't you tell me?
> You've seen me shrinking
> away! I didn't know! I was
> ignoring it!

> HEIDI
> I know. That's why I didn't
> want to tell you. You seemed
> so damn happy. I didn't want
> to be the one to ruin it for
> you.

> BILLY
> (bitterly)
> Oh, yeah, sure.
> (imitating her voice)
> Billy, you were great in bed
> last night and I never loved
> you more and, oh, by the
> way, something's eating you
> up inside—

> HEIDI
> (suddenly screaming)
> Stop it! Do you hear me?
> Just stop it!

> BILLY
> (a long beat, then in a
> small, ashamed voice)
> I'm sorry.

> HEIDI
> (another beat as she
> recovers, then)
> It's all right. It's hard on

all of us.
            (a beat, then)
I've talked to Mike Houston.
He says you should go to a
clinic so they can run some
metabolic tests—

                BILLY
          (cutting her off)
Tests aren't going to do any
good. Nothing is except—

He suddenly bites his tongue, stopping himself.
Heidi looks at him.

                HEIDI
Except what?

Billy stares up at her, his eyes flooding
with even more hysteria, panic, and above all
else, fear, blind, cold, gut wrenching fear.
He suddenly blurts it out.

                BILLY
The old Gypsy cursed me.

                HEIDI
          (staring at him like
              he's nuts)
What?

                BILLY
          (wildly)
Well, what other explanation
is there? Mike Houston
says nothing's wrong with
me, I eat eight thousand
calories a day, don't do any
exercise, and <u>still</u> I lose
weight! And it's all your—

He suddenly falls silent, Heidi staring at
him.

                    HEIDI
          All my what?

                    BILLY
            (a beat, then bursting
              out with it)
          Fault! There, I've said it!
          If you hadn't been doing
          that to me in the car—

                    HEIDI
            (yelling back at him)
          Billy, you were driving not
          me! Besides, if you didn't
          like what I was doing, why
          didn't you tell me to stop?
            (a beat, then
              reasserting self-
              control)
          Oh, Christ, what's wrong
          with us? We're both talking
          crazy. You've got to go to
          that clinic. Mike says the
          tests will definitely tell
          us what's wrong—

Billy abruptly rises, pushing past her out the
door.

INT. SECOND-FLOOR HALL - NIGHT

Billy strides down the hall toward the stairs.
Heidi appears from the bathroom, looking after
him.

                    HEIDI
          Billy, where are you going?

                    BILLY
          (shouting back over his
              shoulder)
     To talk to somebody who
     might believe me.

                    HEIDI
     Who?

But he doesn't reply, disappearing down the
stairs.

Heidi runs after him as Linda sticks her head
out of her door, looking after her parents.

INT. ENTRANCE WAY - NIGHT

Heidi appears at the top of the stairs.

She stares down at her husband as he slips on
his coat.

                    HEIDI
          Billy, who are you going to
          talk to?

                    BILLY
          Cary Rossington. He was in
          on it, too.

                    HEIDI
          In on what?

                    BILLY
          The cover up, for Christ
          sake. That's why the old
          Gypsy cursed me. For killing
          his wife and then covering
          it up.

                    HEIDI
          Billy, you've got to stop
          this

But Billy is no longer listening. He's reaching
for the front door, Heidi yelling after him
one last time.

                    HEIDI
          Billy!

No answer, but the slamming of the door as
Billy goes through it. Heidi stares after him,
not knowing whether to laugh or cry. Linda
appears beside her at the top of the stairs,
looking up at her mother.

                    LINDA
          What's wrong with dad?

Heidi stares at her for a moment, then suddenly
takes her in her arms, and holds her tight,
not knowing what to say.

                                        CUT TO:

EXT. JUDGE CARY ROSSINGTON'S HOUSE - NIGHT

The house is even more expensive and plush
than Billy's. He pulls up in his Jag, hopping
out and hurrying to the door.

He knocks on it.

Leda Rossington, Cary's fifty-some, patrician
wife, opens it.

She has a Martini in her hand, a very big
Martini.

                    BILLY
          Leda, is Cary—

                    LEDA
               (quickly)
          He's not here. He's,
          he's been called back to
          Minnesota. His sister is
          very ill.

                    BILLY
          That's interesting.
          Especially since Cary
          doesn't have a sister. I
          drew up his will, remember.

She stares at him, her upper lip curling like
she's just discovered a very distasteful bug
beneath her feet.

                    LEDA
          Go away, Billy. I don't want
          to answer any questions.

She starts to close the door in his face.

In desperation, Billy sweeps back his overcoat,
showing her his diminished bulk.

                    BILLY
          Look at me, Leda. I've lost
          almost a hundred pounds. A
          <u>hundred</u> pounds!

She gasps as she sees his ribs sticking out
through his shirt, but then quickly recovers.

Her voice is like a blast of Winter air.

                    LEDA

Was it the Gypsies?

                    BILLY
                 (stiffening)
          What do you know about the
          Gypsies?

                    LEDA
          Answer me first. Was it the
          Gypsies?

Billy swallows hard, then answers with a nod
of his head.

                    BILLY
          Yes. I think so. A curse.
          Something like a curse.
                 (a beat, then)
          No, not something
          like. That's bullshit
          equivocation. I think I've
          had a Gypsy curse laid on
          me.

                    LEDA
                 (a beat, then with a
                  chilling smile)
          Come in, Billy.

She steps back.

Billy enters.

She closes the door behind him.

INT. ENTRANCE WAY - NIGHT

She shoves her Martini into his hand with that
cold brittle smile of hers.

                    LEDA
          Here, you're going to need
          this.

She heads for the living room, Billy following.

The ice cubes clink against the sides of the
glass like the finger bones of the Dr. Houston
skeleton he dreamed about in Fairview.

INT. LIVING ROOM - NIGHT

He stops, the glass in his hand, watching her
mix herself a new drink at the wet bar.

                     LEDA
          He is in Minnesota, but not
          visiting relatives. He's at
          the Mayo Clinic.

                     BILLY
          The Mayo—

                     LEDA
          He's convinced it's cancer.
          Mike Houston couldn't find
          anything wrong and neither
          could the dermatologists he
          went to in The City, but
          he's still sure that's what
          it is.
               (finished making her
             drink, she turns to him)
          I was the one who remembered
          the old Gypsy, the one with
          the half-eaten nose. He
          came out of a crowd at the
          flea market in Raintree
          the weekend after your
          hearing...

Billy straightens with a dry croak, stunned by
what he's hearing.

                    BILLY
          ...and touched him.

                    LEDA
             (stopping, looking at
                    him)
          That's right. I see you've
          been through this yourself.
          Anyway Cary's convinced
          it's skin cancer because he
          couldn't let himself think
          it was anything as penny
          dreadful as a Gypsy curse.
          Of course, he wouldn't look
          in a mirror once it started.
          If he had that might have
          changed his mind.

She abruptly finishes off her drink in one
gulp.

She then goes to the bar, mixing herself a new
one.

Billy watches.

He works up his nerve to ask a question he
really doesn't want the answer to.

                    BILLY
                  (slowly)
          "Changed his mind?" Why,
          what did he look like, Leda?

Leda laughs suddenly, a high-pitched, brittle
laugh filled with kind of memories that slowly
drive one mad.

                    LEDA
          Look like? Why, Billy, I
          thought I told you or that
          you knew somehow.
               (turning to look at him)
          He's growing scales. Cary is
          growing scales.
                    (a beat, then)
          No, that's not quite right.
          His skin is <u>turning into</u>
          scales. He's become a case
          of reverse evolution, a
          sideshow freak. He is
          turning into a fucking human
          alligator!
                    (a beat, then calming
                       down)
          He chartered a plane to fly
          to Minnesota. Did I tell you
          that? Because he can't bear
          to have people look at him.
          At the end before he went,
          his hands were like claws,
          his eyes were two - two
          bright little sparks of blue
          inside these pitted scaly
          hollows, and his nose—

She finally runs down, bursting into tears.

Billy sets his drink aside and goes to her
side, reaching out to her.

                    BILLY
          Leda, I'm so sorry

She suddenly whirls on him.

Her hatred chokes her face, pure, naked,
unadorned, murderous hatred.

                    LEDA
                 (screaming)
        Don't touch me, you, you fat
        pig! If it hadn't been for
        you hitting that old lady,
        none of this would have
        happened. Do you hear me?
        It's all your fault. <u>Yours!</u>

She backs him across the room, Billy stumbling
back, horrified by her rage.

                    BILLY
        But I didn't mean to—

                    LEDA
        Who cares! It was your
        fault! <u>You</u> hit her, not Cary

Billy turns and flees for the door.

She stumbles after him, sloshing gin as she
goes.

EXT. ROSSINGTON HOUSE –NIGHT

He smashes out the front door, and leaps into
his Jag, flooding his car in his hurry to be
gone as Leda appears in her doorway

She screams at him loud enough to wake the
dead.

                    LEDA
        Come back in another couple
        of weeks, Billy! Come back
        when you've lost another
        forty or fifty pounds. I'll
        laugh and laugh and laugh—

The ignition finally catches and Billy tears
out of there, leaving a spray of gravel and a
weeping woman, suddenly very old, behind.

                              DISSOLVE TO:

EXT. FAIRVIEW MUNICIPAL COURTHOUSE - DAY (IN
BILLY'S DREAM)

Billy and Heidi break free from Judge Rossington
and Leda, leaving them behind with Police Chief
Hopley as they walk toward their car.

Suddenly Tadzu Lempke appears out of nowhere,
brushing Billy's face with his nicotine stained
fingertip and whispering to him in that voice
from beyond the grave.

                    LEMPKE
          Thinnerrrrrr—

Suddenly Hopley detaches himself from Cary
Rossington and Leda, hurrying over to confront
Lempke.

                    HOPLEY
          Hey, what are you doing
          here?

                    LEMPKE
             (smiling thinly)
          I just came to see that
          justice was done—

                              SMASH CUT TO:

INT. BILLY'S ROOM - NIGHT (BACK INTO REALITY)

Billy sits bolt upright in his bed, Heidi

asleep beside him, staring into the darkness.

His face is alive with hope.

                    BILLY
          Of course! Hopley! Hopley
          was in on it, too!

He snaps on a light, reaching for the phone.

He stops as his eyes hit the alarm clock.

Four in the morning.

Too late to call.

He relaxes.

                    BILLY
          Tomorrow. I'll see him
          tomorrow

He flicks off the light, settling back into
bed, staring up at the ceiling, totally awake.

We hear the thoughts tumbling about in his
head as he thinks.

                    BILLY (V.O.)
                 (to himself)
          But what good's Hopley
          going to do me even if he
          is cursed. He can't take it
          off. Only one person can do
          that—
                 (a beat, then)
          Lempke! I've got to find
          Lempke. It's my only chance,
          my only chance, my only—

His eyes slowly flutter closed as he finally
falls asleep.

                              DISSOLVE TO:

EXT. RIBBONMAKER LANE -DAY

A street of cute saltboxes, not as plush as
Billy's street, but still real nice.

Billy's Jag pulls to a halt in front.

INT. JAG - DAY

Billy is on his car phone, talking as he eyes
Hopley's house.

                    BILLY
          Hello, Kirk. It's Billy. I
          know this is kind of sudden,
          but I want to take a little
          time off from work—

                    PENSCHLEY (V.O.)
               (obviously thrilled by
                    the idea)
          Hey, take as much time as
          you need, Billy-boy. A
          month, two, whatever. I can
          handle the cases.

Billy's face darkens as he half mutters to
himself.

                    BILLY
          What's wrong? Don't want me
          hanging around the office
          looking the way I do?

                    PENSCHLEY (V.O.)
          What was that? What'd you
          say, Billy?

                    BILLY
          Nothing. You remember my
          accident a month ago?

                    PENSCHLEY (V.O.)
          You mean the old Gypsy
          woman?

                    BILLY
          That's right. You think you
          could use that wonderful
          detective agency of yours to
          find out where the Gypsies
          are now?

                    PENSCHLEY (V.O.)
          Hell, yeah. I told you
          they're the best in the
          business. You want the whole
          band or just one Gyp?

                    BILLY
          Just one. The husband of the
          woman I killed. His name was
          Lempke, L-e-m-p-k-e.

                    PENSCHLEY (V.O.)
          Got it. What's wrong? You
          worried about a civil suit?

                    BILLY
          No, I just want to talk to
          him, that's all. When do you
          think you'll have something
          for me?

                    PENSCHLEY (V.O.)
          Knowing these guys, in
          twenty-four hours. You take
          as much time off as you
          need, you hear me. Talk to
          you later.

The phone goes dead, Billy hanging up, muttering
angrily to himself.

                    BILLY
          Prick.

He slips out the door, slamming it behind him.

EXT. HOPLEY'S HOUSE - DAY

He walks up to Hopley's front door and starts
banging on it.

Nothing.

He lifts the mail slot and yells through it.

                    BILLY
          Hey, Duncan, it's Billy
          Halleck. I just came from
          the station house. They said
          you were home sick.
                    (no answer)
          C'mon, Duncan, I know you're
          in there!
                    (nothing but silence;
                     Billy stares at the
                       door)
          All right, don't answer me,
          but at least listen.
                    (pressing his lips to
                       the door)
          A few weeks ago I hit an old

                    Gypsy woman. Now I'm losing
                    weight and I can't stop. If
                    it keeps up, I'm going to
                    look like the Human Skeleton
                    in a carny sideshow.
                         (still no answer; Billy
                              plows on)
                    And Judge Rossington
                    presided at the hearing and
                    declared there was no case.
                    He's developed some weird
                    skin disease, and you know
                    what I think? I think we
                    were both cursed by that old
                    Gypsy. What do you think,
                    Duncan?
                         (no answer; Billy
                         presses his ear even
                         closer to the door)
                    Duncan, are you there?

A voice suddenly answers from behind the door,
thin and papery and really dreadful sounding.

                    HOPLEY (O.S.)
                    So what do you want me to do
                    about it?

Billy recoils from the door in surprise.

Recovering, he presses his lips back close to
it.

                    BILLY
                    Nothing. Only—has anything
                    happened to you?

                    HOPLEY (O.S.)
                    Why?

                    BILLY
          Because if it has, I have an
          idea of something we can do
          about it.

The lock turns. Feet can be heard shuffling
away. Billy pushes at the door. It slowly
creaks opens. He steps inside.

INT. HALL - DAY

The hallway is dark, almost pitch black. Billy
sees a bathrobe clad form disappearing into a
room at the end of the hall. He moves after
it.

INT. STUDY - DAY

It's just as dark in here, all the shades
pulled. Billy appears in the doorway, peering
inside. Duncan Hopley is hunched in a corner
behind his desk, his form cloaked in shadows,
not even his face visible. A tensor lamp sits
on the desk, shining down on the desk top, its
pool of light the only illumination.

Billy looks at Hopley, trying to see him
through the darkness.

                    BILLY
          He touched you, too, huh?

The form grunts and nods at a chair in front
of the desk. Billy sits. The form stares at
him from the darkness.

                    HOPLEY
          What's your idea?

                    BILLY
We go after him, the old
Gypsy. We ask him to take
the curse off
          (Hopley gives a short
               derisive bark of a
                    laugh)
No, wait, listen. It wasn't
my fault, damnit. My wife
was giving me a—was doing
something to me in the car
when the old woman appeared
from nowhere. That's why I
hit her—

                    HOPLEY
You were behind the wheel.
That's all the Gyp cares
about.

                    BILLY
But it was the old woman's
fault, too. She ran out of
nowhere right in front of
me—

                    HOPLEY
Did she really run, Billy?

                    BILLY
          (taken aback, a beat,
               then)
All right, she walked,
but so what? She came out
between two parked cars.
Nobody could have stopped in
time.

                    HOPLEY
What about the drinking,

Billy? How sober were you
really?

                    BILLY
Completely. So I'd had a few
drinks at the club. So what?

                    BILLY
If you'd given me the bloody
breathalizer it would have
shown I was sober—

                    HOPLEY
          (cutting him off with a
               dry chuckle)
But I didn't, did I? So I
got mine. Just like you're
going to get yours.

Billy looks up at the figure cloaked in
shadows, trying to pierce the gloom with his
eyes and failing.

                    BILLY
Got yours? What do you mean?

                    HOPLEY
You really want to see? All
right, I'll let you see.

He slowly leans forward and lifts the tensor
light so it shines directly into his face.

Billy gasps.

Hopley's face is a harsh alien landscape.
Malignant red pimples the size of tea saucers
grow out of his chin, his neck, his arms, and
the back of his hands.

Smaller eruptions rash his cheeks and forehead:
his nose is a plague of blackheads. Yellowish
pus oozes in weird channels between bulging
dunes of black ingrown beard.

Blood trickles here and there, and from the
center of it all, helplessly embedded in that
trickling red landscape, are Hopley's bulging,
trapped eyes.

Billy pales as he stares, barely restraining
the urge to gag.

                    BILLY
          Oh, Christ, Hopley, I'm
          sorry.

                    HOPLEY
          (turning the lamp away)
          Don't be. Yours is going
          slower, but you'll get there
          eventually.

                    BILLY
          Not if I get to him first.
          Sure, it was my fault, but
          it was <u>all</u> our faults,
          yours, Cary's, my wife's,
          even the old Gypsy woman.
          How can he blame any one of
          us? It was fate!

Hopley slowly claps his hands together in
sarcastic applause.

                    HOPLEY
          Great closing summation,
          Halleck. If you were in
          court, I'd vote for you.
          Only you're not in any

court. You're in front of
some wigged out ancient
Gypsy motherfucker who only
cares about one thing:
<u>revenge</u>. He wants his pound
of flesh and from the looks
of you, he's getting that
and a lot more.

                    BILLY
              (a beat, then
               helplessly)
     I, I have to try.

                   HOPLEY
              (a beat, then)
     Yeah? Then why don't you
     take this with you?

He opens a drawer and pulls out his service
revolver, pushing it across the desk to Billy.

He leans into the light with that terrible
face, his eyes alight with hatred, his voice
rising.

                   HOPLEY
     When you find the old fuck
     and he tells you to go to
     hell, why don't you kill him
     with this? And why don't
     you tell him it was me that
     gave it to you? Cause that's
     what I'd do if I could leave
     here. I'd blow his face away
     by chunks, first the eyes,
     then the mouth

Billy can't stand it anymore. He leaps out of
his chair and flees the room.

INT. HALLWAY - DAY

Billy stumbles down the hall toward the front
door, Hopley screaming after him.

                    HOPLEY (O.S.)
          Kill him, Halleck! It's the
          only satisfaction you'll
          ever get cause he's never
          going to take the curse off!
          You hear me? Never!

EXT. HOPLEY'S HOUSE - DAY

Billy shoots out the front door, slamming it
behind him, cutting off that terrible voice.

He races to his car, jumps in and takes off.

                                        CUT TO:

EXT. BILLY'S HOUSE - DAY

Billy pulls up in front of his house.

A brand new four door Lexus is parked in his
driveway next to Heidi's station wagon.

He gets out, giving it a glance on his way to
the front door.

INT. ENTRANCE WAY - DAY

Billy enters, closing the door behind him and
hanging up his coat.

Heidi appears from the living room.

                    HEIDI
        Billy, Mike Houston is here.

                    BILLY
          (giving her a dark look)
        I don't have to ask why, do
        I?

He goes into the living room to face the doctor.

INT. LIVING ROOM - DAY

Dr. Houston rises with a drink in his hand and
a broad, professional smile smeared across his
face.

                  DR. HOUSTON
          Hi, Billy, Heidi tells me
          you're still losing weight.

Billy goes to the bar and pops a beer, turning
to face him with a broad, jovial smile of his
own.

He makes like a golf pro giving his handicap.

                    BILLY
          Broke below two hundred this
          morning. One ninety-eight to
          be exact.

Houston just stares at him poker-faced, the
irony lost on him.

                  DR. HOUSTON
          I know how scared you must
          be, Billy, but if you'll
          just—

                    BILLY
                (losing the smile)
            Cut the crap, Mike. She told
            you about the Gypsy curse,
            didn't she?

                    DR. HOUSTON
                (taken aback)
            Well, yes, she did.
                (then hurriedly)
            But I think such thoughts
            are perfectly understandable
            under the circumstances

                    BILLY
                (bitterly)
            It's all in my head, right,
            Mike?

Houston gives Billy's disappearing body and
pallid, sweaty face a good glance, then shakes
his head.

                    DR. HOUSTON
            No, not this. There has to
            be a medical reason. That's
            why I want you to go to the
            clinic

                    BILLY
            Mike, new tests aren't going
            to show anymore than the old
            tests. Nothing medical is
            wrong with me.

                    DR. HOUSTON
            Look, Billy, I don't think
            you understand. If you keep
            losing like this it will
            only be a matter of days

until you get lesions in the
mouth, heart palpitations,
pneumonia, you name it.
You're also causing Heidi
a great deal of undue
emotional stress—

                BILLY
            (exploding)
Heidi? What about me?
What about the stress I'm
feeling? I'm the one who's
dying, for Christ sake! Not
her!

                HEIDI
Billy—

                BILLY
    (losing it, whirling on
            her)
Shut up! If it weren't for
you I wouldn't be in this
situation!

                HEIDI
    (rolling her eyes at
            him)
Oh, God, not that again.

                BILLY
Yes, that again, and if that
isn't enough, you convinced
me not to tell the truth
in that hearing. If it
hadn't been for you, I would
have told Rossington what
happened.
            (beat)
I would have told him

Hopley didn't give me a
breathalizer. I wouldn't
still be losing weight. I
wouldn't be <u>thinner</u>!

                    HEIDI
          (exploding right back)
     All right, I made a mistake,
     but you were the one who
     lied, not me. Besides, it
     doesn't make any difference
     now. You have to go to the
     clinic.

                    BILLY
     For Christ sake, I can't go
     to any clinic! Don't
     you understand what's
     happening to me yet? I'm
     losing four pounds a day
     no matter how much or how
     little I eat. How much time
     does that give me to find
     the Gypsy? A week, two
     before I'm some kind of
     living skeleton that doesn't
     even have the strength to
     get out of bed and go the
     bathroom on his own.
               (to Houston)
     That's why I can't go to
     some clinic, Mike. I don't
     have the time. I'm going
     to be dead soon, dead of
     starvation!

He whirls, heading for the entrance way.

Heidi and Houston rush after him.

INT. ENTRANCE WAY -DAY

Billy starts up the stairs, Houston and Heidi
behind him.

Houston shouts up after him.

                    DR. HOUSTON
          Look, Billy, let me give you
          something to help you relax

                    BILLY
               (stopping and whirling
                   on him)
          Godamnit, you still don't
          believe me about the curse,
          do you? Well, why don't you
          ask Cary Rossington? Talk
          to his wife. Call Duncan
          Hopley. That's all I ask.
          Just talk to them. They
          can tell you all about it,
          believe you me.

He turns and disappears up the stairs. Heidi
bursts into tears. Houston puts a comforting
arm around her.

INT. BILLY'S ROOM - DAY

Billy slams into his room, standing there,
trying to gather his wits.

The phone suddenly rings. It makes him jump
ten feet. He snatches it up.

                    BILLY
          Yes.

                    PENSCHLEY (V.O.)
          Hey, Billy-boy, the agency
          got a lead on him for you.
          Did I tell you they were the
          greatest or what?

                    BILLY
          How'd they do it so fast?

                    PENSCHLEY (V.O.)
          Computers. This Lempke
          family have left a paper
          trail of criminal charges
          behind them a blind man
          could follow.

                    BILLY
          Family?

                    PENSCHLEY (V.O.)
          Yeah, they're all inter-
          related. Remember that
          Gypsy piece of ass? She's
          his granddaughter and his
          grandson's with him, too. He
          was the one with the bowling
          pins.

                    BILLY
             (grabbing pen and paper)
          Give me what you got.

                    PENSCHLEY (V.O.)
          They went from here to
          Raintree. From Raintree to
          Greeno, and from there to
          Lincoln, Mass—

                    BILLY
          They're heading North along

the sea coast.

                    PENSCHLEY
          Sure looks like it.

                    BILLY
          You sure this is the same
          group every time?

                    PENSCHLEY (V.O.)
          Positive. The agency made
          some calls to the local
          constabularies. For some
          reason people remember the
          hundred-year old guy with
          the big black cancer in the
          middle of his face. Computer
          says they follow the same
          pattern every year. Usually
          hit Boothbay and they're
          always in Bar Harbor for
          Labor Day. Hang on for a
          week and you can meet 'em
          there.

Billy looks at his reflection in the mirror on
the back of the closet door.

He looks ghastly, all sallow skin and sharp
bone, his clothes hanging off him.

He gives his reflection a gallows grin and
murmurs to himself.

                    BILLY
          For some reason, I don't
          think I have the time—

                    PENSCHLEY (V.O.)
          Huh? What'd you say, Billy?

                    BILLY
          Nothing, Kirk. You got any
          mug shots?

                    PENSCHLEY
          Yeah, a ton. You want me to
          send them over?

                    BILLY
          No. FedEx them to the
          Portsmith Hilton, okay. I'll
          be there tonight. And Kirk,
          thanks for all the help.

                    PENSCHLEY (V.O.)
          Hey, don't thank me. Thank
          the Dumbarton Detective
          Agency.

He hangs up, Billy staring straight ahead, his
forehead creasing as he worries out loud, his
eyes flooding with incipient panic.

                    BILLY
          I have to do this on my own.
          But how? What if I can't
          find them

And then he remembers something, a voice in
his head suddenly as clear as a bell.

                    GINELLI (V.O.)
          Anything you need, Billy,
          you just ask! You hear me?
          You just ask!

Billy perks up, slowly smiling.

                    BILLY
          Of course, Ginelli—

He hears the front door suddenly open below, breaking his reverie.

He looks out the window. Below he can see his wife and Dr. Houston in a heated discussion.

He says something.

She nods agreement.

They get into their separate cars and drive away.

Billy stares after them for a moment, and then suddenly launches himself into action, grabbing a suitcase from the closet and beginning to hurriedly pack.

                                        CUT TO:

EXT. THREE BROTHER'S RESTAURANT, HARTFORD, CONNECTICUT - DAY

Billy's Jag sits in front of an up scale harbor side restaurant.

INT. RESTAURANT - DAY

A MAÎTRE D that looks more like a thug conducts Billy through the dimly lit restaurant to Ginelli's booth.

The Mafioso looks up from his plate of steaming pasta with a grin.

                        GINELLI
                Have a seat, counselor. Nice
                to see you.

Billy slips into the plush booth opposite
Ginelli.

He looks around, his eyes probing the gloom.

More thugs can be dimly glimpsed, keeping watch
over their boss from a discrete distance.

                    BILLY
          You own this place?

                    GINELLI
                  (nodding)
          I hate making reservations.
          You lost some weight?

                    BILLY
             (trying to grin and
              barely making it)
          Noticeable even in this
          light, huh?

                    GINELLI
          It don't look so good on
          you. I'll get you some
          pasta, fatten you up.

He raises a hand to signal to one of his men,
but Billy stops him.

                    BILLY
          I haven't got time, Richie.
          I've gotta be moving on.

                    GINELLI
                (really surprised)
          You? No time to eat? You
          must be in real trouble, my
          friend.

                    BILLY
A little. I had a car
accident

                    GINELLI
I heard. Some old Gypsy,
right?

                    BILLY
              (looking at him in
                  surprise)
How'd you know?

                    GINELLI
I keep my ear to the ground.
It's important in my line
of work. What's wrong? One
of the relatives leaning on
you?

                    BILLY
Something like that?

                    GINELLI
And you want me to make 'em
back off?

                    BILLY
No, not yet. It's just that
if—if I'm not able to work
things out by myself—maybe
you could help me?

                    GINELLI
Hey, you did me a favor.
A big favor. And Richie
Ginelli doesn't forget
favors. Ever. You need help,
you give me a ring.

Billy smiles at him. A big smile. Full of relief. He leans across the booth, giving Richie a hug.

                    BILLY
          Thanks, Richie. You don't
          know what this means to me.

                    GINELLI
                (smiling back)
          Hey, I haven't done anything
          for you yet. See how you
          feel after I do. Then thank
          me.

                                        CUT TO:

EXT. MYSTIC SAVINGS - DAY

In Mystic, Connecticut. Billy's Jag is parked out front.

INT. MYSTIC SAVINGS - DAY

Billy stands in front of an American Express Traveller's Cheque dispenser, sticking in one AmEx credit card after another.

The Traveler's Cheques fan-fold out in a pile on the counter.

                    BILLY (V.O.)
          Dear Heidi, By the time you
          read this, I'll be gone. I
          don't know for how long—

                                        CUT TO:

EXT. ROUTE 95 - DAY

The Jag crosses the beautiful border between
Connecticut and Rhode Island.

INT. JAG - DAY

Billy drives, the thoughts tumbling around in
his head.

                    BILLY (V.O.)
          —but I hope when I come back
          all of this will be over.
          This nightmare we've been
          living with.

                                        CUT TO:

EXT. MACDONALD'S, WOBURN, MASSACHUSETTS - DAY

Billy has stopped at a MacDonald's just
underneath the State House dome.

He eats outside, sitting in the open door of
his car, his face thin and haggard, and his
clothes falling off him.

He stuffs one quarter-pounder after another
into his mouth, tastelessly chewing, the food
dribbling unnoticed out of his mouth. People
walk by, giving him a wide berth.

                    BILLY (V.O.)
          I know it's hard for you to
          believe, but I have been
          cursed and I've got to find
          the old Gypsy who did it.

                                        CUT TO:

INT. FACTORY OUTLET CLOTHING STORE, REVERE,
MASS. - DAY

At the check out counter, Billy is buying
the next smaller size clothing. He pays by
Traveller's Cheque.

                    BILLY (V.O.)
          If I can get him to take
          the curse off, we can,
          hopefully, all go back to
          the life we had before any
          of this happened.

Finished paying, Billy walks toward the door.

EXT. PARKING LOT - DAY

Billy opens his trunk, dumping the new clothes
in. He slams it shut and climbs behind the
wheel. His car pulls out of the lot and onto
the street, accelerating away.

                    BILLY (V.O.)
          But if I can't, and
          something should happen to
          me, I want you to know how
          much I love you.

                                        CUT TO:

EXT. PORTSMOUTH, NEW HAMPSHIRE - DAY

Billy's Jag approaches the bridge, the signs
reading, "I-95, North, Maine, Prince Edward's
Island, The Maritimes." Billy takes the exit
ramp into Portsmouth proper.

INT. JAG - DAY

The thoughts continue to tumble through his
head.

                    BILLY (V.O.)
          Losing weight like this
          brings out the worst in me
          - down to one eighty -nine
          this morning - and sometimes
          I wish you were down here in
          hell with me.

                                        CUT TO:

EXT. PORTSMOUTH HILTON - NIGHT

Billy drives into the underground parking
garage.

INT. RECEPTION DESK - NIGHT

Billy signs in and is handed a Fedex envelope.

He opens it and pulls out the mug shots of
Tadzu, Gina, and Gabe Lempke.

He stares at them, especially the photo of
Tadzu and his malignant nose.

                    BILLY (V.O.)
          The truth is you're
          partially responsible for
          that old woman's death, too,
          and you know it. Whatever
          happens to me, we both
          deserve it.

                                        CUT TO:

INT. BILLY'S HOTEL ROOM -NIGHT

Billy sits at the desk, composing his letter.

> BILLY (V.O.)
> But mostly I'm glad you've
> been spared. Because I love
> you, Heidi, you and Linda.
> Tell her how much I love
> her, too. Love, Billy—

Finished he slips the letter into an envelope, addresses it, and rises, his bulky terry cloth robe flapping open, revealing his rapidly diminishing form beneath. He catches sight of himself in the bathroom mirror. He still has some meat on him, but sagging discolored flesh droops off his body everywhere, arms, stomach, butt, the result of a rapid, inexorable weight loss. He looks gravely ill, hallows beginning to appear in his face, haunted eyes looking out from within deep, dark circles. He collapses on the bed in tears, the letter held in one hand.

                                        CUT TO:

EXT. SEASIDE TOWN - NIGHT

Small, tawdry, cheap, and probably a lot of fun. The Jag cruises down a two-lane road between a municipal parking lot and a pier loaded with rides and arcades.

INT. JAG - NIGHT

Billy suddenly sees something, the vehicles from the Gypsy caravan, all parked in a group in the municipal lot.

EXT. PARKING LOT - NIGHT

Billy swings the Jag into the lot, backing into a space so fast he scrapes bumpers. He gets out, wearing a blue Polyester outfit from the factory outlet.

He takes a deep breath of air, slowly expelling it.

                    BILLY
          I smell you, old man.

From across the way, a high-pitched voices crackles:

                    GINA (O.S.)
          Come one, come all, let
          the Gypsy Chief Guess Your
          Weight and Tell Your Fate!

Billy turns in that direction, hurrying across the road onto the pier.

EXT. PIER - SEASIDE FAIR - NIGHT

Billy pushes through the crowd, stopping in front of a Test-Your-Strength platform with inset floor scales.

Lempke sits in a chair beside Gina as she touts his skills to the crowd.

                    GINA
          Let him guess your weight!
          If he's off by more than
          five pounds—

Billy comes closer, Gina, as if expecting him,

suddenly turns and grins right at him.

                    GINA
          —then you get the doll of
          your choice!

She nods at the three rows of dolls behind
her: one, an Acne-Atrocity doll for Duncan
Hopley, the doll's face the color of a dropped
pizza, an Alligator-Boy doll for Rossington,
a green scaled doll standing upright on two
legs, and finally a Skeleton-Scout for Billy,
a doll that looks like it was modeled after a
starving Ethiopian.

Lempke rises to his feet beside Gina, staring
hungrily at Billy.

                    LEMPKE
          Don't bother to step on the
          scales, mister. I can tell
          your weight from right here.
          One seventy-six, right?
          But next week it'll be one
          forty-four and the week
          after that? Well, we don't
          even want to think about
          that, do we, mister?

                    GINA
               (grinning at Billy)
          You lose, mister, but have a
          prize anyway!

She tosses Billy a skeleton doll, Billy blocking
it with a forearm, and looking up to see her
pulling her slingshot and ball bearings from
a fold of her skirt. He whirls, taking off at
a shambling run. Gina leaps off the platform,
dashing after him, Lempke left behind on the

platform, laughing and laughing.

EXT. TWO-LANE ROAD - NIGHT

Billy dashes across the road for the parking lot, Gina in close pursuit.

His breath comes in ragged gasps now, his face sheened with sweat. He can't keep it up, not in his weakened condition. From the corner of his eye he sees her stop, raising that deadly slingshot.

A Fairview black and white suddenly screeches to a halt in front of him.

The passenger door is flung open, Duncan Hopley staring out at him with his ruined, dripping face. He screams at Billy.

                    HOPLEY
          Get in!

Billy hops in the front seat, slamming the door shut just as a ball bearing smashes into the window, shattering the glass into a million spidery cracks. The black and white takes off, roaring down the road.

INT. FAIRVIEW POLICE CAR - DAY

Billy turns to Hopley, nodding back toward the pier.

                    BILLY
          Thank God, you decided to
          come. Lempke's back there.
          We have to get him alone—

                    HOPLEY
          The time for talk is gone,
          Billy-boy. Long gone, at
          least for me.

                    BILLY
          What do you mean?

Hopley suddenly pulls his service revolver
without answering, jams it into his temple,
and pulls the trigger. The side of his head
blows off, splattering Billy with blood and
gore. Billy screams as Hopley slumps over his
wheel, the car racing ahead, out of control.

Billy looks out the front window. They are
speeding directly toward a huge eighteen-
wheeler with "Danger, Highly Flammable" signs
stuck all over it.

Billy screams again and lunges for the wheel,
trying to shove Hopley's body out of the way.

EXT. TWO-LANE ROAD - NIGHT

Too late. The cop car slams into the eighteen-
wheeler, both of them going up in the biggest,
fieriest explosion you've ever seen.

                                   SMASH CUT TO:

INT. HOTEL ROOM - DAY (BACK INTO REALITY)

Billy snaps bolt upright in his bed with a
scream, his face and bony, trembling body
covered with sweat.

He's no longer in the Portsmouth Hilton; this
is another hotel and he's lost more weight,

easily another thirty pounds.

He's starting to look a lot like the doll in his nightmare. He reaches for the phone, dialing a number with shaking hands.

Heidi answers on the other end of the line.

Super up "EIGHT DAYS LATER."

>   HEIDI (V.O.)
>   Yes.

>   BILLY
>   Heidi, did you or Mike talk
>   to Hopley?

>   HEIDI (V.O.)
>   Billy, where are you—

>   BILLY
>   (CUTTING HER OFF)
>   Just answer the question,
>   damnit!

>   HEIDI (V.O.)
>   Duncan Hopley committed
>   suicide yesterday. Shot
>   himself with his revolver.

Billy rolls over in bed, hopelessly looking up at the ceiling.

>   BILLY
>   Oh, my God—
>   (a beat, then back into
>   the phone as he sits up)
>   Heidi, I need help. I'm down
>   to one fifty-three—

                    HEIDI (V.O.)
          Oh, Billy, please, come
          home—

                    BILLY
                  (EXPLODING)
          For Christ sake, don't you
          believe me yet? Didn't
          someone see Hopley's face?

                    HEIDI (V.O.)
          Mike did. After what you
          said he went over to the
          house with the coroner. He
          said it was just a bad case
          of acne, Billy, that's all.

                    BILLY
                  (stunned)
          It couldn't be, it just
          couldn't be...

                    HEIDI (V.O)
          Billy, Mike's not going to
          lie about it.

Billy lets the phone dangle from his suddenly
limp hand, staring off at nothing, mumbling
to himself.

                    BILLY
          Of course. It's like in
          the werewolf movies. The
          werewolf always returns to
          normal when he's dead.
                  (back into reality)
          Heidi, what about Leda
          Rossington? Did you talk to
          her?

                    HEIDI (V.O.)
          Right after you left. She
          denies ever having seen you
          that night.

                    BILLY
          Of course, she would. She
          hates me, but maybe Cary
          doesn't. What about Cary?
          Have you talked to him?

                    HEIDI (V.O.)
          He's dead, too. He jumped
          out of a window at the Mayo
          Clinic.

                    BILLY
          Well, doesn't that prove
          anything? They're both dead,
          for God's sake!

                    HEIDI (V.O.)
          Mike says it's perfectly
          understandable. Hopley was a
          cop. Cops always have high
          suicide rates, and Leda
          says Cary was dying of skin
          cancer. Billy, you have to
          go to that clinic—

Billy hangs up on her, staring hopelessly at
his emaciated form in the closet mirror.

                    BILLY
          Well, I know how to gain the
          weight back now, don't I?

He puts a finger to his temple and mimes
blowing out his brains. He seems to find this
very amusing because he starts to laugh. He

keeps on laughing until he collapses on the bed in tears.

                                    CUT TO:

EXT. PIER - SEASIDE FAIR - NIGHT

Billy pulls into the municipal parking lot, getting out of his car and staring at the rides and arcades. It's exactly like in his dreams. Super up "TWO DAYS LATER" as he looks around, mumbling to himself.

                    BILLY
          You've been calling to me,
          haven't you, old man? You
          want me to find you—

Shaking his head, he starts walking toward the pier.

EXT. PIER - NIGHT

Billy walks through the arcades and rides, stopping at a Guess Your Weight booth. No Mr. Skeleton doll, just the usual Taiwanese trash. He continues down the pier, passing the Freak Tent with its poster of the Skeleton Man next to Mr. Colossus, heading for the Seven Seas Cocktail Lounge at the end of the pier.

INT. SEVEN SEAS LOUNGE - NIGHT

This is strictly a locals hangout. Billy enters, blinking his eyes to adjust them to the lack of light. He heads for the nearest drinker at the bar, an OLD MAN who looks like he is on his last legs. Billy shoves the mug shots of Tadzu Lempke under his nose.

                    BILLY
          Could you help me. I'm
          looking for someone. A
          Gypsy. Name's Tadzu Lempke—

The old man just shakes his head without
glancing at the pictures, ignoring Billy.
Farther down the bar, another old man turns to
him. His name is ENDERS and he looks like his
last legs gave out long ago.

                    ENDERS
          Teddy? You mean Teddy
          Lempke?

Billy hurries to his side, staring at him
anxiously.

                    BILLY
          You know him?

                    ENDERS
          Maybe. Big hole right here?

He points to the side of his nose. Billy nods,
excitement and hope flooding his eyes as he
flashes the mug shots. Enders takes a glance
and nods.

                    ENDERS
          Yeah, sure, that's him. He
          and his tribe were here a
          couple of days ago. Hadn't
          seen him since I worked
          the Ferris wheel, ten,
          maybe twenty years ago.
          Then suddenly there he was,
          standing right in front of
          me. Hadn't changed a wink
          except for that nose of his.

Enders finishes off his beer. The BARTENDER, a big, beefy man instantly appears, setting another beer in front of Enders.

He looks at Billy inquiringly, but Billy shakes his head, paying for Enders' beer.

His eyes never leave this old man whose last legs gave out long ago.

The bartender retreats to the end of the bar, keeping an eye on Billy. Enders is still locked into his memories, tears popping into his eyes.

                    ENDERS
          You know what he said to
          me? Said "Say hello to your
          wife from Teddy." Told him
          my wife was dead, and he
          just grinned and said not to
          worry, that I'd be seeing
          her soon. Funny thing is,
          I think the son-of-a-bitch
          meant it.

Enders tries to repress a shiver and fails. The bartender reappears, looming over Enders protectively as he looks at Billy.

                    BARTENDER
          Maybe you'd better move on,
          mister. You look like bad
          luck waiting for a place to
          happen.

                    BILLY
          Just a second, please.
               (back to Enders)
          Did you see where the

Gypsies went when they left
here?

                    ENDERS
          Sure did. I was watching
          them. Out Route Twenty-Seven
          and then right on One.

                    BILLY
          Thanks. Thanks a lot—

Billy stumbles toward the door, Enders suddenly
turning and yelling after him.

                    ENDERS
          Be careful, mister. Teddy
          knows you're coming or I
          wouldn't be here talking
          to you. Damn Gyp knows
          everything!

                              DISSOLVE TO:

EXT. HIGHWAY 1 - NIGHT

Billy pulls his car to a halt on the soft
shoulder. He gets out, staring down at the
gully below.

The Gypsies are camped there, all the scruffy
vehicles pulled in a circle around a huge,
roaring fire. Billy murmurs to himself.

Super up "THREE DAYS LATER."

                    BILLY
          Here I am, Lempke. Ready or
          not.

Taking a deep breath, he begins a slow walk

down the slope toward the gully below.

EXT. GYPSY CAMP - NIGHT

The Gypsies sit around in their lawn chairs, the women pasting Green Stamps, the men drinking and laughing, the children practicing picking pockets. A huge fire burns in the middle. Billy suddenly appears between two vehicles, slowly walking toward the fire. As he passes, people stop talking, the entire camp slowly falling silent as they turn to watch him.

Billy stops in the middle, staring about him at the silent faces. An old woman darning a sweater forks the sign of the evil eye at him. Others join her. Gina suddenly appears on the opposite side of the fire, staring at Billy. He stares back as she yells over her shoulder.

                    GINA
          Ta mig, Mamma! Va dybbuk!

Tadzu Lempke appears out of the darkness behind her, Gabe behind him. The old man stops, staring at Billy, seemingly totally unsurprised to see him there. Gina whirls back to Billy, screaming at him.

                    GINA
          You no understand our lingo,
          mister? I say you kill my
          grandma! I say you are a
          demon and we should kill
          you!

She suddenly leaps forward, spitting right in Billy's face.

Billy stands there, letting the warm white

spittle run down his chin, looking back at her.

                    BILLY
      I'm not a dybbuk. Not a
      demon, not a monster. What
      you see is all I am.

He raises his arms, his long overcoat flapping open, revealing a t-shirt and shorts beneath, and beneath that the skeleton of a body, hardly any skin left on him at all. Back lit by the fire, he looks like a huge, malnourished, white moth. Lempke steps forward, staring at Billy.

                  LEMPKE
      What you are is what you
      deserve to be, what I made
      you. You know what we
      call you in our language?
      "Skumade igenom. It mean
      "White Man From Town," but
      it also mean like it sound.
      Ignorant scum. Go now, White
      Man. Go back to your town.
      Our business is done.

He starts to turn away, but Billy suddenly steps forward, screaming at him.

                  BILLY
      No, it is _not_ done! I
      haven't gone through all
      this, lost all this weight,
      traveled all these miles
      to have you suddenly turn
      and walk away. You put this
      curse on me. I want you to
      take it off.

Lempke stops, turning back to face him.

                    LEMPKE
          Why? You kill my wife, you
          walk away. Happen all the
          time to us. We go into
          towns, we only Gypsies,
          they do whatever they want
          to us. Filthy Gypsies, they
          say, who care about filthy
          Gypsies? Well, I care and I
          take care of it. Now leave
          us.

Billy steps forward, pleading with the old man.

                    BILLY
          But it wasn't my fault.
          My wife was, was doing
          something to me in the car—

                    LEMPKE
          I know what she do to you.
          You think I not see? I am
          Tadzu Lempke, leader of the
          Gypsies. I have the gift of
          second sight!

The Gypsies nod and murmur assent among themselves. Billy ignores them, his eyes drilling into Lempke.

                    BILLY
          All right, she shouldn't
          have been going down on
          me in the car. It was my
          fault. I let her. But your
          wife walked out between two
          parked cars. There was no

way I could have seen her.
Nobody could have. Don't you
understand? What you've done
to me isn't fair. It isn't
just!

Lempke stares at Billy for a long moment, his
face filling with a rage all his own.

He suddenly steps forward, screaming at him.

                    LEMPKE
          I not curse you for killing
          my wife. I curse you for
          getting off! No trial, no
          inquest, not even—what
          you call it—a suspended
          license. Is that fair? Was
          that your justice? You use
          your influence, white man's
          influence, to escape what
          was right. So I use Gypsy
          justice. It not like white
          man's laws. It simple. Blood
          for blood. Like this!

Gabe and the other man stop, letting Billy go
and stepping back, suddenly fearful.

Lempke looks at Billy, that same fear in his
eyes now.

These people believe in curses and with good
reason and Billy knows it.

He raises his thin wasted hands up to either
side of his face, splaying the fingers like
some talk show host asking the audience for
their applause.

                    BILLY
          You think men like me don't
          have the power to curse?
          We have the power. We're
          good at cursing once we get
          started, old man. Don't make
          me start.

He turns, beginning to point a finger at Lempke.
Gina suddenly steps forward with a scream of
fear, sweeping the slingshot up, drawing the
cradle back, and releasing all in one smooth
gesture. A liquid gleam streaks through the
air, a ball bearing, and tears right through
the middle of Billy's open palm. Billy slowly
turns to look at it in shock. He has a huge
hole right in the center of his hand. He can
see Gina and Lempke staring at him through it,
the firelight flickering on the other side.
Then the pain hits him. He doubles over with a
shriek, grabbing his bleeding hand, the blood
running down the front of his coat. Gina steps
forward, screaming at him.

                    GINA
          Enkelt! Get out of here,
          eyelak! Get out of here,
          killing bastard!

Billy slowly rises, everyone in the circle,
Gabe, Gina, and Lempke falling silent to watch
him. Staring directly at Lempke, Billy raises
his injured hand and slowly closes it into a
fist. His face grimaces in pain, but he makes
it, squeezing hard. Blood runs from between
the fingers, dripping on the ground.

                    BILLY
          The curse from the white
          man is on you, Mr. Lempke.
          They don't write about it in

               books, but I'm telling you—
               it is on you!

His eyes suddenly roll back in his head, and
he faints, his Mr. Skeleton man body falling
across the roaring fire, sending sparks
shooting high into the black night sky.

                                    DISSOLVE TO:

INT. MOTEL - NIGHT

A cheap motel room. Billy sits bare chested in
a chair, his body shrunken and wasted, every
rib sticking out, his eyes sick and feverish.

He has a wet towel wrapped around his injured
hand.

It is soaked with blood.

He is on the phone, listening to it ring on
the other end as he croaks to himself.

                    BILLY
          C'mon—

A voice suddenly answers.

                    MAÎTRE D (V.O.)
          Three Brother's Restaurant.
          Our specialties tonight are
          linguine with Marinara sauce

                    BILLY
               (interrupting)
          This is Billy Halleck. Let
          me speak to Mr. Ginelli,
          please.

                    MAÎTRE D (V.O.)
              Who did you say's calling?

                         BILLY
              Halleck, Billy Halleck.

The man abruptly drops the phone, silence
ensuing. Then a familiar voice comes on the
line, obviously happy to hear from him.

                      GINELLI (V.O.)
                 Billy! How you doing,
                 counselor? Gain any weight
                 back yet?

Billy stares at himself in the closet mirror.
If he had the energy his eyes would widen in
terror. He's gone beyond Mr. Skeleton man.

The only thing left with any flesh on him
are his legs and it looks like the curse is
starting on them.

The rest of him is just a hundred and thirty
some odd pounds of skin and bone.

He slowly shakes his head.

                         BILLY
                 No, I'm afraid not, Richie.
                 In fact, things aren't going
                 very well at all.

                      GINELLI (V.O.)
                 That time has come, huh?

                         BILLY
                 Yeah, it's come, Richie. I'm
                 hurt. I need a doctor. Bad.

                    GINELLI (V.O.)
                 (concern flooding his
                        voice)
                 Where are you?

                       BILLY
                 Frenchman's Motel. Boothbay
                 Harbor, Maine. Room twenty-
                 one.

                    GINELLI (V.O.)
                 Okay, you stay right there,
                 you hear. I'll have someone
                 there by morning. He's not
                 a doctor, but he's pretty
                 close.

                       BILLY
                 Thanks, Richie. Thanks a
                 lot.

                    GINELLI (V.O.)
                 Hey, what are friends for?

He hangs up, Billy slowly doing the same.
Then the pain and exhaustion, his skeletal
condition, all overcome him and he passes out
on the bed, his hand wrapped in the blood
soaked towel hanging over the side of the bed.

It slowly begins to drip on the cheap puke
colored carpet.

                                         CUT TO:

EXT. FRENCHMAN'S BAY MOTEL - DAY

An anonymous in-season place with double-
decked wings of identical rooms.

Billy's Jag stands in the parking lot.

Next to it is an idling taxi, the driver leaning on it, leafing through a newspaper.

He glances toward one of the rooms on the lower level.

INT. BILLY'S ROOM - DAY

FANDER, Ginelli's "almost doctor," unwraps the bloody towel from Billy's hand.

Fander is a small man, prematurely grey. He works out of a country doctor's bag, gauzes, disinfectants and scissors laid out neatly on the bed.

Finished cleaning the wound, he can't resist the opportunity to raise Billy's hand and peer through the hole at him.

                    FENDER
          A ball bearing, huh? That's
          a first for me.

                    BILLY
                (numbly)
          I never felt this kind of
          pain before.

                    FANDER
          There's a reason for that.
          I worked on cadavers in med
          school that looked healthier
          than you.

                    BILLY
          Can you give me something?

                    FANDER
          Codeine'll put you in a
          coma. Darvon'll send you
          into cardiac arrhythmia.
          Looks like I just flew a
          hundred miles to prescribe a
          grain and a half of Empirin.

He goes through his bag, coming up with a
bottle of pills.

                    FANDER
          And these are mine, but you
          need 'em more. Potassium
          tablets.

                    BILLY
          Are they gonna help the
          pain?

                    FANDER
          No, but they're gonna help
          you not go into cardiac
          arrest. Do yourself a favor
          - give up diet sodas.

He gets up, inadvertently brushing against
Billy's newly bandaged hand. Billy howls in
pain, almost passing out. Fander ignores him,
packing his little black bag.

                    FANDER
          Oh, I almost forgot. You're
          gonna have a visitor
          tomorrow.

                    BILLY
          Who?

Fander heads for the door, ignoring the

question.

                    FANDER
          Take that Empirin and get
          some rest or you're not
          gonna have the strength to
          answer the door.

He lets himself out without another word,
Billy staring after him.

                                   TIME CUT TO:

INT. MOTEL ROOM - ANOTHER DAY

Billy sleeps on the rumpled bed. He's thrown
a light blanket over himself. It does nothing
to hide his bony frame.

There's a loud pounding on the door.

Billy tries to rise, but doesn't make it. He
yells at the door, his voice hoarse and thin.

                    BILLY
          Who, who is it?

                    GINELLI (O.S.)
          Billy, open the door, you
          asshole. It's me, Richie.

Billy finally makes it to the door and opens
it. Richie Ginelli stands there in his tailored
suit, a Tupperware container in one hand, a
bottle of Chivas in the other.

He stares at Billy, hardly able to believe his
eyes. He slowly shakes his head.

                    GINELLI
          You shoulda called me
          earlier, Billy. A lot
          earlier.
                    (he holds out the
                     container)
          Cannoli. I had 'em made
          special for you. Very
          fattening.

Billy takes the container, Ginelli entering
and closing the door behind him.

Billy smiles at him, hardly able to believe
his eyes.

                    BILLY
          I didn't expect you to come
          yourself, Richie.

                    GINELLI
                    (smiling)
          Yeah? Well, friends deserve
          personal attention. Know
          what I mean?
                    (holding up the bottle
                     of Chivas)
          Wanna deaden your gums?

                    BILLY
                    (shaking his head)
          Think I'll stick to my
          Empirin. I'm really glad to
          see you, but I don't know
          what you're gonna be able to
          do.

Ginelli pours a shot into a motel room glass
and throws himself on one of the single beds.
He smiles up at Billy.

                    GINELLI
          You let me be the judge of
          that. Now start talking and
          don't stop till you've told
          me everything.

                                        CUT TO:

EXT. HARDWARE STORE - BOOTHBAY HARBOR - DAY

An up scale store for people who like to buy
the best in nuts and bolts.

INT. HARDWARE STORE - DAY

Billy skulks in the aisles, trying not to be
seen by the other customers. He wears layers of
clothes, double shirts and trousers, anything
to add to his non-existent bulk.

At the register, Ginelli pays for two cardboard
boxes of stuff with crisp fifties. The GIRL
CLERK takes the bills, nodding at Billy as she
speaks in a low voice.

                    GIRL CLERK
          Hey, mister, your friend—he
          a long distance runner or is
          he, you know, sick?

Ginelli collects his change, picks up the
boxes, and flashes her a smile, showing off a
couple of grand of orthodontia work.

                    GINELLI
          He's a picky eater.

He heads for the door, Billy tagging along
with a lowered head.

EXT. STREET - DAY

They stop by Billy's Jag, Billy buying a newspaper from a vending machine.

He grabs a couple of copies, throwing a glance at Ginelli. He's putting the boxes in a trunk already full with grocery bags.

                    BILLY
          What is all that stuff?

                    GINELLI
          Tools of the trade.

They climb into the car.

INT. JAG - DAY

Billy starts wadding up the newspaper and shoving it under his shirt and down his trousers. Ginelli watches.

                    GINELLI
          What're you doing?

                    BILLY
          Trying to be inconspicuous.

                    GINELLI
                  (laughing)
          Hate to tell you. It's not
          working.

Billy stops, looking at him. He breaks into laughter, too, but it quickly turns into a coughing jag. Ginelli stares at him worriedly, starts the car, and takes off.

                                        CUT TO:

INT. MOTEL ROOM - NIGHT

Ginelli is on the phone, his face darkening as
he listens. He doesn't like what he's hearing.

INT. BATHROOM - NIGHT

Billy steps onto the scale, his body draped in
a heavy terry cloth bathrobe, a box of Vanilla
Wafers in one hand. Ginelli enters, peering
down at the numbers on the scale. They read
122.

Ginelli takes off Billy's robe, revealing a
body that would give even a mother nightmares.
It is all bone held together by flesh stretched
so taut it looks like it will tear at any
second. Bones pop out everywhere.

Billy, indeed, at last looks like Mr. Skeleton
Man.

Ginelli holds out his hand, snapping his
fingers. Billy gives him the cookie box.

The two men watch as the scale drops to 119.

Billy's face falls with it.

                    BILLY
          Yeah, who was I kidding.

                    GINELLI
              (a beat, then)
          Ever hear of something
          called "Committal in
          Absentia?"

                    BILLY
            (his legal mind still as
             sharp as ever)
          Oh, sure. It means
          somebody's committed to the
          loony bin without being
          examined—

He grinds to a halt as the meaning of Ginelli's
question dawns on him. His face falls further.

                    BILLY
          Oh, Christ, you don't mean

Ginelli slowly nods. Billy's face suffuses with
a killing rage. He becomes almost apoplectic.

                    BILLY
          Houston couldn't have done
          it without Heidi! My wife
          did this to me! My fucking
          wife!

                    GINELLI
          Yeah, well, there's
          something else, too.
            (Billy looks up at him,
             waiting)
          I hear she's been spending
          a lot of time with this Dr.
          Mike Houston. You think—?

He stares at Billy, waiting for an answer. The
implication slowly registers with Billy.

                    BILLY
          You mean that anything could
          be going on between them?
          No, no, of course not.

                    GINELLI
          Then relax. You got nothing
          to worry about. By the time
          the order goes through,
          this will either be over or
          you'll be dead.

                    BILLY
           (with a gallows grin)
          Yeah, right.

Ginelli chuckles and gives Billy a wink,
leaving the bathroom.

Billy leans back against the wall, thoughts
swirling in his head.

                                        CUT TO:

INT. HOTEL ROOM - MOHONK - NIGHT (IN BILLY'S
MIND)

Heidi and Billy have just finished making love.

She lays by his side, staring happily at him,
Billy looking back.

                    HEIDI
          That was wonderful. I must
          be a nymphomaniac. I don't
          think I could go a week
          without making love.

                                   CUT BACK TO:

INT. MOTEL ROOM - DAY (BACK INTO REALITY)

Billy snaps out of it, muttering to himself.

                    BILLY
          No, she couldn't. She just
          couldn't—

He stands there, still lost in thought,
obviously not so sure. Oh, no, not so sure at
all.

                              DISSOLVE TO:

EXT. BILLY'S HOUSE - NIGHT

Sheathed in darkness. The sounds of fervid
love making can be heard from the second-story
bedroom.

INT. BILLY'S ROOM - NIGHT

Heidi and Mike Houston make love in Billy's
bed, Heidi underneath him, he thrusting into
her with greater and greater abandon, her
fingernails digging into his shoulders, sweat
beading her face as she approaches climax.

                    HEIDI
          Oh, no, don't stop, don't
          stop!

                              SMASH CUT TO:

INT. GINELLI'S RENTAL CAR - NIGHT

Billy snaps awake with a dry gasp to find
himself sitting in a stopped car, Ginelli
looking at him.

                    GINELLI
          We're here, Billy. You all
          right?

Billy turns, looking out the window.

EXT. ROAD - NIGHT

Ginelli has pulled the car to a stop by the side of the road.

In the gully below can be seen the Gypsy encampment, all the old cars and campers pulled around a huge, roaring fire. Sentries can be glimpsed keeping guard.

INT. CAR - NIGHT

Billy turns back to Ginelli, nodding jerkily.

                    BILLY
          Yeah, fine. Just dreaming.

Ginelli starts to get out, a paper bag in his hands.

Billy starts to do the same thing. Ginelli stops, looking at Billy's wasted face and body.

                    GINELLI
          Are you kidding? You
          couldn't walk ten feet
          without having a heart
          attack.

Billy sags back, realizing he's right. Ginelli reaches for the door again.

Billy grabs him with a thin, palsied hand.

                    BILLY
          You're—not gonna hurt
          anybody, are you?

> GINELLI
> No. But, Billy, if I'm gonna
> help you, you don't get to
> ask that question again.

Ginelli flashes him a murderous smile and gets out. Billy stares after him as Ginelli disappears into the darkness, muttering to himself.

> BILLY
> I did curse you, Lempke, I
> just didn't know it.

EXT. ENCAMPMENT - NIGHT

Ginelli emerges from the darkness, slipping past the vehicles drawn into a circle, peering into the windows as he passes. He stops by one car, reaching through the open window.

He withdraws a filthy jacket discarded by one of the Gypsies. He slips it on, wrinkling his nose at the smell, and, picking up his paper sack, disappears into the darkness.

EXT. BARBED-WIRE DOG PEN - NIGHT

Outside the encampment. Ginelli emerges from the darkness, looking around for sentries.

There are none. He squats in front of the pen, looking at the pit bulls inside. They look back at him, one of them growling low and deep.

Ginelli grins at them, holding out a cuff of his stolen jacket for them to smell.

                    GINELLI
          What do you say, fellas? Do
          I stink like a Gyp? Well,
          what fucking Gyp ever gave
          you steak for supper?

He pulls a steak from his bag, holding it up.

The dogs come to their feet, their attention
snagged. Ginelli grins.

                    GINELLI
          So who wants strychnine? And
          who gets the uncut heroin?

He throws the steak into the pen, following it
with the others from the bag. The dogs attack
the meat ferociously.

He rises, pinning a pre-written note to the
cage. It reads, "The White Man from Town says
take off the curse!" He turns and walks away as
the pit bulls continue to devour the poisoned
meat.

                                        CUT TO:

EXT. ROAD - NIGHT

Ginelli's rental Ford whips down the highway.

INT. RENTAL FORD - NIGHT

Ginelli's behind the wheel, whistling
tunelessly, obviously quite satisfied with
himself. Billy throws him a look.

                    BILLY
          What now?

                    GINELLI
          We find The Man.

                    BILLY
          What man?

                    GINELLI
              (throwing him a grin)
          Not what man. The Man. One
          who'll be willing to do a
          small job for us. At the
          right price, of course.
                (catching sight of
              something in his rear
                  view mirror)
          Shit!

                    BILLY
           What?

He turns, looking back. A beat up pickup is
riding their tail. Whatever color is left
leaves Billy's face.

Ginelli yells at him.

                    GINELLI
          Get down.

Billy scrunches down in the seat as Ginelli
turns off the road into the nearest store
parking lot.

EXT. SEVEN/ELEVEN - NIGHT

The Ford pulls to a stop in front of a 7/11.

INT. FORD - NIGHT

Billy watches the pickup speed on down the
road, its tail-lights disappearing into the
night.

                    BILLY
          Looks like we're safe.

                    GINELLI
            (his eyes elsewhere)
          Yeah, you just never know.

He gets out of the car, Billy watching as he
walks toward an old Chevy Nova parked to one
side of the lot.

EXT. SEVEN-ELEVEN - NIGHT

Ginelli stops, looking into the Nova. It's
owner, FRANK SPURTON, is asleep behind the
wheel.

He's a down-at-the-heels twenty-five year old
with a two-day stubble. Ginelli raps on the
window with a shout.

                    GINELLI
          Hey, wake up, kid! I Gotta
          job for you!

Spurton wakes with a jerk, rolling down the
glass and looking up at him.

These are eyes that have been in trouble with
the law before.

Ginelli smiles when he sees them.

                    GINELLI
          What's your name?

                    SPURTON
          Spurton. Frank Spurton.

Ginelli reaches inside his coat pocket and
withdraws a wad of money. A big wad.

                    GINELLI
          Okay, Mr. Frank Spurton.
          How'd you like to earn some
          money?

Spurton, fully awake now, climbs out of the
Nova. His eyes are on the wad.

                    SPURTON
          I don't do nothin' that goes
          on videotape.

                    GINELLI
          Hey, it ain't nothin' like
          that. There are some Gypsies
          camped out back up the road.
          They're gonna be leaving
          tomorrow. You find out where
          they're going and call me.
          That's all.

Ginelli counts out nine fifties from the wad,
and gives them to Spurton. He follows it with
a number he's jotted down. Spurton looks at
it, then at Ginelli.

                    SPURTON
          What name should I ask
          for in case someone else
          answers?

                    GINELLI
          Don't worry. I'll answer.

He turns and heads back for the Ford and Billy.

INT. FORD - NIGHT

Ginelli slips behind the wheel, Billy looking
at him.

                    BILLY
          What happened?

                    GINELLI
          I found The man.

He starts the car, and pulls out of the gas
station.

Billy stares out the window at Spurton as they
pass.

EXT. SEVEN/ELEVEN - NIGHT

Spurton's mouth drops open as he gets a glimpse
of Billy's skeleton like face. It's a vision
from hell.

His mouth drops open in sudden horror as he
watches the car pull onto the highway and
accelerate into the night.

INT. CAR - NIGHT

Billy turns to Ginelli.

                    BILLY
          Everybody look like that

                    when they see me?

                         GINELLI
                        (nodding
                      sympathetically)
                These days, Billy, these
                days.

EXT. ROAD - NIGHT

The Ford accelerates down the highway.

                                        DISSOLVE TO:

EXT. BILLY'S HOUSE - DAY

Early morning sunshine dapples the house.
Fervid lovemaking can be heard coming from the
second story.

INT. BATHROOM - DAY

Heidi and Mike Houston make love standing
up in the shower. He bangs away at her with
everything he has, Heidi clawing the walls in
growing excitement, starting to scream as she
climaxes, water raining down on them both.

                         HEIDI
                Oh, God, don't stop, don't
                stop

                                        SMASH CUT TO:

INT. MOTEL ROOM - DAY

Billy snaps away with a gasp, his pallid,
skeletal face slicked with sweat. Ginelli lays

on the other bed, turning from his paperback
novel to Billy.

Early morning sunshine pours through the
window.

                    GINELLI
          You all right?

Billy collects himself, nodding, obviously
not wanting to talk about it.

                    BILLY.
          Yeah, fine. Just another
          dream. What are we waiting
          for now?

                    GINELLI
          A FedEx delivery and a phone
          call.

The phone rings.

Ginelli smiles and picks it up.

                    GINELLI
          Yeah?

                    SPURTON (V.O.)
          They're at a small farm off
          Route Ninety-Two. Can't miss
          'em, but I think they made
          me.

                    GINELLI
          If I were you, friend, I'd
          get the fuck away as soon as
          I could. And lose my number
          on the way.

                    SPURTON (V.O.)
          Yeah, you're probably right.

The line goes dead in Ginelli's ear. Ginelli
hangs up, Billy looking at him.

                         BILLY
          What?

                        GINELLI
                (smiling contentedly)
          Now all we need is the FedEx
          delivery.

                                        CUT TO:

EXT. MOTEL - DAY

A FedEx van pulls to a lateral stop in front
of the motel. A delivery man, no more than
a pimply faced kid gets out, carrying three
packages. One of them is large and oblong.

INT. MOTEL ROOM - DAY

Billy watches TV, trying to shove cheese and
crackers down his throat without throwing up.
Ginelli can be heard showering in the bathroom.

There is a knock at the door. Ginelli yells to
Billy from the bathroom.

                    GINELLI (O.S.)
          Sign for me, will ya, Billy!

Billy slowly rises, going to the door, and
opening it. He hardly has the strength to do
that anymore. The FedEx kid stands there. He
loses his color when he sees Billy, unable to

stop staring at him. He finally snaps out of it.

                    KID
          Didn't mean to stare,
          mister. Just I've seen
          pictures of people who look
          like you.

                    BILLY
          (signing the receipt)
          Yeah? Where?

                    KID
          (proudly)
          Buchenwald. My grandpa
          liberated it.

He shoves the packages into Billy's hand and walks back to his truck, Billy staring after him for a moment before he turns and dumps the packages on the bed. Ginelli emerges from the bathroom in a robe, toweling his hair dry.

He looks down at the packages with a smile.

                    GINELLI
          Well, well, well—

He tears into one, but Billy is no longer paying attention. He is staring out the open motel door. When the FedEx van pulled away, it revealed a car on the other side of the lot. It is a Chevy Nova and it has "White Man From Town" written on its side in shaving cream.

Billy staggers out the door, crossing the lot toward the Nova. Ginelli looks up from his packages to stare after him.

                    GINELLI
          Hey, Billy—

Then he sees the Nova, too. He follows after
Billy.

EXT. MOTEL PARKING LOT - DAY

Billy stops by the car, peering in the
driver's side window. Ginelli stops by his
side, following his gaze. Frank Spurton lies
inside, a precise hole in the center of his
forehead, dried blood crusting the edge. It
could easily have been made by a ball bearing.

Above it, "Never!" has been written in blood
in small, precise hand painted letters. In the
young man's lap is the body of a decapitated
capon. It's wide-eyed head pokes out of
Spurton's mouth.

Billy raises his head, looking nervously
around the lot.

                    BILLY
          I think it's time for us to
          move on.

Ginelli nods, the two men backing for their
room, their eyes darting everywhere.

                                        CUT TO:

EXT. BARN AND FARMHOUSE - NIGHT

Modest, but neat, the house nineteenth century
clapboard painted white. Ginelli's Ford is
parked in front. There is a glimmer of light in
the second-story. Super up "TWO DAYS LATER."

INT. BEDROOM - NIGHT

Billy stares out the window at a field below.
He's so bony now he looks like he must clack when
he walks. The lights of the Gypsy encampment
can be seen.

                    BILLY
          They're down there, huh?

He turns away from the window to watch Ginelli
unwrapping his packages and laying their
contents on the bed.

They are a spring-loaded knife, industrial
strength strapping tape, and a jar of lamp
black. Ginelli attacks the large, oblong
package without answering. Billy looks about
the house nervously.

                    BILLY
          What about the, ah, people
          who own this place?

                    GINELLI
          Mr. and Mrs. Theodore
          Norcross?
                (suddenly grinning)
          They're spending a free
          weekend at the Ritz-Carlton
          in Boston.

He pulls a Soviet Kalashnikov machine gun from
the oblong box, holding it up. It is enormous.
Billy looks at it worriedly.

                    BILLY
          Listen, Richie, my wife
          gives me a blow-job and so
          far four people are dead.

> This thing can't escalate
> anymore.

Ginelli blackens his face and hands, pockets the tape, shoulders the machine gun, and turns to Billy.

                    RICHIE
          Billy, they killed that kid
          to show their contempt for
          me. Things like that I take
          personally.

He turns for the door. Billy rises, grabbing his arm, too weak to stop him. His face is tortured.

                    BILLY
          Please, don't—

                    GINELLI
               (a beat, then)
          All right, I won't for now.

He pulls free and disappears out the door, Billy staring helplessly after him.

EXT. FARM HOUSE - NIGHT

Ginelli slips out the door, walking down the sloping hill toward the Gypsy camp below. Billy can be seen in the room above, his face pressed to the glass, watching.

INT. BEDROOM - NIGHT

Billy falls into a chair, too weak to move. He mutters miserably to himself between suddenly chattering teeth.

                         BILLY
              Oh, God, what have I done—

EXT. DIRT ROAR - NIGHT

A car pulls up slowly and quietly, its headlights off, parking on the side of the road leading to the Gypsy camp. As the DRIVER gets stealthily out, Gabe suddenly leaps on his back, struggling with him.

Just as quickly Gabe slips off again with a low laugh. The Driver gives Gabe a buddy-punch on the arm, then both men lean into the trunk, taking out a caged and muzzled Pit Bill. The Driver hefts the cage over his shoulder and walks away, Gabe staring after him as he disappears into the darkness.

Ginelli suddenly emerges from the bushes behind Gabe, and slams him on the back of the head with the butt of the Kalashnikov. Gabe slumps to the ground, Ginelli kneeling beside him and quickly binding him with the strapping tape. Finished, he shoves a note into Gabe's unconscious hand, and turns, fading into the night.

EXT. GYPSY CAMP - NIGHT

The Gypsies gather around the Driver as he clips the ID collar off the dog. The children tease the dog. It tries to snap at them through its muzzle. Everybody laughs and claps.

Lempke watches from the open door to his trailer, then turns back inside.

EXT. ROCKS - NIGHT

Ginelli appears out of the darkness. He lies prone on a rock outcropping, sighting down on the camp below with the huge machine gun.

INT. LEMPKE'S TRAILER - NIGHT

Lempke counts out crumpled bills with one hand, the other occupied rolling a quarter back and forth between the knuckles.

INT. FARM HOUSE BEDROOM - NIGHT

Billy stares out at the camp, waiting, hardly daring to breathe.

EXT. LEMPKE'S TRAILER - NIGHT

A gunshot suddenly blasts the night and one of the trailer's tires explodes. Another gunshot. A second tire explodes.

INT. TRAILER - NIGHT

The entire trailer suddenly lists forward, threatening to dump Lempke out of his chair.

Things spill from the shelves and counter. Shouts erupt outside.

All hell is breaking loose.

EXT. GYPSY CAMP - NIGHT

Gypsies, frantic with fear, pile out of their trailers and tents, half-dressed, shouting to each other as gunshots rip the night and bullets whistle over their heads.

EXT. ROCKS - NIGHT

Ginelli sights in on what remains of Lempke's camper, and opens fire again. The rest of the tires explode.

INT. FARMHOUSE BEDROOM - NIGHT

Billy listens to the loud staccato of automatic fire, squeezing his eyes shut, shaking his head and muttering to himself.

                    BILLY
          Oh, sweet Jesus

EXT. GYPSY CAMP - NIGHT

Lempke throws open the door to his now flattened camper, stepping out into the middle of the camp, people rushing everywhere. Bullets continue to whizz overhead. Lempke just stands there, searching the darkness for the muzzle flash. His people rush forward to protect him. The gunfire changes direction and bullets smash the car directly in front of him, demolishing it. His people hit the dirt. Lempke just stands there, still searching for those muzzle flashes.

INT. FARMHOUSE BEDROOM - NIGHT

Billy becomes agitated as he listens to the gunfire, starting to hyper-ventilate. One hand goes to his chest. His heart is skipping beats. He rises, staggering toward the hallway.

                    BILLY
          No, stop

EXT. GYPSY CAMP - NIGHT

Several of Lempke's people grab him, hustling
him toward the protection of an old Cadillac
limousine parked to one side. It suddenly
explodes, riddled with gunfire, the windows,
headlights, body pocked with bullets. Lempke's
people drop to the ground, trying to bury
themselves in the dirt.

The old man turns, staring up at the rocks,
his eyes drilling into the darkness.

EXT. ROCKS - NIGHT

Ginelli stops firing, staring down at the
camp below. Lempke is staring directly at
him, standing there, refusing to flinch. It's
almost like the old man can see him in the
dark. It sends a shiver up the Dago's spine.

EXT. GYPSY CAMP - NIGHT

Lempke suddenly raises a hand, pointing to
where Ginelli lies.

Several of the Gypsy men rise to their feet,
shooting in that direction. A blood-curdling
scream cuts the night. Somebody has been hit.
Bad.

INT. FARMHOUSE - SECOND-FLOOR HALL - NIGHT

Billy staggers down the hall for the stairs,
the scream ringing in his ears.

                         BILLY
              No, please, stop

INT. STAIRS - NIGHT

Billy appears on the stairs, trying to
negotiate his way down the steps. He is too
weak and his legs give out, spilling him the
rest of the way.

EXT. GYPSY CAMP - NIGHT

Gina comes to a stop beside her grandfather,
grinning up at the rocks, the rest of the
Gypsies cheering as they hear the scream die.
She jumps up and down with bloodthirsty joy.

                         GINA
              He's dead, old-papa! The
              eyelak is dead!

She rushes toward the rocks, most of the rest
of the Gypsy camp following. Two of the younger
men lock their hands together, making a seat
for Lempke.

They carry him up the hill after the others.

EXT. ROCKS - NIGHT

Gina reaches the top of the rocks, looking
around, the other Gypsies scampering up behind
her.

She suddenly freezes, staring down at a body
bathed in moonlight. It is her brother, Gabe.
He had broken free of the strapping tape and
was headed back for the camp when his people
shot him by mistake. The other Gypsies gather

around as Gina slowly kneels by his side, taking Ginelli's note from his hand. She silently reads it. It says "Take it off!" and below that a phone number.

She suddenly throws it aside, lifting her head and screaming into the night.

                    GINA
          Never! You hear me, White
          Man From Town? Never!

She dashes up the hill, disappearing into the night after her brother's killer. A moment later, Lempke, carried by the two young men, appears out of the darkness. one glance at Gabe's body and he looks at the others. Real fear has suddenly entered his eyes.

                   LEMPKE
          Gina, where's my Gelina?

One of the men points off into the darkness after the girl. Lempke suddenly screams at him.

                   LEMPKE
          Find her! Eingolt! Eyelot!
          Hurry!

The Gypsies scatter into the darkness, terrified of the old man who stares after them with the eyes like burning coals.

EXT. WOODS - NIGHT

Gina slips from the rocks into the woods, searching the darkness around her. She has her slingshot and ball bearings ready in her hand. Suddenly Ginelli steps out of a tree in front

of her, the machine gun aimed at her heart.
She jerks to a halt, staring at him, hatred
pouring from her eyes.

                    GINA
          You! You killed my brother!

She leaps for him, her rage blinding her to
any danger, her fingernails extended like
claws. Ginelli sidesteps and kicks her feet
out from under her. She drops to the ground,
stunned. Ginelli jams the barrel of his rifle
into her neck, pressing down hard. She glares
up at him, no terror in her face, nothing but
unreasoning, maniacal hatred.

Ginelli grins down at her.

                    GINELLI
          Just as crazy as your
          grandpa, ain't you? Tell him
          to take it off.

                    GINA
             (spitting the words out
                  at him)
          Your friend is a pig and he
          die thin. But you die first,
          you bastard!

                    GINELLI
             (leaning in, still
                  grinning)
          Anything you say, honey.
          Only tell him tomorrow
          night, I kill one more
          person: you! You tell your
          filthy old Gyp of a grand-
          dad that.

She suddenly comes alive, snarling as she tries to scramble to her feet He steps back, slamming her across the side of the head with the rifle butt. Gina rolls to the ground, unconscious. Ginelli stares at her like he's ready to off her right there, but then he hears the Gypsies approaching, softly calling her name. He disappears into the woods.

INT. FARMHOUSE - LIVING ROOM - NIGHT

Ginelli bursts through the front door to find Billy semi-conscious at the foot of the stairs.

                    GINELLI
          Billy?

He presses two fingers to Billy's wrist, checking for a pulse. Not finding one, he breaks a tiny ampule of ammonia under Billy's nose. The skeletal man opens a groggy eye, staring up at Ginelli. Ginelli grins at him.

                    GINELLI
          We're almost there, Billy,
          almost there.

He scoops Billy up in his arms, heading for the door and his waiting car outside.

                              DISSOLVE TO:

EXT. BANGOR, MAINE - DAY

A nice enough town if you like state capitols. An I-Hop sits on a busy downtown street.

INT. INTERNATIONAL HOUSE OF PANCAKES - DAY

A pay phone rings. Ginelli, who's been standing alongside waiting, answers. Billy sits in a booth, staring at the nearest wall. The layers of clothing he wears do nothing to hide his scarecrow frame. He is now literally nothing but skin and bone, his eyes burning coals lost in dark, deep sockets.

A waitress appears, putting a fresh mound of pancakes in front of him. Billy is too weak to respond. He just sits there, staring at nothing as Ginelli hangs up the phone and returns to the booth. The waitress looks up at him as he approaches.

                    WAITRESS
          Mister, take your friend to
          the hospital. Nobody oughta
          die in a pancake house.

                    GINELLI
               (with a big grin)
          I just made an appointment
          with the man who can cure
          him.

He looks down at Billy for a reaction, but Billy is too far gone. He passes out instead, beginning to slide under the booth. The waitress and Ginelli catch him just in time.

                                        CUT TO:

EXT. GREAT WHITE WATER TOWER PARK - DAY

A weird landmark of white-washed wood, with lattice work and a spiraling enclosed stairway. Some kids are running under-manned

scrimmages in the grassy park below. A would-
be QUARTERBACK rears back for a long pass, his
would-be RECEIVER going out for a long one,
backing up and backing up—brushing past Billy,
knocking the pathetically frail man backward
onto a bench. The Receiver stops, looking at
him apologetically.

                RECEIVER
      Oh, listen, mister, I'm
      sorry

He breaks off, staring at Billy, his mouth
dropping open. Billy has never looked worse:
he sits sprawled on the bench, his head back,
his eyes closed, his breath a rattle, his bony
hands clacking spasmodically like castanets.

The Receiver is still staring at Billy as the
Quarterback comes dashing up. He takes one
look at Billy and drags his buddy away.

              QUARTERBACK
      Come on, Mickey, I got some
      Mac-Attack coupons from my
      idiot brother—

The two boys run away, Billy sitting there,
wheezing away.

Ginelli comes out of the brush behind the bench,
walking to a stop above Billy. He glances
down, putting his jacket around Billy's razor
thin shoulders.

              GINELLI
      I'm parked right over there
      behind the hedges. I'll be
      watching everything. Okay?

                    BILLY
              (his voice hardly a
                  whisper)
            Richie thanks—

                   GINELLI
          I owed you, but you really
          want to thank me? Get this
          old bastard.

He turns and walks away, disappearing into
the shrubbery. Billy slowly nods off, his
breathing so light and shallow it's hard to
tell if he's still alive.

                                    DISSOLVE TO:

EXT. FAIRVIEW - DAY (IN HIS NIGHTMARE)

Billy's back in Fairview, the Fairview of the
Living Dead. Only they're not living anymore.
All the starving people are dead, their
emaciated corpses lying about in the street and
on the sidewalks, Billy, equally as starved,
staggering along, staring at them with wide
vacant eyes. The vulture with Lempke's face and
rotting nose suddenly lands on his shoulder,
pecking at his neck, tearing what little flesh
he has left loose. Blood courses freely down
his shirt. Peck, peck, peck the horrid bird
goes as it whispers in his ear.

                  LEMPKE (O.S.)
            Wake up, White Man From Town

                                    SMASH CUT TO:

EXT. WATER TOWER PARK - DAY

Startled, Billy's eyes snap open. He finds

himself staring at Tadzu Lempke and his rotting
nose. He clears his throat, managing to gasp
out a few words.

                    BILLY
          I'm awake.

His eyes zero in on Lempke's cancer riddled
nose. Dark lines now radiate out from the
black hole and across most of his runneled
left cheek. Lempke smiles, seeing his gaze. He
touches his nose.

                    LEMPKE
          Cancer. I die soon. You like
          that? It make you hoppy?

                    BILLY
          No. No, of course not.

                    LEMPKE
          Don't lie. There is no
          need. It make you hoppy, of
          course, it make you hoppy.

                    BILLY
          None of it makes me happy.
          I'm sick about it all.
          Believe me.

                    LEMPKE
          I don't believe nothin' no
          white man from town ever
          told me. But you sick, oh
          yeah. So I brought you
          something. It gonna fatten
          you up real good.

He stares down at the something in his lap.
Billy follows Lempke's gaze. A pie in a

disposable aluminum pie plate sits there.
Innocuous enough, but Billy pales when he sees
it anyway. Lempke grins at him.

                    LEMPKE
          You looked scared. It is too
          late to be scared, white man
          from town.

The old man withdraws a pocket knife, opens
it, and cuts a slit three inches long across
the top of the pie.

He lays the knife on his lap and hooks his
misshapen thumbs over opposing sides of the
plate and pulls.

The slit opens, gaping up at Billy, showing
a swimming viscous fluid in which dark things
float like blood clots.

Lempke continues to pull and release as he
talks, Billy's gaze fixed to the evil looking
slit in the pie that alternately gapes and
closes.

                    LEMPKE
          So you have made yourself
          believe that what happened
          to my Suzanne is nobody's
          fault, not yours, not your
          friend's, not even God's.
          Or you tell yourself it is
          everybody's fault, mine,
          yours, your wife's, my
          Suzanne's, all of us. You
          tell yourself you can't be
          asked to pay for it -there
          is no blame, you say. But
          you are wrong, white man

from town. <u>Everybody pays
when the guilty get away
with it.</u>
          (pulling the pie open
          and closed, open and
          closed, Billy staring at
          it, mesmerized)
Because you won't take
blame - not you, not your
friends -I stick it on you
like a sign. For my dear
dead wife that you kill.
Then your friend comes.
He poisons dogs, shoots
gun in the dark, kill my
grandson, threaten to kill
my granddaughter. Take it
off, he say, no, never, say
my Gelina. But I say, yes.
Because if I don't maybe she
die, too. So I stop it here.
I take off the curse if your
friend get out of here.

                    BILLY
               (nodding)
He'll get out.

Lempke stares at him for a moment, then nods
at his bandaged hand.

                    LEMPKE
All right, then unwrap your
hand.

Billy slowly unwinds the bandages from his
wounded hand. He holds it up. The wound looks
liverish, the edges pulling together in a vain
attempt to close the hole. Lempke hands Billy
the knife.

                    LEMPKE
          If you want to be rid
          of this curse, this
          "purpurfargade ansiket," you
          let your blood run into the
          pie. You understand?
                    (Billy nods; Lempke
                      smiles)
          Then do it. Now!

His thumbs tighten again, spreading the slit
in the pie.

Billy hesitates for only a second and then
pushes the blade of the knife deep into his
scabrous wound.

It opens immediately, blood splattering into
the slit of the pie.

Lempke closes his eyes, muttering in Rom, the
Gypsy language.

Billy continues to dig at his wound, more
blood gushing into the pie. Lempke finally
opens his eyes, looking up at him.

                    LEMPKE
          Enkelt! Enough.

He plucks the knife from Billy's hand. Billy
lays back against the bench, exhausted. His
eyes slowly fall to the pie, widening in sudden
amazement.

As he watches the slit in the top closes until
the pie looks like it was never sliced open.

He looks down at his hand.

The wound is gone, nothing to indicate a ball bearing ever tore through his hand except for a jagged white scar.

He looks back down at the pie.

It is pulsating now, quietly rising and falling as though something living is trapped inside, breathing in there, trying to get out.

And it is, too—the "purpurfargade ansiket," the Gypsy curse.

Billy looks back up at Lempke.

> BILLY
>
> But how?

> LEMPKE
>
> You give curse to pie. You
> take weight now. But in
> a day, twenty-four hours
> zactly, you start to fall
> back. Only this time there
> be no stopping it. Unless...

> BILLY
> (stunned)
> Oh, my God. You mean...

> LEMPKE
>
> Zactly. Someone must take
> curse from pie before it go
> back into you. Someone must
> eat it. You got someone?

A beat, then Billy slowly nods, a cold hatred leaking into his eyes and congealing his face.

> FLASH CUT TO:

INT. BILLY'S BATHROOM - DAY

Mike Houston banging away at Heidi and Heidi
loving every moment of it, clawing the walls,
her face wreathed in ecstasy, water running off
her as she gets closer and closer to coming.

                                    CUT BACK TO:

EXT. PARK -DAY

Billy snaps out of it, slowly turning to Lempke
with an expression that even sends a shiver up
the old Gypsy's spine.

                    BILLY
          Yes, I have someone

                    LEMPKE
          Good for you, bad for them,
          but the curse is still
          yours. If you should change
          your mind—

                    BILLY
               (quickly)
          I won't.

                    LEMPKE
          But if you should, you eat
          pie, curse leave them and
          come back to you.

                    BILLY
          I told you. I won't take it
          back. Not once I've given it
          to—

He falls silent, enjoying the dark, terrible
thoughts running through his mind.

Lempke watches him, interrupting his reverie.

                    LEMPKE
          All right, have it your own
          way. Only remember this.
                    (beat)
          <u>Justice is justice and there</u>
          <u>no escaping it. Not for any</u>
          <u>of us, not now, not never!</u>

He abruptly rises and walks away, Billy staring after him until he's disappeared into the trees.

Slowly Billy stands, the pulsating pie in his arms, and starts back toward where Ginelli said he'd be waiting.

EXT. STREET - DAY

Billy comes through the shrubbery toward his Jag, looking around for Ginelli.

He's nowhere to be seen.

Billy slides the pie in the back, climbing in the front seat, muttering to himself.

                    BILLY
          Now where the hell is he—

INT. JAG -DAY

Billy sits on the passenger side, looking around the empty car, still muttering to himself.

                    BILLY
          He must have left a message—

He searches the seat and floor.

Nothing.

Still searching, he opens the glove compartment.
A handful of ball bearings spill into his lap
and after the bearings comes Ginelli's severed
hand, holding still more ball bearings. Billy
stifles a scream, staring at the severed hand
in horror.

Bloody strips of flesh dangle from the wrist.

He collapses back in his seat, his eyes squeezed
shut in grief, trying not to scream and just
barely, but only barely, making it.

                                        CUT TO:

EXT. REST AREA - DAY

Billy has pulled off the interstate into a
rest area. He is on a pay phone. Ginelli's
severed hand sits in front of him, wrapped in
a road map.

                    LINDA (V.O.)
                (jumping up and down
                  with excitement)
            Daddy, are you okay?

                    BILLY
            I'm still pretty thin,
            honey, but I'm gonna be
            fine. I'm coming home
            tonight, but I don't want
            you to tell your mother. I
            want it to be a surprise,
            okay?

                    LINDA (V.O.)
          Yeah, sure.

                    BILLY
          Great. And I want you
          to spend the night at
          Georgia's.

                    LINDA (V.O.)
                    (protesting)
          Daddy!

                    BILLY
          There are some things I
          need to talk to your mother
          about. Now promise me
          you'll spend the night with
          Georgia.

                    LINDA (V.O.)
                    (rattling on)
          What do you want to talk to
          her about? That court order
          she got? I know all about
          it. I heard her talking to
          Dr. Houston—

                    BILLY
                    (with a growl)
          Linda—

                    LINDA (V.O.)
                    (giving up)
          Oh, all right, I'll spend
          the night at Georgia's.

                    BILLY
                    (smiling)
          Thanks, honey. Now let me
          talk to your mother.

                    LINDA (V.O.)
                  (yelling back)
        Hey, mom, dad's on the line.

Heidi almost immediately picks up on the
extension.

                    HEIDI (V.O.)
          Billy, is that you?

                    BILLY
          Yes, and I'm fine. I'm
          coming back in a couple of
          days.

                    HEIDI (V.O.)
                (her voice flooded with
                      joy)
          Oh, Billy, that's wonderful.
          What happened?

                    BILLY
          I found the Gypsy and you
          know what he did when I
          asked him to take off the
          curse? He said ''What
          curse?"
                (he laughs, a very
                forced laugh that's just
                a bit too hard)
          That's when I realized that
          you and Mike were right. It
          was all in my head. I've
          been gaining weight ever
          since.

                    HEIDI (V.O.)
          Oh, Billy, that's the best
          news

                    BILLY
     —but before I can come back
     you have to get in touch
     with Mike Houston, and tell
     him you've changed your mind
     about the committal order.

                    HEIDI (V.O.)
     Oh, Billy, I'm sorry about
     that. You were just acting
     so crazy.

                    BILLY
            (to himself, smiling
               nastily)
     I understand. Just tell
     him to have the Res Geste
     declared null and void. I
     don't want to get arrested
     as I cross the state line.

                    HEIDI (V.O.)
     Billy, you sound so cold.
     You're not mad at me, are
     you?

                    BILLY
            (that nasty smile
             getting broader)
     No, of course not. I'm just
     tired, that's all. See you
     at the end of the week.

He hangs up, and walks back toward his car.
On the way he drops the severed hand into a
trash bin.

INT. JAG - DAY

Billy hops behind the wheel, twisting to look

in the back seat. The pie sits there, quietly
pulsating. Billy smiles at it grimly. Then he
starts the car and puts it in gear.

EXT. REST AREA - INTERSTATE -DAY

The car pulls out of the rest area onto the
interstate, heading back toward Connecticut.

                                        CUT TO:

EXT. BILLY'S HOUSE - FAIRVIEW - NIGHT

The house is well lit up, Heidi's station
wagon in front. Billy's Jaguar pulls to a halt
behind the station wagon.

INT. JAGUAR - NIGHT

A smile slowly spreads Billy sits there,
staring at the house across his face. It isn't
a nice smile. Grabbing the pie in the back
seat, he slips out of the car.

EXT. BILLY'S HOUSE - NIGHT

Billy does a slow walk to his house, disappearing
inside with the pie in his hands.

INT. ENTRANCE WAY - NIGHT

Billy stops in the darkened hallway. He flicks
on the light, calling up the stairs.

                    BILLY
          Heidi!

Heidi appears with a rush at the top of the

stairs, staring down at him, her face flooding
with joy.

                    HEIDI
          Billy! I thought you weren't
          coming home for a few days—

                    BILLY
                  (smiling)
          Couldn't stop myself from
          seeing you.

She comes down the stairs to hug him, but
is stopped by his appearance. He is still
perilously frail.

                    HEIDI
          Billy, you're still so thin—

                    BILLY
          And totally exhausted. You
          mind if I turn in?

He comes up the stairs a few steps, she down
a few more.

They are very close.

                    HEIDI
          Linda went to Georgia's for
          the night. I'll sleep in her
          room so I won't disturb you.
            (a beat, then in a rush)
          Billy, I really am sorry
          about the committal order,
          but I thought

                    BILLY
          I understand.

                    HEIDI
                (hopefully)
        You do?

                    BILLY
            (smearing a smile across
                his face)
        Of course. You did what you
        thought was best for me.

A beat, then he loses control of the smile.

It starts to look a lot more like a gallows
grin.

                    BILLY
        But it doesn't make any
        difference. Or at least it
        won't by tomorrow.

                    HEIDI
            (stepping back in sudden
                fear)
        Tomorrow? What do you mean?
        Billy, what's wrong?

Billy spends a moment getting the smile back.

It's pretty weak, but it covers the rage and
hatred.

                    BILLY
        Nothing. Just exhaustion
        talking. Look, a peace
        offering.

He raises the pie, distracting Heidi. Her gaze
falls on it, her eyes widening. The pie never
looked more scrumptious.

                    HEIDI
          Oh, strawberry, my favorite
          kind.

                    BILLY
          Here, why don't you have a
          piece while I get ready for
          bed.

He gives her the pie and leans forward, giving
her a peck on the cheek and an even bigger
smile.

                    BILL
          I just know you're going to
          love it.

He goes up the stairs, Heidi staring after
him for a few beats before heading for the
kitchen, and the fridge.

INT. BILLY'S BEDROOM - NIGHT

Billy enters the bedroom, starting to undress
for bed.

He hears noises below, the scraping of a
kitchen chair, the rattle of silverware.

Heidi is eating a piece of the pie. He calls
out.

                    BILLY
          How is it?

Heidi's yell echoes up from below.

                    HEIDI (O.S.)
          Delicious.

He flops back on the bed, turning off the light, staring up at the ceiling, a grim smile on his face.

                              DISSOLVE TO:

EXT. BILLY'S HOUSE - DAY

The house is smothered in early morning sunshine.

INT. BILLY'S BEDROOM - DAY

Billy rolls over in bed, slowly waking up.

Linda suddenly appears in the doorway, looking in at him, panic struck.

                    LINDA
          Dad, I just came in and
          something's wrong with mom!

Billy sits upright, trying to hide his smile.

                    BILLY
          Really? What?

                    LINDA
          I don't know, but I've got
          the same problem. Look.

She reaches up, grabbing hold of her ear, and literally tears it from the side of her head. Blood follows, gushing down her neck in a torrent. She holds out the ear, looking down at it in the palm of her hand as though there's nothing surprising about seeing it there. Her face scrunches up, tears beginning to pour from her eyes as the blood continues to run.

                    LINDA
          Look, daddy, it just fell
          off!

                              SMASH CUT TO:

INT. BILLY'S ROOM - DAY (BACK INTO REALITY)

Billy sits bolt upright in bed, his face
sheened with sweat. He spends a moment getting
control of himself.

                    BILLY
          Just a dream, that's all.
          Just a dream—

He throws back the covers, grabs his robe and
throws it over - his skinny frame, staggering
for the door.

INT. HALL - DAY

He enters the kitchen. He smiles. Then, we see
Billy suddenly freeze. He is staring at a young
girl's purse. Inside is an album, Bon Jovi. He
approaches, pulling out a wallet, even though
he already knows what he will find. The wallet
says: Property of Linda Halleck, reward if
found.

Linda's in the house! He whirls, heading for
the kitchen.

INT. KITCHEN - DAY

He enters the kitchen to find his wife and
daughter finishing off a piece of the pie, a

fourth of it gone. He looks at his daughter, and the pie with sick dread. Heidi rises, oblivious, and puts the plates in the sink.

                    HEIDI
          Good morning, darling.

Heidi rinses them off. When Billy speaks, it's in a dry, cracked voice.

                    BILLY
          What are you doing home?

                    LINDA
          I wanted to give you a kiss
          before I went to school. I
          love you, daddy. We'll talk
          later.

She gives him a quick kiss on the cheek, grabs her schoolbooks, and disappears out the back door. Billy slowly turns his sick eyes to Heidi.

She is putting the dishes into the washer.

                    BILLY
          Why'd you let her have a
          piece of that pie?

                    HEIDI
          Oh, Billy, I know it isn't
          the best breakfast in the
          world, but it is your
          homecoming.

She continues to stack dishes, Billy staring at her, Lempke's words suddenly tumbling through his head.

                    LEMPKE (V.O.)
          Everybody pays when the
          guilty get away with it.
          Everybody!

Billy looks up at Heidi.

Sanity slowly floods back into his eyes, maybe
for the first time since this all began.

His voice becomes clearer, stronger.

                    BILLY
          Heidi, I want to apologize
          to you.

Heidi looks at him, her eyes welling up as she
see the sincerity in his face.

                    HEIDI
          For what?

                    BILLY
          All that stuff I said about
          hitting the old Gypsy woman.
          It wasn't your fault.
          Neither was fixing the case
          so I got off scot free. I
          did all that.

                    HEIDI
          I know, darling. You were
          just sick for a while,
          that's all. I love you, you
          know.

She wipes away the tears and gives him a kiss.
Billy stares at her, slowly smiling back.

It's the first honest smile he's had in a very

long time. It's sweet and sad and filled with
love.

                    BILLY
          Yeah, I know. There was
          never anything between you
          and Mike Houston either, was
          there?

                    HEIDI
          What do you mean?

                    BILLY
          Nothing. My mind's just been
          playing strange tricks on
          me, that's all.

                    HEIDI
          Mine's been doing the same
          thing. When you came in last
          night, I actually thought

                    BILLY
          What?

                    HEIDI
               (with a laugh)
          That you wanted to kill me.
          Can you believe it? I'll
          take a shower and fix you
          some breakfast. You need all
          the calories you can get.

She gives his skinny middle a playful pinch
and heads for the door. He calls after her.

                    BILLY
          Heidi
               (she stops, turning
               back)

I really love you, too.

                    HEIDI
              (her smile growing)
          I know.

She disappears out the door, heading for the
stairs. Billy stares after her for a moment,
and then slowly turns, looking down at the
pie.

It has begun to pulsate again, almost as if
it's calling to him. And it is and he knows
it. More Gypsy words tumble through his head.

                    LEMPKE (V.O.)
          You change your mind, you
          eat pie, curse leave them
          and come back to you.

Billy slowly picks up the pie, cutting a huge
piece and slipping it on a desert plate.

He looks at it, the dark chunks like blood
clots swimming in the viscous fluid.

He grins.

It's a lopsided grin, maybe a little crazy,
but also filled with relief and resignation.

This is a man who's finally accepted his guilt
and the sentence.

                    LEMPKE (V.O.)
          Justice is justice and there
          no escaping it. Not for any
          of us, not now, not never!

Billy slowly chomps down on the pie, carefully

chewing before he swallows.

His smile grows as he slips another piece on
his fork.

THE END

Stephen King's
THINNER

ADAPTED FOR THE SCREEN BY

MICHAEL MCDOWELL

INT. CONNECTICUT TURNPIKE - DAWN

A thick mist obscures the roadway and adjacent shoulder. O.S. the loud sound of distant engines whinnying, panting - clearly out of tune.

Headlights begin to come out of the mist. What emerges is a caravan of older cars, dented trucks with camper shells, and twenty-year-old motor homes.

Leading the procession is a '57 Pontiac with wide-stripe white side walls.

The cortège exits the interstate.

CU: the road sign. It reads: FAIRVIEW, CONNECTICUT.

                                        CUT TO:

EXT. COUNTRY ROAD - EARLY MORNING

The mist has risen and the line of cars, their lights still on, makes its way down the two-lane highway past a succession of big old comfortable houses, set back on generous wooded lots. One of these is...

THE HALLECK HOUSE - a well-maintained Cape Codder with lots of add-ons and a long driveway.

                    BILLY HALLECK (O.S.)
              My Lord! Looks like a Gypsy
              caravan!

                                        CUT TO:

INT. BATHROOM - HALLECK HOUSE - EARLY MORNING
- CONT ACTION

BILLY HALLECK, naked, stands at a high bathroom
window, watching the ragged procession. He's
nearing forty, dignified, not un-handsome,
but distinctly fat.

                    BILLY
          I bet it is! Honest-to-God
          Gypsies!

In discomforting Close-Up, the CAMERA moves up
a body that is heavily fleshy, if not actually
obese. Hairy flesh legs with knees like Parker
House Rolls rise into hips like old goose-down
pillows, flabby arms showing a golfer's short-
sleeved tan line terminate in two pudgy hands
manipulating a small vanity mirror.

As Billy puts his left foot on a sturdy, old-
fashioned scale, there's a short knock on the
bathroom door.

                    HEIDI HALLECK (O.S.)
          How many eggs you want?

                    BILLY
          Three!

His right foot mounts the scale BOOOINNNNG.
The needle lurches over the top.

                    BILLY (CONT'D)
          Make that two.

Billy holds up...

THE ROUND VANITY MIRROR -

so that it reflects the reversed numbers on the scale: 277. It's easier for Billy to use the mirror than to stretch his head forward enough to see the numbers directly over the mound of his belly. Billy gets off the scale and reaches for a bathrobe hanging on the back of the door.

CU: the label reads XXX LARGE.

Billy puts on the robe, and then stands in front of the mirror. He pokes and prods the ample flesh around his waist.

                    BILLY
              (to himself; ironic)
          I gotta get a haircut.

                                        CUT TO:

INT. KITCHEN - HALLECK HOUSE - MORNING

Billy is eating a breakfast of eggs, bacon, buttered toast and marmalade, grapefruit heaped with sugar, coffee, and milk.

Heidi is filling out her grocery list on a computer set up on a corner of the counters.

She stands and reaches deep in one of the cupboards, coming up with a six months-old package of Cheetos.

                    HEIDI
          Billy, it's bad enough you
          keep going off your diets,
          but when you hide your
          junkie food, it attracts
          bugs.

                    BILLY
          Sorry Heidi, I was just
          trying to put 'em out of
          sight. What's for dinner?

                    HEIDI
          Spaghetti and Italian
          meatballs. But are you going
          to be back from New Haven?

LINDA HALLECK enters.

Linda, Billy and Heidi's 17-year-old daughter,
is pretty, smart, and much more attuned to her
father than to her mother.

She swipes the last piece of bacon off her
father's plate and places a kiss on his cheek.

                    LINDA
          So - you gonna get Mister
          Mafia off his murder charge?

Before Billy can reply to this flippant
question, Heidi interrupts.

                    HEIDI
          Don't call him Mister
          Mafia. It's bad enough your
          father's defending a man
          like that - we don't need to
          make jokes about it.

Billy puts down his fork and speaks with
aggravated patience:

                    BILLY
          I wouldn't have taken on
          Ginelli's case if I weren't
          absolutely convinced that he

is innocent.
              (beat)
Of this particular charge.

Linda takes a half-piece of her father's toast
and wipes up some fried egg with it.

                  LINDA
                (to Heidi)
          Teacher's meeting today.
          You want to pick me up at
          eleven?

                  HEIDI
          I didn't forget.

Linda swallows off the remainder of her
father's coffee and heads for the door.

                  LINDA
                (teasing)
          So if you don't get Mr
          Ginelli off, is the Mafia
          gonna rub us all out?

                                        CUT TO:

INT. COUNTRY CONVENIENCE STORE - MORNING

A small, old house has been discretely converted
into a 6am-11pm convenience market for upscale
Fairview. Billy picks up a magazine, two
newspapers, and a foil-wrapped egg sandwich.

At the point-of- sale rack, he hesitates,
then hurriedly picks out an 8-ounce bar of
chocolate. Right ahead of him in line is JUDGE
CARY ROSSINGTON, a distinguished 50 year old,
who is purchasing a carton of cigarettes.

                    ROSSINGTON
          Georgia, last time you threw
          in a free lighter.

The desk clerk, GEORGIA - a high-school girl -
obliges, along with the man's change.

                    BILLY
          Morning, Judge. Hello,
          Georgia.

                    ROSSINGTON
          How long is that trial gonna
          go on, Billy?

                    BILLY
          Why? You and Leda need some
          competition out on the
          links?

                    ROSSINGTON
          Yeah, and you need a little
          exercise.

                    GEORGIA
          Did you want this, Mr
          Halleck?

Georgia holds up the candy bar. Billy grabs it
and stuffs it in his pocket.

                    GEORGIA (CONT'D)
          So is that Mafia guy gonna
          go free? Linda said-

                    BILLY
          Linda says too much.

                    ROSSINGTON
          Oh Jesus -

The Judge stands at the door with his bag.

                    ROSSINGTON
          We've got a whole damned
          tribe of Gypsies out here!

                    BILLY
          I was right!

ROSSINGTON'S POV THROUGH THE GLASS DOOR-

of three Gypsy trucks parked across the street.

                    GEORGIA
          Those guys are Gypsies?! For
          real?!

Georgia goes to the end of the check-out
counter. Billy joins the Judge at the door.

                    ROSSINGTON
          Yeah. I had a run-in with
          'em when I was with the
          A.G.'s office. Twenty-two
          years ago.

                    BILLY
          They're not coming to
          Fairview to live.

                    ROSSINGTON
          They're not even going to
          stay the night.

The Judge exits. Billy returns to the counter
for his purchases. The door signal sounds, and
Billy and Georgia look up to see...

A GYPSY WOMAN -

pushes through the door. She's about 35, thin, angular, her bleached yellow hair showing an inch-and-a-half of black roots. With her is a SMALL GIRL, about five, with a large birthmark disfiguring her face.

The Gypsy Woman glances at Billy, then heads directly for Georgia.

                    GYPSY WOMAN
          Put this here please.

Before Georgia can react, the Gypsy Woman snags some Scotch Tape from the register, and tapes a business card to the counter. Georgia cranes to read it:

CU: THE CARD

                    GINA
          AT THE SIGN OF THE UNICORN
          GINA KNOWS YOUR PAST
          GINA TELLS YOUR FUTURE

The Little Girl pours a handful of sticky pennies onto the counter, and reaches for a pack of gum high on a counter display. The display starts to topple, but Georgia grabs it. Out of the corner of his eye, Billy catches a movement of the Gypsy Woman's arm as if she had just swiped bills out of the register.

To distract, the Gypsy Woman's smiles mysteriously at Georgia:

                    GYPSY WOMAN
          Gina can tell you your
          secret name.

                    GEORGIA
          What's a secret name?

The Gypsy Woman and the Little Girl are heading for the door.

                    GYPSY WOMAN
          A secret name is the one
          that' s written on your
          soul.

The Little Girl looks at Billy very seriously, then follows her mother out.

                                        CUT TO:

EXT. COUNTRY STORE - MORNING

Billy is getting into his car when he sees...

THE LITTLE GYPSY GIRL -

peeling an 8-oz chocolate bar, tossing the wrapper onto the ground. Behind her, some TEEN-AGED GIRLS are giving the Gypsy Woman money in exchange for a couple of red plastic flowers.

The Little Girl, as if feeling Billy's glance on her, looks up and grins.

                                        CUT TO:

EXT. NEW HAVEN - MORNING

Halleck's car passes over a long bridge arching over a scummy river, flowing between grimy docks and smoke stacked factories.

INT. HALLECK'S CAR - SAME TIME

As he finishes off the fried egg sandwich

he stuffs the wadded wrapper in the bag. He reaches into his pocket for his candy bar. When he doesn't find it there, he starts looking everywhere for it. The car starts to swerve into the wrong lane. He regains the wheel, then thinks for a moment.

                    BILLY
          That little Gypsy girl stole
          my candy bar!
                    (beat)
          Hell, she needed it more
          than me.

                                        CUT TO:

EXT. NEW HAVEN COURT HOUSE - MORNING

Establishing shot.

Billy pulls into the parking lot, exits the car with his briefcase and the Country Market bag filled with trash. He tosses it into a trash basket, when a large black limousine pulls up behind him.

The BODYGUARD Driver hops out and opens the rear door for...

RICHIE GINELLI -

nearing 50, slight and sinewy, discreetly Italian. He's been dressing well for a long time.

Ginelli has appeared stalwart and poised in worse situations than this simple indictment for attempted murder.

Richie is a strong, old-fashioned man but with

sudden, impish, irresistible grin.

                BILLY
Morning, Richie.

              GINELLI
Now I've been thinking,
Counselor - what this is all
about is - you. You're the
one who's gonna decide if I
spend the next twenty years
at home or in jail.

                BILLY
Doesn't that depend on the
jury?

              GINELLI
What it's all about, Billy,
is you and what you say in
there - cause the jury knows
I probably did some bad
things in my past. You gotta
make 'em believe I didn't
shell out thirty-seven
thousand dollars to knock
off the only honest Union
leader on the East Coast.
Like I said - what it's all
about is you... And one more
thing...

Billy and Ginelli stop at the front door of
the court house.

Ginelli suddenly grins and throws one arm
around his lawyer's shoulder.

With the other he cheerfully squeezes and
kneads Billy's stomach.

                    GINELLI (CONT'D)
                Gotta rub the Buddha belly
                for luck.

                                        CUT TO:

INT. COURTROOM - DAY

Medium-sized. Its carved-wood splendor faded
a while back. There are a number of Trial
Junkie SPECTATORS and a mixed attentive JURY
sits 'in its BOX.

On the bench sits JUDGE PHILIPS, a graying
taciturn jurist known for running a "tight
ship".

The PROSECUTOR is a painfully thin man - gaunt
in contrast to Billy who sits across the aisle
from him with Ginelli.

                    JUDGE PHILIPS
                I think that'll be all, Mrs
                Boynton. Thank you.

MRS BOYNTON - a middle-aged secretary type -
gets down from the stand.

                    JUDGE PHILIPS
                Mr Halleck, was this your
                last witness for the
                defense?

                    BILLY
                Well, your Honor...

Billy looks anxiously towards the back of the
courtroom.

Just then the doors are pushed open and DEEVER

enters.

This private investigator is 30 and pretty beefy and black.

Grinning, Deever hurries down the center aisle, hands Billy a file folder, and then exits just as quickly. Billy glows with satisfaction, but it's clear his client has no idea what's going on.

                    BILLY
               (grinning)
          I have just one more, your
          Honor.

The Prosecutor shuffles through his papers for his prepared witness list.

                    BILLY (CONT'D)
          I'd like to call Mr Max
          Duganfield to the stand.

Immediate eruption of astonishment in the courtroom.

The Prosecutor's mouth falls open.

                    GINELLI
               (low)
          You better know what you're
          doing.

                    BILLY
               (low)
          You got to let me run with
          this one, Richie.

Across the aisle, the Prosecutor is nearly apoplectic.

                    PROSECUTOR
          Your Honor, I object to
          this.

                    BILLY
          Your Honor, the Defendant
          has a right to face his
          accusers.

Judge Philips motions down to the two attorneys.

                    JUDGE PHILIPS
          Approach the bench,
          counselors.

Billy and the Prosecutor walk to the front of
the Judge's bench.

Judge Philips places his hand over the
microphone before him.

                    JUDGE PHILIPS
                    (to Billy)
          Mr Halleck, are you certain
          that you want this witness
          to testify?

                    BILLY
          Quite sure, your honor.
          If my client paid someone
          thirty seven thousand
          dollars to have this man
          killed, I want to hear him
          state it in open court.

                    PROSECUTOR
          I object. Mr Duganfield
          isn't on the Defence's
          subpoena list...

                    BILLY
            (to the Prosecutor)
        He was on our original list.
        We were unable to serve him
        because you and the Feds had
        him in hiding.

                  PROSECUTOR
        For his own safety, your
        honor.

Judge Philips sits back in his leather chair
and speaks to the open court.

                 JUDGE PHILIPS
        Call Max Duganfield to the
        stand.

                   BAILIFF
        Mr Max Duganfield!

The Private Detective Deever throws open the
back doors of the courtroom.

MAX DUGANFIELD enters.

Ginelli rolls his eyes in bewilderment, but
Billy gives him a reassuring wink.

                              CUT AWAY TO:

EXT. DOWNTOWN FAIRVIEW - DAY

Focused around a large well-manicured town
common, the shopping area of Fairview is
compact of scale, zoned for architectural
consistency and a two-story ceiling.

The vehicles of the Gypsy caravan take up
the parking spaces on two sides of the Town

common.

The Gypsies themselves are everywhere. They've unloaded aluminum loungers, set up hibachis, and virtually taken over the Common.

SUSANNA Lempke, a very old Gypsy woman stands at a concrete water fountain, bathing two very young children.

A young dark haired Gypsy male; GABE, is juggling four Indian Clubs, grinning and yelling "Hay!" every time he hurls a club high into the air.

GINA Lempke, sultry and sexy and young only in years, is setting up an easel by the central fountain.

                    GABE
        Gina!

The girl produces a sling shot from her rear pocket and tosses it to Gabriel, who adds the sling shot to his juggling routine. After several rounds he shouts out.

                GABE (CONT'D)
        Hay!

... and tosses the weapon back to the girl.

Gina steps back from the easel, now covered with a paper bulls-eye target.

Walking thirty feet away, she produces three steel ball bearings from her pocket and shoots three quick bull's eyes.

Several of the local Boys crowd around her,

clamoring to try their skill.

                              CUT BACK TO:

INT. COURTROOM - DAY

Billy is examining the witness Max Duganfield.

                    BILLY
          Mr Duganfield is there
          anyone else beside my client
          who might want to see you
          dead?

Ginelli rolls his eyes.

                    PROSECUTOR
          Objection, your honor.

                    JUDGE PHILIPS
          Why?
                    (to Billy)
          Go on.

                    DUGANFIELD
          Possibly. Any number of
          people.

Reaction in the courtroom.

                    BILLY
                    (rapid fire)
          Would this be the first time
          someone has paid to have you
          killed?

                    DUGANFIELD
                    (reluctant)
          Well, three years ago -

                    BILLY
          Who was it Mr Duganfield?
          Who took out a contract on
          your life three years ago?

                 PROSECUTOR
          OBJECTION!

                 DUGANFIELD
          Well it was my wife but -

                 PROSECUTOR
          Your Honor!

Too late. Pandemonium in the courtroom.

                 DUGANFIELD
          - but we've reconciled.

The Jury are all grinning at Ginelli.

                                   CUT TO:

EXT. MAIN STREET - DAY

A CHRYSLER NEW YORKER crashes a yellow light
turning to red, and two opposing vehicles blow
their horns sharply.

INT. THE NEW YORKER

Heidi is behind the wheel and Linda rides
shotgun.

                    HEIDI
          Be careful today. Leda
          Rossington called and said
          the town is _filled_ with
          Gypsies.

Heidi is driving hard, and Linda braces for safety.

                    LINDA
          Mom, put on your seatbelt.

At a turn that corners the town common, Heidi whips the wheel sharply. Just as she plows over the crosswalk...

A YELLOW FRISBEE -

careens off the windshield. A ten-year-old GYPSY KID rushes out into the street, chasing the frisbee.

Heidi slams on the brakes, and barely misses hitting the boy. The New Yorker stalls.

RESUME EXT. DOWNTOWN FAIRVIEW .

The Gypsy Kid retrieves the frisbee. Then, suddenly taking on a limp, the Kid staggers up and pounds on the closed driver's window of the New Yorker.

RESUME INT. NEW YORKER

Nervous and frightened, Heidi is trying to start the car again. She doesn't even look at the Gypsy Kid beating on the window.

                    HEIDI
          Gypsy trash! -

                    LINDA
          Mom! You nearly ran over
          him!

                    HEIDI
                  (angry)
          Why doesn't he go away?!

                    LINDA
          What if he's hurt?!

The engine starts. Heidi stamps the accelerator.

RESUME EXT. DOWNTOWN FAIRVIEW

Heidi swerves the Chrysler into the first available space she sees - a metered space next to a Black-and-White Cop Car in front of the Fairview City Hall.. Just as Heidi and Linda get shakily out of the car...

DUNCAN HOPLEY -

the Chief of Police of Fairview - comes down the steps of the Town Hall. Hopley is 35ish and trim. There are pocks on his cheek and the back of his neck - the result of bad acne in his youth. Hopley joins Heidi and Linda as they gaze in amazement at the transition the Gypsies are making to the Town Common.

                    HEIDI
          You're the Chief of Police,
          Duncan. Why don't you do
          something about them?!

                    DUNCAN
          Judge Rossington and I are
          already working on it,
          Heidi.

                                        CUT TO:

INT. CROSSED PATHS BOOKSTORE - DAY

From the Home Computer <u>Father's Day Special</u> display, Heidi selects a floppy disk program called "The Big Byte Computer Diet Plan." Preparing to leave...

                    HEIDI
          Linda?

Linda waves from the check out counter. Heidi approaches and sees that Linda is holding a book called <u>The World of the Gypsy: Myth and Reality</u>.

                    HEIDI
          I hope you haven't already
          bought that.

The STORE OWNER - fifty and fastidious with a curling white moustache - starts taking care of Heidi's single purchase.

                    STORE OWNER
          She charged it to you.
                    (beat)
          You know, when I was living
          in Woodstock the Gypsies
          came through and stole the
          silver out of every house on
          Shakepainter Road.

Linda's sense of fair play is offended.

                    LINDA
          How do you know it was them?
          It could have been anybody!

The STOCK CLERK - young and handsome - pops up with an armload of books.

                    STOCK CLERK
          They train their children to
          pick pockets and they're all
          over Paris!

                    LINDA
                  (Annoyed)
          Oh, they're just homeless!

Linda stalks out with her book, indignant
against the anti-Gypsy bigotry.

The Store Owner shakes his head as he hands
over the charge slip for Heidi to sign.

                    STORE OWNER
          Know what I hate most? They
          always try to touch you...

                                        CUT TO:

EXT. DOWNTOWN FAIRVIEW - DAY

Linda stalks back to the car. She's just about
to open the door when a hand is laid on her
arm.

                    LINDA
          Look Mom the Gypsies are
          just

She turns and finds herself face to face
with...

TADZU LEMPKE -

an ancient Gypsy with skin the color of a
nicotine-stained knuckle. He wears a loose,
shiny suit over an angular body. His hands are
like claws, his neck like taut rope. His eyes

are sunken, his lips are cracked and bitter.
But most repellent of all is...

LEMPKE'S CANCEROUS NOSE -

the rotting ruin of what was once a hooked beak
of considerable size. But now it's broken,
turned permanently to one side.

It's discolored, nearly purple, with tiny
hemorrhaging veins.

Rot has destroyed most of one nostril and is
now working on the other.

                    LEMPKE
          Pardon me miss -

Linda tries to draw away from Lempke, but
his grip on her arm is tight. He shows her a
folded scrap of white paper.

                LEMPKE (CONT'D)
          I have a prescription...

He's just about to press it into her hand, when
Heidi, suddenly appears and, to get rid of
him, presses a five-dollar bill into Lempke's
hand.

                    HEIDI
          Excuse me. Linda, we have to
          go.

Heidi opens the car door and shoves Linda
inside.

                                        CUT TO:

INT. NEW YORKER

As Heidi drives away, Linda sits beside her,
shocked.

> LINDA
> What happened to that man's
> nose?!

CUT TO:

EXT. THREE BROTHERS RESTAURANT - DAY

The best clam joint on the entire Connecticut
Coast.

It's got great food because buying the very
best is one way to disguise how much money
laundering is going on.

Ginelli and Billy sit in a picturesque corner
of the restaurant, nearly empty in the after-
lunch lull.

Ginelli savors Linguine with Clam Sauce while
Billy is wolfing down a meal that looks like
lunch and dinner combined.

> GINELLI
> What this is really all
> about, Billy, is I owe you a
> big one. You believed in me.

> BILLY
> Or I wouldn't have taken the
> case.

> GINELLI
> Christ, Counselor, you
> not only got me off, you

even solved the fucking
crime! How'd you know about
Duganfield's goddamn <u>wife</u>?!

                    BILLY
Well I know a little bit
about husbands and wives...

                    GINELLI
You and Heidi have had your
troubles but she never paid
anybody 37-K to... ah - take
care of you...

                    BILLY
How did you know we were
having trouble?

                    GINELLI
I keep my ear to the ground.
But you and Heidi are back
on track, right?

INT. LAW OFFICES - DAY

                                        CUT TO:

JILLIAN, Billy's secretary, stands at the top
of the stairs in the second floor offices
of Greely, Penschley, Kinder, and Halleck.
Billy comes huffing and puffing up the steps,
and actually has to pause once in the single
flight of stairs.

                    JILLIAN
They're coming this
afternoon to fix
the elevator. And
congratulations, you made
the noon news!

Billy finally makes it up. His face is red and
he's heaving for his breath. Jillian supports
him for a moment, and whispers, grinning:

                    JILLIAN (CONT'D)
          The guy really was innocent,
          wasn't he?!

KIRK PENSCHLEY - one of Billy's partners -
opens his office door. He's a selfish, bottom-
line Horndog.

                    PENSCHLEY
          Well, you pulled it off,
          Billy. And I didn't think
          you would.

                    BILLY
          Thanks, Kirk. Always glad to
          have your support.

Billy's about to go into his office, but
Penschley pulls him over.

                    PENSCHLEY
          I want to show you
          something. You're not going
          to believe this.

                                        CUT TO:

EXT. TOWN COMMON - DAY - <u>BILLY & PENSCHLEY'S
POV</u>

The Gypsies look as if they've homesteaded the
place. Already the trash bins are overflowing.
The men have set up card and domino tables.
Two Gypsy Women are washing out diapers in the
fountain. The kids are running wild.

                    PENSCHLEY (O.S.)
          Look at em! Like vermin in a
          potato storage locker!

The CAMERA PULLS BACK to show we're in
Penschley's second-floor office, with Penschley
and Billy looking out adjoining windows.

                       BILLY
                     (ironic)
          Lowering the property
          values?

                     PENSCHLEY
          You want 'em camping out in
          your front yard?

Penschley grins, and points out the window.

                       BILLY
          You're in luck, Penschley.
          Here comes the cavalry.

EXT. DOWNTOWN FAIRVIEW - DAY

A number of people - among them Judge Cary
Rossington - stand on the steps of the
courthouse, watching as...

DUNCAN HOPLEY -

the Chief of Police, walks across the street
to the Common, where he is met by Tadzu Lempke,
the ancient Gypsy with the cancerous nose.
Chief Hopley presents a summons to Lempke

                      LEMPKE
          Mister Rossington - he don't
          forget met

                    HOPLEY
          It's <u>Judge</u> Rossington,
          Lempke.

ANGLE ON LAW BUILDING -

showing Billy and Penschley just visible in
the second-floor windows.

                    BILLY
          I'm gonna take off now.
          Heidi and I are going up
          to Mohonk for the weekend.
          Celebrate the end of all
          this Ginelli business.

                    PENSCHLEY
          She been on your case again?

Billy doesn't answer. Billy's about to turn
away, but Penschley stops him and points out
the window.

               PENSCHLEY (CONT'D)
          You see that piece of Gypsy
          ass over by the blue van?

POV OUT THE WINDOW -

of the Gypsies sullenly packing to leave the
Conmen.

The sultry Gina is helping her decrepit
grandmother, SUSANNA Lempke, up into the
fortune telling van.

BACK TO SCENE -

Penschley fishes a quarter from his pocket,
and gives it to Billy.

                    BILLY
          Yeah. What about her?

                  PENSCHLEY
          Give her that quarter
          and ask her to raise her
          skirt...

RESUME EXT. TOWN COMMON

As if she's heard the two men talking about
her, Gina looks up at the windows on the second
floor of the law building.

The two figures of Billy and Penschley quickly
withdraw.

EXT. COURT HOUSE - DAY - MOMENTS LATER

Billy is unlocking his car and about to get
in it. Judge Rossington and Chief of Police
Hopley converge on him.

                  ROSSINGTON
          I heard you did good work up
          in Hartford today, Billy.

Billy nods towards the Common. The Gypsy
vehicles have started to take off.

                    BILLY
          You two have been busy as
          well.

                  ROSSINGTON
          They're not gone yet.
          They've rented a field from
          Lars Arncaster.

                    HOPLEY
          And I'm gonna have a little
          talk with Lars.

When Hopley and Rossington move off together,
Billy is about to get into his car, but he is
startled when he sees...

GINA -

looking   directly   at   him,   and   smiling
lasciviously. Billy turns away, but a young
GYPSY BOY blocks his path.

                  GYPSY BOY
          Give me a quarter mister
          and my sister'll show you a
          trick.

Startled, Billy produces the quarter Penschley
gave him.

The Gypsy Boy, with a grin, holds it up between
his thumb and forefinger.

Lightning quick, Gina pulls out her slingshot,
plugs a ball bearing into the pocket, and
fires it -

BLASTING THE QUARTER -

out of the boy's grasp. Gina grins at Billy
with derision.

                                        CUT TO:

INT. KITCHEN - HALLECK HOUSE - LATE AFTERNOON

Heidi is filling thermoses with coffee, milk,

Diet Coke, etc. Linda sits at the table looking
through the Gypsy picture book.

                    HEIDI
          And promise me you and
          Georgia won't go near the
          Gypsies.

                    LINDA
          What do you want? Cross-My-
          Open-Heart Surgery?

                    HEIDI
          I'll consider it an
          anniversary present.

                    LINDA
          Happy anniversary. I
          promise.

Billy enters. Heidi has finished with the
thermoses.

                    BILLY
          Promise what?

                    HEIDI
          Nothing. Ready?

                    BILLY
              (nods yes)
          Leave the thermoses here.

                    HEIDI
          So every time you finish off
          a bag of potato chips we can
          stop for a Pepsi?

                    BILLY
          Leave the potato chips too.

                    LINDA
          Is this diet gonna be for
          real?

Billy grimaces ruefully.

                    BILLY
          I saw what I looked like on
          television.

                    HEIDI
          So did everybody in town.
          Let's go.

Billy and Linda exchange a sympathetic glance.

                                        CUT TO:

EXT. MOHONK - EARLY EVENING

A grand resort hotel in the Catskills, catering
to old-line upscale Wasps. A long, impressive,
but inviting building with a lake to one side
and a rocky mountainside to the other, and
forest in the back.

                                        CUT TO.:

INT. BILLY AND HEIDI'S ROOM - MOHONK - EARLY
EVENING

Billy and Heidi are dozing on a rumpled four-
poster bed. Billy's size makes him modest even
in front of his wife of twenty years, and he
wears a thin loose kimono-like robe.

Billy stirs, smiles lecherously at his sleeping
wife, and slowly sits up against the head of
the bed. When he starts to pull Heidi head-

first towards his lap, the flaps of his thin
robe inch slowly open.

                    BILLY
                 (apologetically)
          I feel how much I weigh...

                    HEIDI
                 (umnmnppph)
                    BILLY
          I've got to lose some.
          Because right now...

He slowly draws himself up in the bed. Heidi
remains stationary, and her head slowly rolls
down Billy's belly until it comes to rest
right in his crotch.

                BILLY (CONT'D)
          ...if we did it missionary
          style, you'd suffocate.

He waits expectantly for Heidi's response.
None comes.

                BILLY (CONT'D)
          But I can think of some
          alternatives.

He gently puts his hand behind her head, as if
to press it into his crotch. Suddenly, Heidi's
head snaps up. She's wide awake, and she gives
him a passionless, unappreciative stare. Billy
gives up entirely.

                    BILLY
          We ought to go downstairs,
          or they'll give our table
          away.

                                        CUT TO:

INT. DINING ROOM - MOHONK - NIGHT

No cuisine minceur here.. If you order roast
beef, it comes with gravy. And the iced tea
has real sugar in it. Billy and Heidi sit at a
table alone together, with special anniversary
flowers between them.

                    BILLY
          I'm gonna get a huge bonus
          this year. Because of the
          Ginelli case. What would you
          like?

                    HEIDI
          I'd like you to put it aside
          for Linda's education.

                    BILLY
          Of course, but what would
          you like?

A WAITER comes by pushing a pastry cart filled
with fresh, fattening delicacies. Billy eyes
it greedily.

                    HEIDI
                  (smiling)
          Lose some weight. That'd be
          a nice gift.

Billy grimaces, but waves the cart away.

                                        CUT TO:

EXT. COUNTRY ROAD - FAIRVIEW - DAY

A two door Mustang drives slowly down the road,

pausing at several of the rural mailboxes.

INT. MUSTANG

Georgia (the clerk at the Country Store) is driving, Linda's riding shotgun. The book on Gypsies is open on her lap. It's marked with numerous torn scraps of paper.

                    GEORGIA
          If your mother finds out, I
          did not kidnap you. This was
          all your idea.

                    LINDA
          I'm gonna write my Senior
          paper on the Gypsies. This
          is research.

Up ahead is the Gypsy camp. The Gypsies have settled down in a fallow pasture next to a pretty nasty-looking fresh produce stand with a sign reading <u>Arncasters Vegetables - Worms Too.</u>

                    GEORGIA
          Anything in there about
          gypsy aphrodisiacs?

Linda immediately starts searching.

                                        CUT TO:

EXT. MOHONK NATURE TRAIL - DAY

Billy and Heidi are working their way through a gentle upward-sloping forest.

After a year of VCR aerobics, Heidi's fine -

Billy huffs and puffs and pants and drips.

When they reach a picnic area Heidi finally stops and pushes Billy down onto a bench.

                    HEIDI
          You have to be careful,
          Billy. You're not used to
          this kind of exercise.

                    BILLY
          Yeah. I don't know why I'm
          trying to climb a mountain.
          Yesterday I couldn't get up
          a single flight of stairs.
                    (beat)
          I could have a heart attack
          - any time.

                    HEIDI
          That's right. If you don't
          do something you might
          not be alive to see Linda
          graduate in the spring.

                                        CUT TO:

EXT. GYPSY CAMP - DAY

The Gypsy vehicles are arranged in a wagon-train circle.

A number of curious TOWNSPEOPLE - most of them teenagers and young down-scale couples - are present, their vehicles parked for two dollars just outside the encampment.

A COBALT BLUE MICROBUS -

in the Gypsy circle is adorned with a Lady

and Unicorn and the legend: MISS GINA / THE
PROPHETESS.

The back doors are open, and concrete block
steps lead up to a curtained entryway.

Beside the steps, sitting in a folding aluminum
chair, is SUSANNA Lempke, the very old gypsy
woman.

Her skin is dark and well-weathered and she
wears a child's 5-and-10 plastic beret in her
grizzled hair.

Georgia is hanging around, a little uncertainly.
She smiles at Susanna.

                    SUSANNA
          You like chocolate?

Susanna proffers a dingy box of home-made
candies. Georgia shakes her head no.

                    GEORGIA
          I'm waiting for my friend.

                                   CUT TO:

INT. MICROBUS - DAY - SAME TIME

Every square inch of metal has been covered:
with India-print sheets, with surplus wall-
to-wall carpeting, with swags of heavy fringe,
with drapery fabric.

There are two low chairs for the use of Gina's
older or joint-stiffened customers, but the
gypsy fortune-teller and Linda sit on pillows
on the floor.

The light is misty and dim.

Linda pushes a bill across the floor.

                    LINDA
          Five dollars...?

                    GINA
          And a quarter.

                    LINDA
          I don't have any change.

Gina hands Linda a quarter.

                    GINA
          Here. Put it in my hand.

Perplexed, Linda does so. But then she figures
it out.

                    LINDA
          You just wanted me to touch
          you.

Gina smiles and spreads a deck of cards on the
carpeted floor.

                    GINA
          Pick out five.

Linda turns over the first: the Jack of
Diamonds.

                    GINA (CONT'D)
          That's you.

Linda then turns over the King of Diamonds.

                    LINDA
          My father?

                    GINA
          He loves you very much.

Linda turns over a very lowering Queen of
Clubs.

                    GINA (CONT'D)
          And your mother did not want
          you to come here today.

                    LINDA
          Wow this is great!

Linda turns over a fourth card: the four of
clubs.

Gina startles and suddenly looks very serious.

                    LINDA (CONT'D)
          What's wrong?

                    GINA
          Nothing.

Linda starts to turn over the fifth card, but
Gina stops her.

                    LINDA
          But you said five - oh okay.
          So what does the Four of
          Clubs mean?

                    GINA
          Nothing.
                    (beat)
          You have to ask me some
          questions.

                    LINDA
          Okay - ah - should I apply
          early admission to Vassar?

                    GINA
          What? No. Something
          important.

Gina looks at the palm of Linda's hand.

                    LINDA
          College is crucial. So will
          Vassar accept me if I apply
          -

                    GINA
              (suddenly somber)
          That's not something you're
          gonna have to worry about...

                                        CUT TO:

EXT. COUNTRYSIDE - LATE AFTERNOON

Billy's Chrysler is almost alone on this
beautiful stretch of eastern Connecticut road.

INT. CHRYSLER - LATE AFTERNOON

Billy's driving, and they're a little closer
to town now.

Heidi rouses herself from a nap. .

                    BILLY
          We were at Mohonk exactly
          one year ago, too. Know what
          that proves?

                    HEIDI
                 (mumbles)
          What...?

                    BILLY
          It proves we made it through
          another year.

                    HEIDI
          I wasn't so sure we'd make
          this one.

                    BILLY
                 (alarmed)
          Isn't everything all right?
          I thought our truce was
          working beautifully.

Heidi is fully awake now, and trying to recover.

                    HEIDI
          Of course it is. And it
          looks like you're finally
          getting serious about losing
          some weight. You were real
          good, the whole weekend.
          You've lost some already.

                    BILLY
          Come on, Heidi, give me a
          break.

                    HEIDI
          After all these years, you
          think I don't know your
          body?

Heidi reaches over and pulls down Billy's
zipper.

                        BILLY
                       (laughs)
              Hey what are you doing?

                        HEIDI
              Thought maybe you could
              use a little positive
              reinforcement.

She goes down on him.

                                              CUT TO:

EXT. DOWNTOWN FAIRVIEW - LATE AFTERNOON

The old Gypsy limousine - an ancient up-graded
Cadillac hearse - is parked at the curb in
front of the drugstore.

INT. PEARL DRUGGIST'S - LATE AFTERNOON - SAME
TIME

Tadzu Lempke stands across the counter from the
DRUGGIST, minutely questioning the DRUGGIST
about the bill for his prescription.

The Druggist can't take her eyes off Lempke's
rotting nose.

                        DRUGGIST
              No, no, I don't understand
              what it is you don't
              understand.

The Druggist starts to examine the bill again.

Meanwhile, Lempke gives a satisfied look
towards...

THE FRONT OF THE STORE -

where the old woman Susanna Lempke is with a LITTLE BOY of five. Susanna points at...

A TALL RACK OF GREETING CARDS -

The Little Boy goes over and spins the rack so hard that the cards start to fly off onto the floor. Two CLERKS rush over. Meanwhile...

IN ANOTHER AISLE -

GINA grabs fistfuls of different sized Batteries and shoves them into hidden pockets of her skirt.

                                   CUT BACK TO:

INT. CHRYSLER - OUTSKIRTS OF FAIRVIEW - LATE AFTERNOON

Heidi is still administering her positive reinforcement. Billy is breathing deeply, and pressed back against the seat, holds his arms straight out and grasping the wheel.

                                        CUT TO:

EXT. DRUGSTORE - LATE AFTERNOON

The two Clerks firmly escort Susanna and the Little Boy out the front door of the Drugstore.

Susanna protests volubly and confusingly, and the Little Boy tries to hide some candy he stole.

                                        CUT TO:

INT. CHRYSLER - ON MAIN STREET - LATE AFTERNOON

Billy's getting closer to ecstasy His hand's
on the back of Heidi's head - to keep it out
of sight as she bobs up and down in his lap.

> BILLY
> We're getting there... We're
> getting there... Don't
> worry... Nobody around...
> Oh that feels... Oh Heidi
> I love you and this one's
> going to -

Then just as he starts the Ejaculation Groan...

                                        CUT TO:

EXT. DRUGSTORE - LATE AFTERNOON

The Clerk makes a grab for the little Boy's
stolen candy, but he sprints away across the
street.

Susanna now becomes strident against the two
Clerks and backs towards the curb.

Behind the Clerks, Gina slips out of the store,
nods to the old woman, and then slips way.

Susanna laughs, turns, and starts to squeeze
between two cars parked close together.

                                        CUT TO:

INT. CHRYSLER

Billy is panting. Heidi remains face down in
his lap for a beat, then starts to raise her

head.

But just then...

                    BILLY
          Oh that was -

BILLY'S POV THROUGH THE WINDSHIELD -

Susanna Lempke appears suddenly, rushing out
into the street from between the parked cars.

Billy shouts, shoves Heidi aside, slams the
brake, and jams the horn. A SICKENING CRUMP of
metal against flesh.

RESUME EXT. DOWNTOWN FAIRVIEW.

The Chrysler's horn sounds shrill and long.
The car skids left and then right, as the back
tires strike the broken body of the old gypsy
woman.

RESUME INT. CHRYSLER

Heidi jerks her head up out of Billy's lap.
She stares all around in bewildered shock.

                    HEIDI
          Billy, we're in the middle
          of town! Did you run over
          something?!

                    A VERY SLOW DISSOLVE TO:

INT. KITCHEN - HALLECK HOUSE - EARLY MORNING

In sharp contrast to the earlier breakfast,
the atmosphere now is heavy and somber.

Billy and Heidi are dressed as for a funeral.

Linda, heavy-lidded and still in pajamas,
tries to bury her face in a coffee cup.

> LINDA
> So how come you get a trial
> so quick?

> BILLY
> It's not a trial. It's a
> coroner's inquest in Judge's
> Chambers.

> LINDA
> (difficult)
> I know it was an accident,
> but... I mean... what's the
> worst that could happen to
> you?

> HEIDI
> (sudden)
> Your father plays golf with
> the judge. When the Chief of
> Police got a divorce, Billy
> handled it! <u>Nothing</u> is going
> to happen to your father!

> LINDA
> You mean you're gonna get
> off totally?!

> BILLY
> (defensive)
> There's nothing to get off
> from. I'm not guilty. I
> didn't do anything.

Linda says nothing, but her silence is pointed

and sad.

Heidi's look is grim and angry.

                                        CUT TO:

EXT. COURTHOUSE - LATE MORNING

Establishing.

INT. JUDGE'S CHAMBERS - MORNING

Judge Rossington - sans robe - sits upright behind his desk. His hands are peaked fingertip-to-tip in front of his heart.

Heidi Halleck shares a leather couch with a STENOGRAPHER using a TV-Tray for her machine.

Duncan Hopley, in uniform, occupies a straight chair by the door.

Billy is squeezed into a narrow club chair, exposed and alone against a case of law books. The Judge is concluding for the record:

                    ROSSINGTON
          Then - to sum up: It was
          daylight. Mr Halleck's
          vehicle was proceeding at
          proper speed. The Chief of
          Police administered the
          breathalyzer test himself.

                    HOPLEY
          Billy was totally clean. Ah
          - the reading indicated that
          Mr Halleck had probably not
          consumed any alcohol within
          the previous 48 hours.

Heidi is both humiliated and bored.

Finally she can't stand it any more, gets up, and slips out.

The Judge continues reading his decision from notes already prepared and typed out.

                    ROSSINGTON
          And interviews made with
          witnesses at the scene
          of the accident indicate
          that the woman - Susanna
          Lempke - totally ignored the
          crosswalks and ran out into
          the street between parked
          cars looking in neither
          direction as she did so.

                    HOPLEY
          We re-painted the cross-
          walks last month.

                    ROSSINGTON
          (with a look-at Hopley)
          Therefore the Court finds
          no grounds whatever for
          bringing any charges against
          William Halleck in the
          matter of the accidental
          death, on the 9th inst., of
          Susanna Lempke.

Billy holds his breath.

                    ROSSINGTON (CONT'D)
                    (quiet)
          Case dismissed.

                                        CUT TO:

INT. COURTHOUSE LOBBY - MORNING

Heidi is waiting by the front doors, when LEDA
ROSSINGTON enters.

Leda is the straight-backed straight-haired
upper-class wife of Judge Rossington.

                    LEDA
          Was everything taken care
          of?

                    HEIDI
          Leda, I don't want to talk
          about this ever again -

The Stenographer suddenly joins the two women,
and reports with snide glee:

                    STENOGRAPHER
          Don't worry. He's totally
          off the hook.

The Stenographer points out the window at the
Town common.

                    STENOGRAPHER (CONT'D)
          You know how much it cost
          to clean that place up, and
          they were only there one
          afternoon?

                    HEIDI
          Could we talk about
          something besides the
          Gypsies?

                    STENOGRAPHER
          Anyway, they're moving on.
          Old man Arncaster owed

                    somebody some money, and
                    he found out that loan was
                    gonna be called in unless he
                    kicked the Gypsies off his
                    land.

Now the Judge appears and takes Leda's arm.

                         ROSSINGTON
                    Leda, let's go have lunch.
                    Alice, keep your mouth shut.

Alice goes off in one direction, the Judge
and Leda in another. Billy comes out of the
men's room, adjusting his trousers. Instead
of waiting for him, Heidi goes out the front
doors.

EXT. COURTHOUSE - MORNING

The Gypsies' Limo is parked off to the side.
Billy, alone, comes out of the court house.
Heidi waits halfway down the front steps.

                         BILLY
                    Where'd you go?

                         HEIDI
                         (sour)
                    Billy, let's just get out of
                    here.

She heads down the steps in front of him.

                         HEIDI (CONT'D)
                         (coldly ironic)
                    I'll drive.

Heidi goes around, unlocks the car, and gets

inside. As Billy waits for her to unlock the passenger door, from behind him...

> LEMPKE (O.S.)
> Sir...

Billy turns, and faces...

LEMPKE -

who smiles grimly, drawing apart his narrow cracked lips. He lifts one gnarled, yellowed hand, and softly brushes his knuckles against Billy's cheek. He whispers:

> LEMPKE
> Thinner...

> HEIDI (O.S.)
> Billy?

The passenger door is pushed open from inside. Billy looks down into Heidi's annoyed and impatient face.

> HEIDI
> Come on. Get in.

Billy whips back around, but the old Gypsy is gone. The Gypsy Limo glides silently past. Lempke's voice echoes in Billy's head.

> LEMPKE (O.S.)
> Thinner...

Billy touches his cheek.

> CUT TO:

EXT. ARNCASTER FARM - DAY

The Gypsies are decamping. Like a funeral
cortège, the caravan files slowly out of the
field and onto the highway. Duncan Hopley and
his deputy RAND stand with Arncaster, the
farmer who rented his land to the Gypsies.

Arncaster is counting out bills and reluctantly
handing them to the old Gypsy Lempke.

                    ARNCASTER
          I'm not counting today. You
          get that back too.

Lempke pockets the money without reply or
thanks.

                    HOPLEY
                 (uncomfortable)
          Look Lempke, I'm very sorry
          about what happened to your
          wife.

                    LEMPKE
          My wife? Your friend Mister
          William Halleck killed my
          daughter!

                    DEPUTY RAND
          That old woman was your
          daughter?!

                    LEMPKE
          Susanna was my baby. I had
          five girls.

                    HOPLEY
          How old are you, Lempke?

Lempke raises a hand into the air, as if he were going to count on his fingers.

                    HOPLEY
          What is that supposed to
          mean?

But Lempke only smiles. As he lowers his arm, his fingers brush Hopley's cheek.

The old Gypsy leans forwards and whispers something to Hopley.

Rand moves forward as if to back up his chief.

                 DEPUTY RAND
          On your way, Mister.

Lempke shrugs, pulls back, and enters the Gypsy Limo, which pulls up the last in the line of vehicles exiting the field.

Hopley, still distracted by what just happened, watches the Limo drive slowly off.

Then he leans down to pick up a coarse blanket the Gypsies left behind.

But beneath it...

THREE BANTAM ROOSTERS -

are arranged neatly side by side. They've been freshly killed.

                    HOPLEY
          God damn it, Arncaster! Did
          you know they were fighting
          cocks?!

                    ARNCASTER
          Knew they were fighting
          dogs. But these birds didn't
          die in the ring.

                      RAND
          How do you know?

Arncaster picks up one of the dead birds. Its
heads flops over on a broken neck.

                    ARNCASTER
          'Cause somebody wrung their
          necks.

                              DISSOLVE TO:

INT. BASEMENT, HALLECK HOUSE - DAY

In the finished basement, next to a dusty $900
home Nautilus machine, Billy stands profile in
front of a full-length mirror.

Despite some distortion, it's clear Billy's
lost weight - about ten pounds.

He's bunching the waist of his trousers
together at his stomach.

When he lets go...

HIS PANTS DROP COMICALLY TO THE FLOOR -

Billy steps out of the trousers and onto an
ancient set of bathroom scales with a broken
base. The scales are so tilted he has difficulty
keeping his balance. He peers down at the
figures.

                         BILLY
                      (uncertain)
            Two... Seventy... Four...
            Jesus I must have lost more
            than... Oh two-<u>sixty</u>-four!
            That's more like it.

He gets down off the scale, pulls a pair of
out-grown trousers from a storage rack and
starts to get into them. But then he stops and
peers at the scales again.

He drops his too-big trousers onto the scale
and with his foot rubs the dust off - men big
as Billy like to avoid bending over a lot.

                      BILLY (CONT'D)
            Christ! That's two-sixty-
            one!

Suddenly, the door at the head of the stairs
opens, and Heidi's form is silhouetted in the
rectangle of light above Billy.

                         HEIDI
            Billy? Michael Houston is
            here!

                         BILLY
            Coming!

He pulls on his old pants, cinches the belt,
and picks up his golf clubs.

                                        CUT TO:

INT. KITCHEN, HALLECK HOUSE - DAY - MOMENTS
LATER

When Billy comes through with his golf clubs,

Heidi is leaning on the counter, fiddling with
her computer.

A cigarette is burning in an already filled
ashtray. Billy reaches past her to take a large
sack of potato chips out of the cupboard.

                        HEIDI
               (not looking at him)
            Did you weigh yourself?

                        BILLY
            Two-sixty-three.

Heidi punches the number into the computer.

                        HEIDI
            That's fourteen pounds in
            twelve days.

                        BILLY
               (beat)
            Yeah, I finally found a diet
            that works.

He starts to scarf down potato chips.

Car Horn sounds O.S. He starts out, but...

                        HEIDI
            Billy, maybe you're losing
            weight because you feel
            guilty for causing the death
            of that old woman.

Billy whirls round, astonished.

                        BILLY
            And you don't?

                    HEIDI
          I wasn't driving.

Billy is both astonished and appalled by
Heidi's attitude.

                    BILLY
          Right. So that's why you've
          taken up chain smoking
          again?

Billy stalks out.

Heidi angrily stubs out her cigarette.

                                        CUT TO:

EXT. GOLF COURSE, COUNTRY CLUB - DAY.

Houston makes a neat drive. Billy slices.

                    HOUSTON
          You want a diagnosis of your
          game, Billy? No charge...

Billy doesn't respond.

                    HOUSTON (CONT'D)
          Billy, your game sucks. But
          the exercise is starting to
          do you good.

From the side comes Penschley's sarcastic
voice:

                    PENSCHLEY (O.S.)
          Nothing like a little
          manslaughter acquittal to
          turn a man's life around.

Billy rolls his eyes, and turns to greet... A
FOURSOME - made up of Penschley and his date
(the Court Stenographer), and Cary and Leda
Rossington.

                    LEDA
            (sotto voce, to Cary)
          Why doesn't she shut that
          idiot up?

Embarrassed, the Court Stenographer gives
Penschley the high sign to cool it.

Penschley pulls away from her with a sly Grin.

                  PENSCHLEY
          Listen, you better leave
          me alone or I'm gonna give
          Billy five dollars to run you
          down in that golf cart.

                   BILLY
          Mike, let's get out of here!

Billy pushes a disconcerted Houston towards
the golf cart.

Judge Rossington is annoyed with Penschley's
loud mouth:

                CARY ROSSINGTON
          Penschley, you just can't
          talk about this!

                  PENSCHLEY
          Hey, we're among friends...

Billy speeds away in the golf cart.

                                        CUT TO:

INT. LOCKER ROOM, COUNTRY CLUB - LATE
AFTERNOON

Here the Movers & Shakers of Fairview swagger
and boast like Real Men in front of the sixteen-
year-old Caddies.

Mike Houston goes to his locker, where
Rossington has been waiting for him on a bench.
The Judge raises his shirt.

                    ROSSINGTON
          Michael, look at this, would
          you?

Rossington indicates a raised patch of dry,
reddish, scaly skin over his solar plexus.

Houston barely glances at the place before he
diagnoses:

                    HOUSTON
          Your psoriasis is coming
          back.

                    ROSSINGTON
          Why?

                    HOUSTON
          Stress probably. You send
          the wrong man to the gas
          chamber lately?.

Rossington heads for the shower. Houston looks
round and sees...

BILLY -

standing on the scales.

Embarrassed about his size, he wears a bath towel the way a woman does, covering him below-the-knee to above-the-nipple.

                    HOUSTON
          Looks like you lost a
          little.

Houston grabs the towel off Billy and adjusts the balance weights.

                    HOUSTON (CONT'D)
          259.

                    BILLY
          Hey! I've lost two pounds
          today!

                    HOUSTON
          Before you know it, you'll
          be able to see your balls
          without standing on a
          mirror..

General laughter. Billy grabs his towel back and heads for the showers.

IN THE SHOWERS -

The tiled room is filled with steam.

Rossington scrubs at the patch of rough, darkened skin in the middle of his torso. Billy enters.

                    BILLY
          Cary, I guess I never really
          thanked you for - for taking
          care of me last week.

                    ROSSINGTON
          I didn't tell you what
          happened right after that,
          did I? Leda and I went out
          to lunch that day, and
          when I came out of the
          restaurant, that old Gypsy
          was waiting for me.

                    BILLY
                  (shudders)
          What did he say?

                    ROSSINGTON
          It's not what he said - it's
          what he did. He poked me.
          Right here.

Rossington points at the patch of horny skin
on his solar plexus.

                    BILLY
          Yes - but what did he say?!

                    ROSSINGTON
          I don't know, Billy! The old
          bastard just kept on poking
          at me!

Rossington keeps scrubbing away at his stomach.

                                        CUT TO:

INT. KITCHEN - MORNING

Heidi stands at the counter, smoking to the
last drag as she waits for coffee to be ready.
When the dripping finally stops, she drops
the cigarette down the disposal, washes out
the ashtray, hides the pack, and sprays air

freshener.

INT. BATHROOM - MORNING - MOMENTS LATER

We see Billy's feet on the scales.

O.S. there's a Knock at the door.

                    BILLY
          Coffee smells good!

Heidi opens the door. Billy reaches for the
cup but Heidi holds it back.

                    HEIDI
          What does it say?

                    BILLY
          246.

Heidi peers over at the scales.

                    HEIDI
          245.

Heidi at last hands over the cup.

                    HEIDI (CONT'D)
          You're off Equal and back on
          regular sugar.

Billy tastes the coffee, and pointedly relishes
it.

                    BILLY
          I can taste the difference!

Heidi can't bottle it up any longer:

                    HEIDI
          Billy, you're losing two
          pounds a day!

                    BILLY
                   (forced)
          And I feel wonderful!

You wouldn't know it by his expression.

                              CUT TO:

INT. BILLY'S OFFICE - DAY

Billy has shoved aside all his law books and
papers, and cleared a space for the eight or
nine boxes of Chinese food that he and Linda
are sharing.

It's pouring rain out.

Billy is distinctly thinner.

His clothes hang on him.

Billy and Linda each survey the empty boxes
of Chinese food, then exchange a glance. They
laugh simultaneously.

                    LINDA
          Boy, Dad. Great diet.

                    BILLY
          What's your fortune say?

He's digging out the last noodle from one of
the white boxes.

She opens a fortune cookie.

>   LINDA
>   It says, "You will attend a
>   party where strange customs
>   prevail..." Oh right, Aunt
>   Rhoda.

>   BILLY
>   Don't stay in New York too
>   long. I can't do without our
>   picnics.

Billy cracks open his cookie.

Reads the fortune.

Looks troubled.

>   LINDA
>   So what does it say?

>   BILLY
>   (false courage)
>   "You are surrounded by loved
>   ones."

CU: BILLY'S FORTUNE

It reads simply: THINNER.

>   CUT TO:

INT. PEARL DRUGGIST'S, FAIRVIEW - DAY

Billy's at the dietary shelves, looking at the
weight gain products.

A female Oriental PHARMACIST peers at Billy
over the side of the Pharmacist's Perch.

                    PHARMACIST
          You're starting to look real
          good. Tell me what you're
          using so I can recommend it.

                       BILLY
          Will power.

                    PHARMACIST
          Well, don't lose too much at
          one time. It'll make your
          skin all puffy and pasty.

She disappears and goes to a customer with a
finished package.

                 PHARMACIST (CONT'D)
          Here you go, Chief. I put in
          your first refill too. Looks
          like you'll need it.

Hearing this, Billy turns the corner of the
Pharmacy perch and sees...

DUNCAN HOPLEY'S ACNE-SCARRED FACE -

The Chief of Police has the complexion of an
overweight 13-year-old the day school pictures
are taken.

Blackheads and whiteheads freckle his face and
neck.

They're raw and scarring where he's tried to
shave.

                       BILLY
          Jeez you must be allergic to
          something!

                    HOPLEY
          Yeah, Gypsies.

                    BILLY
                  (alarmed)
          What does that mean?

                    HOPLEY
          This started about a
          month ago - I went out to
          Arncasters place just to
          make sure they were really
          going. They went, but there
          was this goddamn blanket
          they left behind. Like an
          idiot I picked it up and man
          it must have had Gyp Germs
          and Gyp Fleas all over it!

Hopley grabs a canister of anti-itch spray and
heads out.

                                        CUT TO:

INT. KITCHEN- HALLECK HOUSE - EVENING -
MINUTES LATER

Heidi is entering Billy's new weight numbers
into the computer.

Billy himself has been making a batch of frozen
roll-out cookies.

He puts two trays into the oven, then starts
nibbling on what remains of the frozen cookie
roll.

                    BILLY
          Make up your mind. You want
          me fat or you want me thin?

                    HEIDI
          All I know is that sudden
          weight loss is one of the
          Seven Warning Signs.

                    BILLY
          Christ! If I gain weight, I
          have a heart attack! If I
          lose weight, I get cancer!

                    HEIDI
          I ran into Michael Houston
          yesterday. He wants you to
          take a few tests.

Billy makes no reply.

                    HEIDI (CONT'D)
          If you won't do it for
          yourself; do it for Linda.

                              DISSOLVE TO:

INT. HOUSTON'S OFFICE - DAY

The kind of doctor's office that Medicaid
patients never get to see.

It's all mahogany and brass.

A week or so has passed, and Billy's fifteen
pounds lighter.

He has a pallor, and he's starting to look
sick.

He's gobbling Lorna Doone's from a full-sized
pack in his jacket pocket.

                    HOUSTON
          I didn't want to get you in
          here till all the tests were
          back. The shit cards came in
          this morning.

Houston leafs through Billy's file.

He frowns slightly.

                    BILLY
          Tell me the truth, Michael.
          Because I'm getting scared.

                    HOUSTON
          It's the people who aren't
          scared who die young.
                    (long beat)
          Everything looks fine.

                    BILLY
Fine?!

                    HOUSTON
          Everything looks fine. The
          lab ran 23 different tests
          on your blood and they all
          turned out good. Cholesterol
          is down, same with the
          triglycerides. You probably
          haven't been this healthy in
          fifteen years.

                    BILLY
          But what about all the
          weight I'm losing?

                    HOUSTON
          You're at 235 -

                    BILLY
          That was a week and a half
          ago! Now I'm down to 212!

                    HOUSTON
          Good! Because 212 is still
          40 pounds over your optimum
          weight.

Billy just shakes his head.

                    BILLY
          It's AIDS, isn't it?

                    HOUSTON
          You're HIV-Negative, and
          we tested twice. Heidi was
          worried about that too.

                    BILLY
          So what do I do?

                    HOUSTON
          Wait a few days. It's a
          little premature to get
          crazy.

                                        CUT TO:

EXT. DOWNTOWN FAIRVIEW - AFTERNOON

Billy and Penschley exit a restaurant and walk
back towards their office. Penschley stops
Billy at a machine that gauges blood-pressure,
pulse, and weight for 50c. Penschley digs into
his pocket for two quarters.

                    PENSCHLEY
          Here you go. Be my guest.

Billy takes the quarters, and pointedly uses them to buy a newspaper in a box next to the weight machine.

> PENSCHLEY (CONT'D)
> What's your secret, Billy?
> Mike Houston give you some
> of his special pills to help
> you shed the lard?

> BILLY
> You know, Kirk, your sense
> of humor sucks.

Before they walk on, Billy has to stop and stick his shirt-tail back in. He even tries to cinch his belt tighter, but he's run out of holes.

> PENSCHLEY
> So let me speak plainly
> - don't wear that suit in
> court this afternoon.

Reluctantly, Billy nods agreement. Penschley walks on while Billy heads towards the door of an upscale men's shop only a few feet away.

CUT TO:

INT. MEN'S CLOTHING STORE - FAIRVIEW - DAY

The OWNER of this small upscale shop is as big as Billy was when we first saw him. Billy is looking through a rack selection of 42" waist trousers, while the Owner tape-measures his waist. He shows Billy the tape.

> BILLY
> You mean I'm down to a 40?

> OWNER
> You can probably take a 38,
> damn you.

> BILLY
> Do you have any scales?

CUT TO:

INT. BACK ROOM - MEN'S STORE - DAY

Billy stands on an industrial scales next to a small loading bay with many boxes for shipping. He shakes his head grimly.

The scales read 211.

> BILLY
> Is this thing accurate?

He's speaking to the Owner, who comes in popping M&M's out of a large bag. He hands Billy a pair of trousers.

> OWNER
> You're gonna need new
> shirts, too.

The Owner looks at Billy closely as he tries on the trousers.

> OWNER (CONT'D)
> This diet you're on - do you
> have to give up liquor?

Billy nods, and reaches for a handful of M&Ms.

CUT TO:

EXT. FAIRVIEW TRAIN STATION - DAY

As a train approaches, Heidi is at the news
kiosk; purchasing a number of Home Computer
magazines. Billy and Linda are saying good-
bye - Billy's lost another ten pounds. His
farewell is so predictable that Linda joins
in:

                    BILLY & LINDA
              Call me when you get there.

They both laugh. Billy places a folded check
in Linda's hand.

                    LINDA
              I'll stay here if you need
              me.

                    BILLY
              You'll see me next week.
              Mike Houston is sending me
              to an incredibly expensive
              Manhattan specialist.

The train arrives. Heidi comes up, and rather
coldly kisses Linda. But Linda is alarmed at
the word specialist.

                    LINDA
              Daddy, what kind of
              specialist?

                    BILLY
              The kind that's going to
              make me fat again. But
              so far, nobody can find
              anything wrong with me.

Linda gets onto the train, smiling and waving

at her parents. Heidi hands Billy a bag of
potato chips.

                    HEIDI
          If there's nothing really
          wrong with you, why do you
          keep losing weight?

                              CUT TO:

INT. LOCKER ROOM, COUNTRY CLUB - LATE
AFTERNOON

Hardly anyone here. The CLUB TRAINER stands
next to the scales.

Billy steps up onto them, and the Trainer
adjusts the weights.

                    TRAINER
          200 even.

Houston comes up, tennis racket over his
shoulder.

                    BILLY
          Is it time to start getting
          crazy? I'm dropping faster.

                    HOUSTON
          That specialist I sent you
          to called today. Let me see
          if I can get hold of him
          right now.

The Trainer grabs Billy's wrist and raises his
arm.

The skin beneath his biceps droops heavy and
loose.

                    TRAINER
          But you'll be looking good
          once we get you on a program
          to take care of these turkey
          wattles.

INT. DINING ROOM, COUNTRY CLUB - EVENING

Billy sits before a table full of dishes -
pretzels, shrimp cocktail, fried potato skins,
and the like. He watches as Mike Houston stops
and speaks to...

LEDA ROSSINGTON -

who is dining and drinking alone.

Then Houston comes over, and stares at the
array of dishes.

                    HOUSTON
          I finally got through to
          that Park Avenue doctor.

                    BILLY
          Good. I don't want to be
          late for dinner. What'd he
          say?

                    HOUSTON
          Good news. It's definitely
          not a tapeworm or any other
          multi-cellular parasite.
          Your immune system is down
          a bit, but you're definitely
          HIV-Negative.

                    BILLY
          Well what's he going to do
          for me?

                    HOUSTON
          He's recommended a clinic.
          And Billy, even if you don't
          want to go, you've got to
          for Heidi's sake. She's
          upset.

He starts to go, but Billy holds him back. He
indicates Leda with a nod of his head.

                     BILLY
          Mike - Leda was eating alone
          last night; too. Is the
          Judge sick?

                    HOUSTON
                  (surprised)
          No! He's just out of town.
          His sister was in a bad
          wreck I think.

                     BILLY
          Cary Rossington is an only
          child.

Houston shrugs and leaves. Billy looks over at
Leda Rossington, thoughtfully.

                                        CUT TO:

INT. UPSTAIRS, HALLECK HOUSE - NIGHT-

IN THE BATHROOM -

Heidi gets out of the shower and steps onto
the scales.

IN THE MASTER BEDROOM -

Billy finishes packing a bag with the few

clothes he has that fit.

He tosses the old Tents-for-Guys wardrobe onto a pile on the floor. Heidi enters in bathrobe.

                    BILLY
          Those don't fit now either.

                    HEIDI
          Well don't just leave them
          there...

                    BILLY
          Would you call Goodwill
          tomorrow?

Billy kicks the clothes into his closet, then gets his keys and wallet.

                    HEIDI
          Are you still going over to
          the Rossingtons? I told you
          - Cary's out of town.

                    BILLY
          He may be back by now.

                                        CUT TO:

EXT. ROSSINGTON HOUSE - NIGHT

Judge Cary and Leda Rossington's place is bigger than the Halleck house, and it's in a more exclusive neighborhood.

Billy stands on the front stoop and rings the bell.

No answer.

He hears a noise above him.

He steps back, sees a shadow pass a second floor bathroom window.

When he rings the bell again, the door is opened immediately, by Leda Rossington.

She finishes off what remains in her Old-Fashioned glass, and then looks at Billy coldly, saying nothing.

                    BILLY
          Leda? I came to see Cary.

                    LEDA
                (calloused)
          He's out of town.

                    BILLY
          Then who's upstairs?

                    LEDA
          Go away, Billy.

                    BILLY
          What's wrong with him, Leda?
          Is he losing weight?

                    LEDA
                (bewildered)
          What?

It's obvious that Leda hasn't even noticed Billy's weight loss.

                    BILLY
          Lost weight, Leda. Like
          me. I've lost over seventy
          pounds.

Leda puts her inebriated attention on Billy.

                              LEDA
                   It doesn't look good on you.

But she lets him into the house.

                                             CUT TO:

INT. ROSSINGTON HOUSE - NIGHT - MINUTES LATER

Billy stands at the foot of the stairs. Leda
comes out of the kitchen with a drink for
Billy, and a re-freshened drink for herself.

                              LEDA
                   You'll need this.

Handing the drink to Billy, she puts herself
on the lowest step and calls:

                         LEDA (CONT'D)
                   Cary! It's Billy Halleck!
                   You want to see him?!

There's no reply. Leda shrugs.

                         LEDA (CONT'D)
                   You're here. Might as well
                   go on up.

Billy starts up the stairs.

INT. SECOND FLOOR HALLWAY, ROSSINGTON HOUSE
- NIGHT

Billy stops on the top landing. Everything's
dark, except for...

THE LIGHT BENEATH THE BATHROOM DOOR -

Billy goes up and knocks softly.

                    BILLY
          Cary, it's Billy. You want
          to come out, or you want me
          to come in?

No response.

                    BILLY (CONT'D)
          I'm coming in. Okay, Cary?

Billy slowly opens the bathroom door. He takes
one step in. The glass slips from his hand,
and smashes on the tiled bathroom floor.

                    BILLY (CONT'D)
          Oh my God ...

INT. BATHROOM

In the bathtub is...

RAWHIDE CARY -

Every square inch of the Judge's skin has
hardened and dried.

It is now cracked like desert clay, the patches
pulling apart to expose raw flesh beneath. His
eyelids have coarsened so that he can see only
through slits; his lips are torn and raw.

                    BILLY
          Oh Cary... I

While Billy stares, Cary awkwardly places a

cigarette between toothless black gums and
lights up with a Bic lighter.

MOMENTS LATER -

Billy is seated on the toilet lid. Still
smoking, Rawhide Cary spritzes his upper body
with a plant sprayer.

                    BILLY
          What is it, Cary?

When Rawhide-Cary replies, his speech is
labored and careful - it's also cold and
bitterly ironic.

                    RAWHIDE-CARY
          We're not quite sure.
                    (beat)
          I went to Mike Houston
          first. Mike decided
          that it wasn't my old
          psoriasis after all - but
          he prescribed some lotion
          anyway. He sent me to
          some idiot Park Avenue
          specialist in New York - a
          dermatologist - who decided
          it wasn't a new strain of
          herpes - but he gave me some
          shots, just in case. And the
          doctors at the clinic in
          Boston decided that it was
          definitely not cancerous -
          but they irradiated me.
                    (beat)
          None of them could stop it.
          When I die, they'll fight
          over who gets to name it.

Rawhide-Cary lights another cigarette.

                    BILLY
          And I know exactly when it
          started. It started the day
          you saved my ass in court.
          The day that old Gypsy
          came after you outside the
          restaurant.

                  RAWHIDE-CARY
          There's something I'm not
          following here.

                    BILLY
          The old man poked you, right
          here -

Billy jabs himself in the solar plexus.

                BILLY (CONT'D)
          And that's where you said it
          started. It started right
          where Lempke touched you.

                  RAWHIDE-CARY
          Oh God, why didn't I think
          of it? I can just call up
          Mike Houston and get him to
          prescribe something that
          works on your basic Gypsy
          curse.

                    BILLY
          Lempke touched me, too.
          That's when I started to
          lose weight. And I can't
          stop, Cary. We're in the
          same boat.

> RAWHIDE-CARY
> Not exactly. You don't have
> to sit in the bathtub all
> day, do you? You go out in
> public, don't you?

> BILLY
> Maybe there's something we
> can do -

Rawhide-Cary stubs out his lighted cigarette
on his stomach.

> RAWHIDE-CARY
> There's something you can
> do, Billy. You can get the
> hell out of my house. And
> don't come back till you've
> lost another seventy pounds.
> So I can see somebody who
> looks as bad as I do. 'Cause
> I need a good laugh.

                                    CUT TO:

INT. BILLY'S OFFICE- LAW OFFICES - DAY

Billy is packing a briefcase full of work.
Penschley slouches on the couch, playing a
hand-held video game.

> BILLY
> It's called the Glassman
> Clinic.

> PENSCHLEY
> Never heard of it. Look,
> don't bother taking that
> stuff with you.

                    BILLY
          I'm only going to be gone
          three days. And that pre-
          school liability case picks
          up again on Tuesday.

                    PENSCHLEY
          Ron Baker's going to take
          care of that. I want you to
          concentrate on getting well,
          understand?

                    BILLY
          I'm not sick. I have a
          nutritional disorder which
          is atypically symptomatic.

                    PENSCHLEY
          Billy, you're shedding
          pounds like a dead dog sheds
          fleas.

                                        CUT TO:

EXT. NEW JERSEY COUNTRYSIDE - DAY

The Halleck Chrysler tools through lovely
woodland New Jersey.

INT. CHRYSLER - DAY - SAME TIME

Heidi's driving, of course. She's grim.

Billy's eating Ritz crackers straight out of
the 16-oz jumbo box.

                    BILLY
          Tell me something, Heidi.

                    HEIDI
          What?

                    BILLY
          Up at Mohonk, the first
          night we were there, you
          refused to - ah - to perform
          the oral sex act on me,
          as we lawyer-types say in
          court.

                    HEIDI
          Billy -

                    BILLY
          - but on the way back from
          Mohonk you grabbed that
          'zipper faster than you can
          say Jack Robinson.
                    (ironic)
          Remember? Just before the
          accident?

                    HEIDI
                    (guarded)
          Yeah. So - ?

                    BILLY
                    (bitter)
          So why did you choose that
          particular moment to ... uh
          ... go down on me?

Billy points to a discreet sign announcing THE
GLASSMAN CLINIC. Through the trees, the clinic
itself is visible: one-story, brick, set deep
among the pines. Privately funded, it's in the
vanguard of nutritional research

Heidi makes a sharp turn into the driveway of

the institution.

                    HEIDI
          What are you trying to say?
          That it's my fault that
          old Gypsy bitch is dead? I
          was the one who blew your
          whistle - so I'm guilty?!
          You're not responsible, and
          I am?! Next it'll be my
          fault you're losing all this
          weight!

                    BILLY
          HEIDI WATCH OUT!

Heidi has to whip the wheel in order to avoid
colliding with a CHARLES RIVER LABORATORY
ANIMALS truck, heading out from the loading
dock.

Heidi slams on brakes, and stops on the road
shoulder.

The truck blows its horn in protest, and passes
on. Heidi leans breathless over the wheel.

                    BILLY
                   (quiet)
          We're there.

                                        CUT TO:

INT. SOLARIUM - GLASSMAN CLINIC - DAY

Billy is in a brightly-colored jumpsuit with
loose legs and loose arms. Ensconced in a lawn
chair among the palms, he's drinking a labeled
Barium Solution through a straw.

A RED-HEADED NURSE is pricking one of his fingers for blood smears.

A SECOND NURSE - burly and bearded - is measuring his arm wattles with calipers.

Heidi is signing documents in triplicate. She looks anxious to be on her way.

                    HEIDI
          What am I signing?

                    BILLY
          In case there's a medical
          emergency... Why don't you
          ask Linda if she can give up
          New York for a few days...?

                    HEIDI
          I don't mind being alone.

                    BILLY
          Heidi, before you go,
          would you mind calling the
          Fairview Police station and
          see if Duncan Hopley is
          around. I really want to
          talk to him.

                    HEIDI
          No, Billy, what you really
          need is to concentrate on
          your problem.
                    (beat)
          Listen, you aren't going to
          be making a lot of calls,
          are you? The whole world
          doesn't have to know you're
          here.

Billy smiles a cold smile.

                                        CUT TO:

INT. BILLY'S ROOM, GLASSMAN CLINIC - DAY

It looks like a businessman's suite in a
Sheraton: roomy, with the sitting room portion
bigger than the sleeping portion. But here the
refrigerator is located, the scales aren't
relegated to the bathroom, there's a table
with computer and printer attached, and the
view of the woods outside is quite lovely.

Billy sits with his feet up on the coffee table,
watching television. Billy's lost another ten
pounds. He's close to his ideal weight, but
his skin's loose, discolored, sagging. He
still moves like a fat man.

He's doggedly plowing through one of several
bowls of snacks laid out in front of him -
each of them on a carefully balanced inlaid
scales.

AT A DESK -

A CLERIC is typing data into a computer. The
heading on the computer and the data both read
DAY 6.

Two DOCTORS enter.

The TALL DOCTOR is senior and solemn.

Second-in-Command is a FEMALE DOCTOR, who's
energetic and constantly smiling.

Billy gets up and meets them halfway across
the room.

                    BILLY
          So? What's the diagnosis?

With a look from the DOCTORS, the Cleric
discreetly exits.

                  TALL DOCTOR
          Hr Halleck, I'd say we need
          about two more weeks with
          you, three at the outside.

                    BILLY
          To cure me or to study me?

                 FEMALE DOCTOR
          Billy, in order to cure
          you we have to study you
          completely.

                    BILLY
          I've been here five days -
          I've lost eleven pounds! I
          may not have three weeks!

                 FEMALE DOCTOR
          And that's the other reason
          you want to stay here! If
          you keep dropping, you can
          expect to develop lesions
          in the mouth, major skin
          problems, and on and on. You
          know what scurvy is? Beri-
          beri?

                  TALL DOCTOR
          You'll find yourself
          extremely susceptible to
          infection - everything from
          a cold to influenza to
          bronchitis to tuberculosis.

<u>Tuberculosis</u>, Mr Halleck.

                    BILLY
And if I stay here, I get
more tests and then you
put me on a life support
system, and you give me even
more tests. But I don't get
cured, right?

                 FEMALE DOCTOR
We don't know what's wrong
with you yet!

                    BILLY
But I do have a good idea...

                                    CUT TO:

INT. HOPLEY'S HOUSE - DUSK

Modest home, landscaped for minimal upkeep
- that is, for a man who lives alone. Billy
- wearing jeans and a t-shirt reading <u>Meat
Me at the Fairview Steak House</u> - get out of
his rental car and goes to the front door. He
rings and knocks at the front door.

                    BILLY
Duncan, open the door!

No response.

                 BILLY (CONT'D)
It's Billy Halleck! Are you
in there?. Are you okay?!

Still no response. Billy starts moving around
the house, peering into the windows. Still
calling out:

                    BILLY (CONT'D)
          Because I'm not! I'm losing
          weight and I'm not on a
          diet!

He rounds the corner of the house. Another
window.

                    BILLY (CONT'D)
          I pig out like I never
          pigged out before and I'm
          still losing two pounds a
          day!

Another window yet.

                    BILLY (CONT'D)
          And it's not Just me,
          Hopley! Cary Rossington -

The window is suddenly jerked open from inside.
Hopley's face and form are dim and indistinct
in the darkness within the house.

                    HOPLEY
          Him too? Well, you might as
          well come on in, Billy ...

                                        CUT TO:

INT. HALLWAY, HOPLEY'S HOUSE - DUSK - MOMENTS
LATER

It's long, dark, windowless, with closed doors
on either side.

Hopley wearing long-sleeves, a high collar,
and gloves, leads the way to the study at the
end. Billy can only see Hopley from the back.

                    HOPLEY
          So the Judge is all dried
          up, hunh? He always was
          anyway. And you finally
          found a diet that works.

                    BILLY
          You don't have to sound so
          glad about it.

                    HOPLEY
          Yeah but you two deserve
          it, 'cause you ran the old
          woman down, and Rossington
          fixed it so you didn't even
          get points taken off your
          driving record.
                    (beat)
          But why'd that old Gypsy
          fuck have to come after me?

                    BILLY
          Probably because you
          testified at the hearing.
          Look - I'm not saying the
          three of us were right, but
          nobody was really lying, and
          the whole thing just wasn't
          our fault!

They enter...

INT. STUDY, HOPLEY'S HOUSE - DUSK -
CONTINUOUS ACTION

Hopley sits at his desk, with his back to the
windows, and the sunset behind him. His face
is in deep shadow, his ruined hands hidden as
well. Billy sits in the interviewee's chair.

                    HOPLEY
          Oh right. I forgot. Susanna
          Lempke was <u>jaywalking</u>!
          You're gonna tell this guy
          his daughter's dead because
          she didn't stop and look
          both ways.

                    BILLY
          Yes! I want to find him and
          confront him and tell him we
          don't deserve this! That's
          why I came to see you. Where
          did the Gypsies go when they
          left Fairview?

Hopley suddenly reaches up and turns on a
lamp.

Revealed in all its lurid glory is...

HOPLEY'S FACE -

a puffed-up landscape of pimples, blackheads,
boils and infected abscesses.

Billy stares in shock and revulsion.

Hopley smiles grimly, but blandly goes on to
answer Billy's question:

                    HOPLEY
          I don't know where the
          Gypsies went. And you've got
          to do this yourself, because
          you are the one who started
          it.

Hopley takes a gun from the desk drawer and
offers it to Billy.

                    HOPLEY (CONT'D)
          Find him Billy! Make him
          take the curse off me, and
          you, and Cary. Then kill the
          bastard and say it's from
          me!

Billy refuses the gun, gets up, and hurries
out. As he races down the hall, Hopley calls
after him.

                    HOPLEY (O.S.)
          It's too late, Billy! You
          know it's too late! But kill
          the bastard anyway!

                                        CUT TO:

EXT. FRONT OF HOPLEY HOUSE - DUSK

Billy flings open the front door and rushes
out to his car. He turns the ignition, slams
it into gear, and takes off driving in a
destructive arc across the lawn.

As Billy drives out of frame, the front door
is pushed softly shut. A beat of silence.
Then, O.S....

A SINGLE SHOT

                                        CUT TO:

INT. HALLECK HOUSE - NIGHT

Halleck comes in the front door. The house
is unlighted, but Heidi has evidently been
waiting on the stairs.

> HEIDI
> Why didn't you stay at the
> clinic?. They wanted you to
> stay!

> BILLY
> Heidi, they weren't helping
> me.

> HEIDI
> Billy, I don't know how to
> take care of you.!

> BILLY
> I'm not asking you to.

Coldly interrupting him, Heidi heads for the
kitchen.

> HEIDI
> I fixed you a snack.

                                              CUT TO:

INT. KITCHEN - NIGHT

Heidi has laid out more than a snack for him:
thick sandwiches, chips and dips, non-diet
sodas, and the like.

As Billy scarfs it down, he leafs through the
books on Gypsies that Linda bought earlier.

Heidi enters, clicking off the remote phone.

> HEIDI
> That was Mike Houston.
> Duncan Hopley committed
> suicide.

                    BILLY
     I'm not surprised. I
     stopped in to see him this
     afternoon, just before I
     came home.

                    HEIDI
                 (bewildered)
     You were over there today? I

                    BILLY
     Lempke - that old Gypsy man
     - he went after Duncan too.

Billy turns to a new chapter in the book on
the table. It's called:

          LOVE PORTIONS AND CURSES
             SECRET GYPSY LORE
                    HEIDI
     Billy are you saying that
     the Gypsies put a curse on
     Duncan Hopley... and on
     you?! And that's why you're
     losing weight?!

Billy indicates the massive amount of food
laid out before him.

                    BILLY
     I'm not on a <u>diet</u>, Heidi.
     And it's not a <u>mental</u>
     <u>disorder</u>, And it's not a
     <u>tapeworm</u>. I've been eating
     like this for over six
     weeks! Six-thousand calories
     a day - at least - and I
     still lose two pounds every
     twenty-four hours!

Heidi sits still for a moment, taking it in.
Then she responds quietly:

                    HEIDI
          You're not talking like this
          to anybody else, are you?

                                        CUT TO:

EXT. METHODIST CHURCH FAIRVIEW - DAY

There's been a memorial service for Duncan
Hopley. Billy and Heidi come out just ahead
of Michael Houston. Heidi goes off and Billy
corners the doctor.

                    HOUSTON
          Billy I saw him! I checked
          him out and yeah he had
          some lesions on the back of
          his neck and so forth but
          he's had acne since - did
          you ever see his yearbook
          picture?

                    BILLY
          But his face...

Houston opens his mouth wide, and sticks his
middle finger up against the roof of his mouth.

                    HOUSTON
          He stuck a .357 right here.
          What face?

                                        CUT TO:

INT. DEN - HALLECK'S HOUSE - TWILIGHT

Billy is sitting up in a recliner, studying

another book on Gypsies. Now there's a stack of them beside the chair.

On the television, Maria Ouspenskaya is giving a Gypsy warning in an old Universal horror film.

Through the windows, outside, we can see Heidi. She been sipping a drink on the patio, at the end of a long hot summer day.

Heidi enters with her empty glass and the remote phone.

> HEIDI
> Do you want to talk to
> someone named Deever?

> BILLY
> Yes! He's helping me do-
> some research...

As she hands Billy the phone, she inadvertently knocks over the pile of books.

> HEIDI
> Let me guess... Is the firm
> paying for this, or does it
> come out of our pockets?

Billy doesn't answer her, but gets right on the phone.

> BILLY
> (into phone)
> Hey Deever - whatever you
> got - why don't you bring it
> straight on over?

Heidi exits into the kitchen.

                    BILLY (CONT'D)
                    (into phone)
          Oh all right, but make it
          first thing in the morning.

He clicks off the phone, and reaches down to
right the books.

He gets a sudden spasm in his chest and he
gasps harshly for breath.

Heidi re-enters with a freshened drink just as
Billy has recovered himself.

                    HEIDI
          Do you mind sleeping down
          here again tonight? It's hot
          and you've become very bony.

                                        CUT TO:

INT. BILLY'S OFFICE LAW OFFICES - MORNING

At his desk, Billy is examining a map of New
England which has been marked with a red route,
with annotations of date and uncertainty.

Across from him is DEEVER - the investigator
who produced Billy's surprise witness in court.

Deever is delivering highlights of his report
on the Gypsies.

                    DEEVER
          Raintree of course, as soon
          as they left here. Then
          Milford, then Greeno - which
          I had never even heard of.
          Then 43 Gypsies totally
          disappear for three days.

                    Turn up in Pawtucket, but
                    now there's 47 of 'em. Then
                    you can't find 'em again -
                    these guys wear real soft
                    shoes.

During this Billy has been going through other
pieces of evidence.

He goes through more photographs of the
various members of the tribe, their vehicles
and plates.

                         BILLY
                    And after that on to...
                    Lincoln, Mass? This the same
                    group every time, you're
                    sure?

                         DEEVER
                    Yeah. For some reason people
                    seem to notice this hundred-
                    year-old guy with a big
                    black cancer in the middle
                    of his face.

Billy abruptly holds up a photograph of Lempke
taken with a telephoto lens.

                         BILLY
                    What else do you know about
                    Lempke?

                         DEEVER
                    For starters? He was a Draft
                    Dodger-
                              (beat)
                    -in World War I.

A button on Billy's phone lights up.

O.S. a faint RING.

INT. RECEPTION, BILLY'S OFFICE - DAY - SAME TIME

Jillian has answered the incoming call:

> JILLIAN
> I'm very sorry, he's busy...
> He's in a meeting at the
> moment.
> (listens)
> Yes, of course I'll take the
> message.
> (listens)
> Yes <u>of course</u> I gave him
> your other messages!

RESUME INT. BILLY'S OFFICE

The Investigator is putting up his notes and charts, preparing to go.

> DEEVER
> But we're less than a week
> behind them now. They
> usually hit Boothbay and
> they're always in Bar Harbor
> for Labor Day weekend. But
> between now and then they
> could be anywhere.

The Investigator goes to the door.

Billy follows.

But as the Investigator reaches for the knob, he is met by a distraught Jillian.

                    JILLIAN
          Billy, it's the Glassman
          Clinic again. This is their
          third call today. Line 2.

As the Investigator exits, Billy grabs the
phone, punches in line two, and barks into it
(as if speaking to Jillian):

                    BILLY
                 (INTO PHONE)
          Tell 'em to go screw the
          fucking cat scan. I'm not
          posing for anybody's Before
          & After shots!

Penschley, having heard from just outside the
door, comes inside.

                    PENSCHLEY
          Hell, Billy, why don't you
          go? Your Bar insurance'll
          take care of everything!

Billy starts to retort, but then an idea occurs
to him. He calms instantly.

                    BILLY
          You're right. I think I need
          to take a little time off.

Penschley grins - he's not sorry to be rid of
his unstable partner.

                                        CUT TO:

INT. BEDROOM - HALLECK HOUSE - MORNING - SAME
TIME

Houston has been giving Billy a cursory check-up here.

While Billy once more tries to find clothes
that aren't too big for him, the doctor sits
on the edge of the bed.

Heidi packs Billy's bag.

> HOUSTON
> It's not about your mind,
> Billy, it's about your
> brain.

> HEIDI
> There's just a chemical
> imbalance - because you've
> lost so much weight. And
> there's no treatment
> involved -

> HOUSTON
> Just testing.

> BILLY
> You two really are in sync
> on this.

> HOUSTON
> It's for your sake...

> HEIDI
> It's for your own good...

> BILLY
> Enough already- you see me
> packing, don't you?

He snaps the case shut.

CUT TO:

EXT. HALLECK HOUSE - MORNING - MINUTES.LATER

Heidi stands in the driveway. Mike Houston is pulling out in his snazzy Porsche so that Billy can get his car out. Billy stops his car alongside the Porsche.

                    BILLY
          Since when did you make
          house calls?

                    HOUSTON
          Wanted to make sure, you got
          off okay, Billy-Boy.

Billy leaves, immediately turning a corner and disappearing.

Houston pulls the Porsche back into the driveway. He quickly gets out and follows Heidi back into the house.

                                        CUT TO:

EXT. THREE BROTHERS RESTAURANT - DAY

Billy's car is parked out in front of the harborside restaurant.

INT. THREE BROTHERS RESTAURANT - DAY

Billy, looking gaunt and nervous, is hurriedly finishing off a large bowl of clam chowder and a larger basket of crackers.

Beside him in this corner booth, Ginelli nurses a cup of black coffee and looks at Billy closely.

                    GINELLI
          You said you wanted to ask
          me something.

                    BILLY
          Yeah, I do.
                    (beat)
          Are you superstitious?

                    GINELLI
          Me? You ask an old wop like
          me if I'm superstitious?
          Growing up in a family where
          my mother and my grandmother
          and all my aunts went around
          Hail-Marying and praying to
          saints you never heard of to
          protect 'em from the Evil
          Eye every time a crow flew
          over the house? You ask me a
          question like that?

                    BILLY
          Yeah. 'Cause I wanna know.

Ginelli sees that Billy is serious. He takes
a breath, and goes on, his voice quite flat
and simple.

                    GINELLI
                    (flat)
          Here's what it's really all
          about, Billy. I believe in
          two things: I believe in - I
          believe in what I can see.
          The other thing I believe
          in? I believe what my
          friends tell me is true. You
          tell me something, William
          Halleck, I believe in it.

                    (Beat)
Heard you had some trouble
over in Fairview. But you
were... protected, right?

                    BILLY
Not entirely. You know the
woman I hit - the one who
died - you know who she was?

                    GINELLI
Old Gypsy crow, right?

                    BILLY
Yeah, she was old. But her
father's still alive. His
name is Lempke, and he made
some trouble for me.

                    GINELLI
And that's what this is
really all about...

                    BILLY
                  (nodding)
Yeah. I'm going after him.
Soon as I leave here.

Ginelli slides out of the booth, followed by
Billy. Billy looks small and weak next to the
robust Ginelli.

                    GINELLI
Okay, but if you find out
you can't handle this thing
on your own - if that old
Gypsy bastard starts making
more trouble, you give me a
call.

They exit the front doors of the restaurant into...

EXT. PARKING LOT - THREE BROTHERS RESTAURANT - DAY - CONT ACTION

Billy heads for his car, pulling out his keys. Ginelli takes the keys away.

                    GINELLI
          When you go after that old
          Gypsy bastard, don't be
          driving the car that killed
          his daughter.

Ginelli hands Billy another set of keys. He points to a solid, but decade- old Oldsmobile.

                    BILLY
          Thanks.

Billy gets his bag from his own car, and then heads for the Oldsmobile.

                                        CUT TO:

EXT. MYSTIC SAVINGS - DAY

In Mystic Connecticut. Billy's Cutlass is parked out front.

INT. MYSTIC SAVINGS - DAY'

Billy stands in front of an American Express Traveller's Cheques dispenser, sticking in one AmEx card after another.

The Traveller's Cheques fan-fold out in a pile on the counter.

                    BILLY (V.O.)
          Dear Heidi: By the time you
          read this, I'll be gone. I
          don't know exactly where,
          and I don't know for how
          long...

EXT. ROUTE 95 NORTH - DAY

The Cutlass crosses the beautiful border
between Connecticut and Rhode Island.

                    BILLY (V.O.)
          ... but I hope that when I
          come back. all of this will
          be over. This nightmare
          we've been living with.

EXT. MACDONALD'S, WOBURN MASSACHUSETTS - DAY

Billy has stopped at a MacDonald's just
underneath the State House dome. He eats outside,
sitting in the open door of the passenger
side. There's a toxic waste treatment plant on
the other side of the ornamental fence.

                    BILLY (V.O.)
          I guess you've realized by
          now that I'm not on my way
          to the Glassman Clinic. The
          fact is, I'm trying to track
          down Tadzu Lempke...

INT. A FACTORY OUTLET CLOTHING STORE, REVERE
MASS - DAY

At the check-out counter, Billy is buying
the next smaller size clothing. He pays by
Traveller's Cheque.

                    BILLY (V.O.)
          The only person who can lift
          the curse is the man who put
          the curse on me.

EXT. FACTORY OUTLET CLOTHING STORE, REVERE
MASS - DAY

Billy's rented Cutlass looks right at home in
this parking lot. Billy opens his suitcase,
tosses out what's there, and puts in the new,
smaller-sized items.

                    BILLY (V.O.)
          Losing weight like this
          brings out the worst in me
          - and sometimes I wish you
          were down in Hell with me.

EXT. PORTSMOUTH NH - EARLY EVENING

Approaching the bridge, with signs reading
<u>95 NORTH - MAINE, PRINCE EDWARD ISLAND, THE
MARITIMES</u>.

                    BILLY (V.O.)
          The truth is, you're
          responsible for Susanna
          Lempke's death too.

EXT. THE PORTSMOUTH HILTON, PORTSMOUTH NH -
EARLY EVENING

Billy's Cutlass heads into the underground
parking garage.

                    BILLY (V.O.)
          Whatever happens to me, we
          both deserve it.

INT. BILLY'S ROOM - THE PORTSMOUTH HILTON -
NIGHT

When the bathroom door opens, steam billows
out. Billy shuffles out the doorway in a thick
terrycloth robe.

As he dries his hair, the sleeves of the robe
slip revealing arms with sagging, discolored
flesh.

                    BILLY (V.O.)
          I love you, Heidi. Tell
          Linda how much I love her.

He spasms with sharp pains in the joints of
his arms.

The brush flies out of his hand.

When he catches himself, his robe falls open
in front.

CU: BILLY'S EXPRESSION OF DESPAIR -

as he sees his naked body reflected in the
full-length mirror.

                    BILLY (V.O.)
          I'll be home as soon as I
          can. Love, Billy...

                                        CUT TO:

INT. KITCHEN, HALLECK HOUSE - NIGHT

Heidi paces with the remote phone. She's
holding Billy's letter.

                      HEIDI
                  (into phone)
            Mike, you're not gonna
            believe this one. Would you
            please come over.
                  (listens)
            Okay, just as soon as you
            can.

She clicks off the remote and heads straight
for the sink.

                      HEIDI
            Damn you, Billy! Damn you to
            Hell!

She crushes the letter and pokes it down the
garbage disposal. Runs water. Flicks on the
switch.

                                        CUT TO:

EXT. SEASIDE FAIR - EARLY EVENING

Small, tawdry, cheap, and probably a whole lot
of fun. The Cutlass cruises the aisles of the
municipal parking lot across Highway 1 from
the arcades and tents. He slams on brakes when
he sees...

THE GYPSY CARAVAN VEHICLES -

all parked in a group here. As one car leaves,
Billy swings into its space so fast he scrapes
bumpers.

Billy gets out, and we see him in his new
K-Mart Blue Light Polyester Special outfit.
He looks over the tops of the cars towards the
Fairground.

                    BILLY
          I smell you, old man...

From across the way, a high-pitched male voice
cackles:

                    LEMPKE (O.S.)
          Guess your Weight and Tell
          Your Fate!

EXT. THE SEASIDE FAIR - EVENING

Next to a Test-Your-Strength column is a
platform with inset floor scales. Lempke sits
in a chair beside Gina, as she touts his skills
to a sparse crowd.

                    GINA
          Guess your Weight! If he's
          off by more than five
          pounds...

Billy comes closer.

But Gina, as if expecting him, turns and grins
right at him...

                    GINA (CONT'D)
          ... then you get the dollaya
          choice!

In the booth behind her are three rows of dolls:
an Acne-Atrocity doll for Duncan Hopley, an
Alligator-Boy doll for Cary Rossington, and a
Skeleton-Scout for Billy Halleck.

                    LEMPKE
          78 pounds. On the day he
          died.

                    GINA
          You lose mister, but have a
          prize anyway.

She tosses Billy the Skeleton Doll. Billy
blocks it with his forearm, then breaks into
a run. Gina puns a slingshot from her pocket,
and then takes off after him.

AT THE TWO LANE ROAD -

Billy pauses to look back before he runs across
to the parking lot. Gina is behind him. She
grins, takes something from her pocket, and
places it in the leather sling.

Billy turns and runs across the two-lane -
right into the path of...

A BLACK MERCEDES -

which bears down on him mercilessly. Billy
stands transfixed in its path. Suddenly he
looks to the side.

GINA-

is about to fire her shiny missile at him.

THE MERCEDES -

continues to bear down on him.

GINA -

releases the ball bearing.

BILLY-ducks and leaps to the side, trying to avoid both.

THE BALL BEARING -

smashes a window in the Mercedes.

The Mercedes skids, and brakes, missing Billy. The passenger door is flung open.

                    ROSSINGTON (O.S.)
            Get in, you idiot!

                    BILLY
            Cary...?

Another window of the Mercedes is smashed. Billy jumps in.

The car takes off. Gina runs into the road and fires another shot.

INT. MERCEDES

Rossington, normal-looking, is driving with a grim smile. The landscape is lushly green and rocky.

                    ROSSINGTON
            What did you expect, Billy?
            We killed his daughter.
            We're going to die.

                    BILLY
            Where are we going?

                    ROSSINGTON
            There's a map in the glove
            compartment.

Billy opens the glove compartment. An Alligator-Boy doll falls out into Billy's lap. When he turns back, Rossington is...

ALLIGATOR-CARY

and his affliction has been carried to a nightmarish extreme. Billy stares in horror. Alligator-Cary grins, and turns the wheel directly into the path of...

AN EIGHTEEN-WHEELER -

barreling down the highway towards them.

                    BILLY
          No!

Billy grabs the wheel and whips it towards the right.

EXT. TWO-LANE ROAD - DAY - CONT ACTION

The 18-Wheeler passes with a blare of horn.

The Mercedes leaps the gravel shoulder and smashes into the cut wall of stone. The Mercedes explodes into flames.

                                    CUT TO:

INT. HOTEL ROOM - MORNING

It was a dream, of course, and Billy snaps upright in bed.

He reaches immediately for his address book and the phone. He unsteadily dials.

                    BILLY
                (into phone)
          Leda? This is Billy Halleck.

                                        CUT TO:

INT. KITCHEN, ROSSINGTON HOUSE - MORNING

Leda cradles the phone on her shoulder as
she fills the dish washer with dirty highball
glasses. Her sarcasm is subtle and bland.

                    LEDA
          Sorry, Billy. Cary cant come
          to the phone right now.
          Yesterday, he drove the
          Mercedes into the side of a
          mountain. Apparently he had
          decided on cremation.

INT. HOTEL ROOM

Billy shakes his head.

                    BILLY
                (into phone)
          Leda, I'm so sorry -

RESUME INT. ROSSINGTON KITCHEN

Leda hangs up the phone. Then...

                    LEDA
          Don't be.

                                        CUT TO:

EXT. SEASIDE FAIR - EARLY EVENING

Exactly as in his dream earlier, the fair is small, tawdry, cheap, and probably a whole lot of fun.

Exactly as in his dream, the Cutlass cruises the aisles of the municipal parking lot across Highway 1 from the arcades and tents.

INT. THE CUTLASS - SAME TIME

Billy shakes his head as he turns the car into the same empty space he had found in the dream.

> BILLY
> (serious)
> I hate dejá vu...

CUT TO:

EXT. SEASIDE FAIR - DAY

Pretty much as Billy saw it in his dream. But the dolls that are prizes at the Guess Your Weight stand are the usual Taiwanese Trash.

Instead of the Weight Guessing platform, there is now...

THE FREAK TENT -

no freaks visible, just the posters, including Mister Skeleton next to The Colossal Man - like Billy After and Billy before.

Someone peers out from behind the cloth curtain of the Freak Tent, but Billy doesn't wait to see who it is.

He strides off down the beach, heading for an old-fashioned cocktail lounge called The Seven Seas.

                                        CUT TO:

INT. THE SEVEN SEAS LOUNGE - DAY.

The tinted windows look out on the Seaside Fair. Billy is showing an old man (ENDERS) the photographs of the gypsies.

When Billy shows the PHOTOGRAPH OF Lempke, Enders queasily turns the picture face down.

CU: THE BACK OF THE PHOTOGRAPH

Info typed on a label identifies the old man as Tadzu Lempke.

                    ENDERS
          How do you say that?

                    BILLY
          Tah-Doush, I think.

                    ENDERS
          Teddy. Knew Teddy when
          he was here twenty years
          ago. Saw him last week.
          Looked exactly the same. He
          remembered me, too. Called
          me by my Secret Name..

                    BILLY
          Secret Name?

                    ENDERS
          You got a name on your birth
          certificate, but a man's
          also got a name tattooed
          in a secret place - on his
          heart maybe, or maybe in his
          groin. Teddy Lempke called
          me Flash - my army name,
          and everybody else who ever
          called me that is dead.

Enders begins to tremble, knocks over his beer
glass.

Billy calls out to the Bartender.

                    BILLY
          Could we have another?
                    (to Enders)
          Go on...

                    ENDERS
          Told me, "Flash - say hello
          to your wife from Teddy."
          I told him my wife was
          dead. "So why you no put
          up gravestone for her like
          good husband?" he says, and
          Mister - I <u>didn't</u> put up a
          gravestone yet.

Enders stares at Billy with tears in his eyes.

The Bartender comes over, protective of Enders,
and very unfriendly towards Billy.

                    BARTENDER
          I want you to get out of
          here. I don't

                    BILLY
     I will. Where'd the Gypsies
     go after they left here?

                    ENDERS
     I watched 'em, Mister! Out
     Route 27 and turned right on
     Route 1.

                    BARTENDER
     Rockland, probably, so get
     out, Mister, 'cause you look
     like bad luck waiting for a
     place to happen.

Billy puts down a twenty and gets up. Enders
starts to get up after him, but the Bartender
holds him down.

Billy heads out.

                    ENDERS
       If you got a secret, Mister,
       don't let Teddy find out
       what it is!

Breaking down, Enders calls after Billy,
nearly frantic:

                    ENDERS (CONT'D)
       He called me by my Secret
       Name and I pissed all the
       way down my leg!

Billy exits, without looking back.

                                        CUT TO:

EXT. FALMOUTH POST OFFICE - DAY

At a window marked <u>General Deliveries</u>, Billy shows the clerk his I.D. and is handed an Express Mail envelope to sign for. Billy's only been on the road a couple of days, and lost about five pounds - but he drags and slumps.

After signing the form for the overnight package, he walks over to an empty counter and rips open the package, removing a file.

                                        CUT TO:

INT. LAW OFFICES - DAY.

Jillian takes her coffee cup and walks away from her desk. Penschley goes up to Jillian's Out Box, thumbs through a second, and removes the Express mail duplicate. He copies down the address, replaces the slip, and goes to his adjoining office. His SECRETARY hands him a note.

                    SECRETARY
          Mr Deever called back. He
          left this number. Isn't
          this the detective that Mr
          Halleck hired?

                    PENSCHLEY
               (obviously lying)
          Never heard of the guy..
               (beat)
          But try him at that number.

                                        CUT TO:

EXT. A USED CAR LOT - NIGHT

It's totally downscale. Chop shop rejects, a
towing service, a vicious Doberman leaping at
the closed driver's window of Billy's Cutlass.
On the passenger side a very FAT BLONDE WOMAN
finishes marking up a map. She hands it inside
the car to Billy, then brings away a $100
Traveller's Cheque.

                                        CUT TO:

EXT. PARKING LOT OF A BURNED-OUT WAREHOUSE -
DAY

A scorched cinder-block shell in the middle
of a vast parking lot. The only car in it is
Billy's. Billy himself, clutching his sheaf
of xeroxes, walks about the empty lot looking
for clues.

                    BILLY
          I smell you, old man.

Billy surveys the detritus of the recently
dismantled Gypsy camp.

                                        CUT TO:

INT. UPSTAIRS HALLWAY, HALLECK HOUSE - DAY

The doors to the Master Bedroom and to Linda's
bedroom are open.

The PHONE RINGS.

Through the open doorway we see Linda as she
lurches for it.

> LINDA
> Hello? ... Hello, is anyone
> there?

Sound O.S. of TOILET FLUSHING. Heidi comes out of the bathroom.

> HEIDI
> Lin? Is that Billy?

> BILLY
> (filtered)
> I don't want to talk to your
> mother.

> LINDA
> (into phone)
> But you'll talk to me, won't
> you?

Heidi suddenly reaches round and grabs the phone out of Linda's hand.

> HEIDI
> Billy, you've got to get
> some help. You can't just-

Evidently at this point, Billy breaks the connection. Heidi slams down the phone and stalks out.

> LINDA
> You don't <u>want</u> Daddy to come
> back, do you?!

Heidi enters her bedroom and slams shut the door.

> CUT TO:

EXT. BOOTHBAY HARBOR - DAY

Quaint, but definitely more upscale than what
we've seen in Maine heretofore.

Next to a high-priced clothing store
specializing in wind breakers, there's a little
lean-to of a shop, with Biff Quigley Owner.

INT. QUIGLEY SEASONAL RENTALS - DAY - SAME
TIME

Biff QUIGLEY's place is a little downscale for
Boothbay Harbor, but that is where the Gypsies
would go.

Quigley himself is also a little downscale for
Boothbay Harbor, too florid for forty, and
with a laugh that is snappish.

Billy sits across from him.

                    QUIGLEY
          Man, I just have to say
          it: You look like an
          advertisement for a vacation
          in Biafra.

                    BILLY
          Thanks. I just wanna know
          if you have seen a troop
          of Gypsies passing through
          here.

                    QUIGLEY
          I can tell you where the
          fucking Gypsies are this
          very minute but it'll cost
          you two hundred bucks.

                    BILLY
          What?

                    QUIGLEY
          Not the information I give
          you, that's a freebie.
          The two hundred's for the
          information that I don't
          give your wife and your
          doctor.

Quigley hands Billy a circular, showing his picture, giving a description and contact numbers for Heidi, Penschley and Houston. There's a $250 reward "for information leading to..."

                    BILLY
          Do you take Traveller's
          Checks?

                                        CUT TO:

EXT. GYPSY CAMP - NIGHT

In a sheltered field near a stand of Maine pines the Gypsy encampment is arranged in concentric circles - the scruffy vehicles form the circle, inside that men and women in aluminum lawn chairs, and centermost a few children around a circle of stones delimiting the communal fire, burning in a hole dug in the earth.

The men are smoking and telling dirty jokes, the women are gossiping and pasting in Green Stamps, and the children are practicing card tricks and pocket-picking.

Suddenly everyone goes silent. Then abruptly

the young woman...

GINA flings herself across the circle, screaming hysterically in Rom - that is, Romish, the secretive language of this nomadic people.

                    GINA
          - ta mig mammal Va dybbuk!
          Ta mig inte till mormor!
          Ordo! Vu' derlak!

With anger and disgust she's pointing at something just outside the circle of flickering light. This fury is directed at...

BILLY -

whom we see when he steps quietly forward into the circle of light. He has a long overcoat wrapped around him. Gina is on him about to attack, but is stopped by a sharp command from behind her:

                    LEMPKE (O.S.)
          So hon laqt, Gina!

Lempke steps into the circle of_ light directly opposite from Billy. Her passion bridled by the old man Gina snarls in Billy's face:

                    GINA
          You don't understand our
          lingo, mister? I say to my
          old papa that you killed my
          old-mamma! I say you are a
          demon and we should kill
          you!

Before she backs away, Gina spits in Billy's face.

This isn't merely a gesture somehow: her spittle is thick and globous.

                    GINA (CONT'D)
          Skummade igenom.

As she stalks away, the old man Lempke comes closer. Billy's tone when he speaks is almost conversational.

                    BILLY
          Skummade igenom - What's
          that mean in Rom? sounds
          like "Ignorant Scum".

                    LEMPKE
          Skummade igenom - yeah,
          that's you. It means "White
          Man from Town."

Billy smiles a grim smile.

                    BILLY
          That's my secret name, isn't
          it? "White Man From Town..."

Lempke is startled, and the Gypsies closest to Billy back slowly away.

                    LEMPKE
          You have no business with
          us, so go away, White Man
          from Town. And we have no
          business with you.

With a dismissive wave of his hand, Lempke turns his back on Billy.

                    BILLY
          I'm not through!

Billy's challenge to the old man's authority astonishes everyone. Lempke turns slowly around, and glares at Billy.

                    LEMPKE
          You are through, white man!
          Because you start something
          and I finish it! You run my
          daughter over in the road,
          white man! Mostly when
          something like that happen
          we turn and we drive out of
          town. But sometimes we get
          our justice.

Lempke snaps his fingers in Billy's face.

Billy snaps his fingers right back, actually flicking the edges of the hole in the old man's face.

                    BILLY
          When the Police Chief blew
          his face off - did that
          bring your daughter back?
          And when the Judge burned up
          inside his car-

                    LEMPKE
          No! Susanna stays in the
          ground! Justice ain't
          bringing back the dead,
          White Man From Town. Justice
          is justice.

                    BILLY
          Fuck your justice. Take it
          off me. Take your fucking
          curse off my head.

Billy grabs the old man by the shoulders and
draws him closer.

Every man in the camp is about to attack Billy -
but they're stopped by a hand sign from Lempke.

                    LEMPKE
          Let go of me or I make it
          worse. So much worse you
          tink I blessed you the first
          time.

At first it looks as if the old man might have
won this round, but suddenly Billy grins his
widest grin.

                    BILLY
          Go ahead. Try. But you know,
          I don't think you can.

Lempke stares back wordlessly.

                    BILLY (CONT'D)
          Because I helped do it to
          myself. Sure, I ran over
          Susanna Lempke and that's my
          fault. But she walked right
          out between two parked cars
          and that's her fault. You
          put a curse on me, and I let
          myself be cursed. Not the
          best balance in the history
          of the world, maybe, but it
          balances. Let it end here.

                    LEMPKE
          I never take it off, white
          man from town. I die widdit
          in my mout.

                    BILLY
          So do it right now! Die with
          the curse in your mouth. And
          let me watch.

For the first time, Lempke himself trembles.
He turns away, and barks a final order.

                    LEMPKE
          Get him out of here.

                    BILLY
          You think men like me don't
          have the power to curse?
          We have the power. We're
          good. at cursing once we get
          started, old man. You don't
          want my curse.

The Gypsies are still and silent, frightened.

Here and there the women make the sign against
the Evil Eye the Men spit.

Lempke pauses on the steps of his van, not yet
going in. Then suddenly...

BILLY -

is wracked by a sudden pain somewhere under
his ribs. He rips open his overcoat to get at
the spasm revealing - ludicrously- that he's
wearing a t-shirt and Bermudas.

Since we last saw his body, he's lost another
fifteen pounds.

It doesn't look good: in places bones show
through, in other places folds of loose skin
bunch and hang. And he stands off-kilter, a

little twisted because of the pain in his
joints.

> BILLY
> I'm leaving, old man. But
> when I go, I'll be leaving a
> curse behind me. The curse
> of the white man from town,
> and it's on you and it's on
> everybody I can see by the
> light of this fire.

There's a flash of movement behind Lempke.

> LEMPKE
> Gina!

Gina steps out of the shadows and into the
light. She raises a slingshot, draws back the
cradle, and sights towards Billy.

> GINA
> Enkelt! Get out of here,
> eyelak! Get out of here,
> killing bastard!

Billy holds up his hand as if that would ward
off her shot.

Gina releases the sling, so quickly and
expertly we barely catch that the missile was
silverish, smooth, globular.

Billy screams in pain, and holds his hand
tight between his thighs. Shaking he pulls his
hand out again and holds it up to the light of
the center fire.

There's a hole in his hand. Right through the
center of the palm.

                              DISSOLVE TO:

EXT. GINELLI HOUSE - NIGHT

Expensive, very up-scale neighborhood. Phone
rings O.S.

                    GINELLI (O.S.)
                      (sleepy)
          Yeah...?

INT. BEDROOM - GINELLI HOUSE - NIGHT

Ginelli's in bed with a buxom blonde, except
in this case she's Ginelli's WIFE. Ginelli's
on the phone.

                    GINELLI
          Fuck late. Tell me what's
          wrong, Billy.

Ginelli gooses his Wife to rouse her.

                    GINELLI (CONT'D)
          Jesus, a slingshot?!

Ginelli's Wife hands him an address book. He
opens it and starts going through it as he
talks to Billy on the phone.

                    GINELLI (CONT'D)
          Okay, Billy, the Better
          Half's gonna make a couple
          of calls.

He points out a couple of names. His Wife nods
and takes the address book into the other
room.

                    GINELLI (CONT'D)
          Yeah, you're welcome, just
          shut up and sit still. I'm
          sending somebody up there
          to look you over. He's not
          a doctor but he's pretty
          damned close.

Ginelli hangs up. To himself:

                    GINELLI (CONT'D)
          Goddamned Gypsy queers.

                                        CUT TO:

EXT. FRENCHMAN'S BAY MOTEL, BOOTHBAY HARBOR
- DAWN

An anonymous in-season place with double-
decked wings of identical rooms. Not many
cars, but one of them is Billy's Cutlass. Next
to it is an idling AIRPORT TAXI.

The DRIVER leans on a front fender, slowly
turning the pages of a newspaper. He glances
towards one of the rooms on the lower level.

INT. BILLY'S MOTEL ROOM - DAWN - SAME TIME

FANDER - Ginelli's "almost-Doctor" - is a
little man, prematurely gray, who works out of
a country doctor's bag.

He has spread out a series of gauzes,
disinfectants, and scissors on a table.

He unwraps Billy's hand - and Billy twists in
terrible pain.

Fander can't resist the opportunity. He peers
at Billy through the hole in his palm.

                    FANDER
          A ball bearing, hunh? That's
          a first for me.

                    BILLY
          I never felt this kind of
          pain before.

                    FANDER
          There's a reason for that.
          I worked on cadavers in med
          school that looked healthier
          than you.

                    BILLY
          Can you give me something?

                    FANDER
          Codeine'll put you in a
          coma. Darvon'll send you
          into cardiac arrhythmia.
          Looks like I just flew six
          hundred miles to prescribe a
          grain and a half of empirin.

He goes through his bag and comes up with a
bottle of pills.

                    FANDER (CONT'D)
          And these are mine but you
          need 'em more. Potassium
          tablets.

                    BILLY
          Are they gonna help the
          pain?

                    FANDER
          No they're gonna help you
          not go into cardiac arrest
          next time you stand up. Do
          yourself a favor - give up
          diet sodas.

As Fander gets up to go, he inadvertently
brushes against Billy's bandaged hand. Billy
howls in pain.

                    FANDER
          Oh, I almost forgot - you're
          gonna have a visitor at noon
          tomorrow.

                    BILLY
          Who?

Fander goes to the door of the hotel room.

                    FANDER
          Take that empirin and get
          some rest or tomorrow you're
          not gonna have the strength
          to answer the door.

                                        CUT TO:

INT. MOTEL - LATE MORNING

Billy's asleep on the rumpled covers of the
bed. There's a light blanket over him, and the
way it falls shows his emaciated, bony frame
beneath.

There's a loud pounding on the door. Billy
rouses, but he's so weak he has trouble getting
up.

                    BILLY
                   (hoarse)
          Who - who is it?

              GINELLI'S VOICE (O.S.)
          Billy, open the door! It's
          Richie Ginelli!

Billy finally makes it to the door, and opens
it. Billy's genuinely glad to see Ginelli.

                    BILLY
          Oh I just figured you'd send
          one of your men...

Ginelli pushes past him with a small bag in
one hand and a bottle of Chivas in the other.

                    GINELLI
          Nah - this I handle myself.
          Wanna deaden your gums?

                    BILLY
          Think I'll stick to my
          Empirin. Thanks for sending
          the doctor - I think he
          saved my life. And I'm
          really glad to see you,
          though I don't know what
          you're gonna be able to do.

Ginelli pours himself a plastic cupful of
scotch, and throws himself onto one of the
single beds.

                    GINELLI
          This time I'm the Counselor.
          Now you tell me all the
          facts.

                                        CUT TO:

EXT. HARDWARE STORE, BOOTHBAY HARBOR -
AFTERNOON

Upscale, for people who like to buy the highest
quality nuts and bolts. Billy is skulking
in the aisles, trying not to be seen by the
other customers. He wears layers of clothing,
doubling shirts and trousers, adding to his
bulk.

At the register, Ginelli has bought two
cardboard cartons-worth of hardware goods.
Whatever they are, they total $215.45 and he
pays the bill with five $50-bills. The GIRL-
BEHIND-THE-REGISTER nods towards Billy, and
in a low voice asks Ginelli:

                GIRL-BEHIND-THE-REGISTER
                Hey mister, your friend - he
                a long distance runner or is
                he, you know, _sick_...

Ginelli puts the boxes under his arms, and
prepares to leave.

                        GINELLI
                He's a picky eater.

                                        CUT TO:

EXT. DOWNTOWN BOOTHBAY - AFTERNOON

Billy watches as Ginelli puts the boxes in the
trunk of the car.

                        BILLY
                What is all that stuff?

                    GINELLI
          Tools of the trade. I got
          to go grocery shopping. Why
          don't you wait here? You
          look tired.

                    BILLY
          I need a sugar fix.

                                        CUT TO:

EXT. CONCESSION STAND, "DOWNTOWN" BOOTHBAY -
DAY

A concession stand on a busy corner. But the
Tourists gathered here are staring at, and
standing back from Billy, who's getting a bag
of candy, a tall shake, and several bags of
natural chips. The CONCESSION GIRL is very
nervous, all too conscious of Billy's appearance
and its effect on her other customers.

                    BILLY
          I think you gave me too much
          change.

                 CONCESSION GIRL
          Look, keep it, and here,
          have another box of candy -
          just take it all across the
          street, okay?

                    BILLY
                 (getting it)
          Okay, sorry, didn't mean to
          put a dent in your profits.

But Billy is already crossing the street. He
goes to a bench where a TEEN AGED GIRL is
reading TV Guide and her father is reading a

thick Boston newspaper.

When Billy sits down the Father and Teen-Aged Girl exchange a glance, and then get up to go. The Father leaves behind several sections of the paper.

>   BILLY
>   You through with these?

>   FATHER
>   (very nervous)
>   Here. You can have the whole
>   thing.

He gives Billy the section he was reading, and then hurries away with his daughter. Billy sighs, gathers up his packages, and the paper, and then heads back for the car.

He doesn't look anybody in the eye.

EXT. "DOWNTOWN" BOOTHBAY - DAY - MINUTES LATER

Ginelli comes out of the grocery store with a couple of sacks of groceries. They go into the trunk, and then Ginelli gets into the car and behind the wheel.

INT. GINELLI'S FORD - DAY - CONT ACTION

Billy is industriously wadding up unfolded pages of the Boston newspaper, and stuffing them under his shirt, down his trousers, and up his pants legs.

He looks absurd, though he seems to be feverishly concentrating.

                    GINELLI
            What are you doing?

Billy sighs. He knows it isn't working.

                    BILLY
            Trying to be inconspicuous.

Ginelli laughs good-naturedly.

                                        CUT TO:

INT. MOTEL ROOM - EVENING

The room is messy. Ginelli peers out the window
as he murmurs quietly on a cellular phone.

IN THE BATHROOM

Billy has taken a shower. With a heavy terrycloth robe on his shoulders, and digging into
a new 2-lb box of vanilla wafers, he steps onto
the scales. Ginelli enters, clicking off the
cellular phone and drops it into his jacket
pocket.

He pours straight Chivas into another plastic
glass, and peers at the numbers on the scales.
The scale reads 124.

Ginelli lifts the robe off Billy's shoulders,
then snapping his fingers, motions for Billy to
hand him the box of vanilla wafers. Guiltily,
Billy hands over the box. The scale drops to
119.

                    BILLY
            Yeah. Who was I trying to
            fool?

                    GINELLI
                   (gently)
          Billy, ever hear of
          something called "Committal
          in Absentia"?

Billy's legal mind is still sharp.

                    BILLY
          Oh sure. It just means
          somebody's committed to a
          mental hospital without
          being examined. It's usually
          invoked when some guy goes
          loony and runs off -

The meaning of Ginelli's question suddenly
dawns on Billy.

                    BILLY(CONT'D)
          Oh great, Heidi thinks my
          mind's been affected by all
          the weight I've lost. Oh
          yeah, and she obviously got
          that pill popping freak Mike
          Houston to sign the order...

Ginelli gently leads Billy to the bed, and
gets him under the covers.

                    GINELLI
          Billy, you do know about
          Heidi and Mike Houston...?

Billy gets it immediately.

                    BILLY
          Oh Christ, you're joking! Oh
          Jesus this is the capper! No
          wonder they're sending out

> wanted posters! Oh this is
> just-

Ginelli doesn't respond to any of this. Rather he goes to the dresser, and starts doing something with half-a-dozen raw steaks he bought earlier.

> BILLY (CONT'D)
> What the hell are you doing?

Ginelli is dousing some of the steaks with liquid from a blue bottle, and others he rubs with a coarse white powder.

> GINELLI
> Hey White Man from Town, you
> never hear of tenderizing
> your red meat?

> BILLY
> Looks like nasty stuff.
> You're not gonna hurt
> anybody are you?

> GINELLI
> No. But Billy, if I'm gonna
> help you, you don't get to
> ask that question again.

                                        CUT TO:

EXT. DARK ROADSIDE - NIGHT

The Ford is pushed out of sight on a logging track. O.S. a Gypsy lullaby.

FARTHER DOWN THE ROAD -

is the line of parked Gypsy vehicles, two

wheels on the asphalt, two wheels on the listing 'shoulder. A young Gypsy SENTRY, with a holstered revolver and Walkman, patrols along the line of cars. When he has passed out of frame; we see...

GINELLI -

creeping along the outside of the Gypsy vehicles, trying the doors of each. He ducks between two of the vehicles when a car passes along the road.

Finally he finds one of the car doors open. He crawls inside.

A MOMENT LATER -

Ginelli crawls out again, wearing a suit jacket much too big for him. He smells the lapel - the coat stinks. He pulls on a pair of pants, and slips into tattered sneakers much too small for him.

The moment he transfers the steaks into the pockets of this tattered jacket, the SENTRY reappears.

But Ginelli is gone.

THE GYPSY ENCAMPMENT -

is as we saw it before, but there are fewer Gypsies about. The Sentry comes into the firelit circle, and is given a large sandwich and bottle of beer.

He leans against a trailer and allows a 10-year-boy to examine his gun.

                                    CUT TO:

A BARBED-WIRE DOG-PEN -

outside the Gypsy camp. There are nine Pit
Bulls inside, all trained to fight on command.
All nine dogs are watching Ginelli's quiet
approach.

                    GINELLI
            Do I stink like a Gypsy,
            guys? Well what fucking
            Gyp ever gave you a steak
            for supper? So who wants
            strychnine? And who gets the
            uncut heroin?

He dumps the poisoned meat over the top of the
fence.

                                    CUT TO:

GINELLI -

dry-smoking a Camel. He sits outside the pen
watching as the Pit Bulls teeter and collapse,
one by one.

He takes out his wallet, removes a hundred-
dollar bill, and writes on it with a felt-
tipped marker:

            The White Man from Town says
            take off the curse.

He rises, goes towards the pen.

Only one of the dogs remains alive.

When Ginelli opens the pen's gate, the dog

lurches...

THE PIT BULL'S BARED TEETH -

clamp down on the $100-bill with the warning
on it.

                                        CUT TO:

EXT. ROAD INTO BAR HARBOR - NIGHT

Two cars on this lonely stretch: Ginelli's
Ford in front, and at an even distance behind
that, a nondescript pick-up.

INT. GINELLI'S FORD - NIGHT

Ginelli's nervous. Looks in the rearview
mirror.

                    GINELLI
          Shit. Could be those fucking
          Gypsies.

He turns off abruptly into the lot of a semi-
rural 7-11.

EXT. 7-11 PARKING LOT - NIGHT - CONT ACTION

Ginelli gets out of his Ford.

The Pick-Up he feared was following him passes
on.

At the rear of the parking lot he notes an old
Chevy Nova - its owner, Frank SPURTON, a down-
at-the-heels 22 year old, is bundled up in his
jacket and asleep behind the wheel.

Ginelli walks over, raps sharply on the window.

                    GINELLI
          Hey, kid, wake up. I gotta a
          job for you.

Spurton sits up startled. Then he rolls down
his window.

                    SPURTON
          What's the word man?

                    GINELLI
          What's your name?

                    SPURTON
          Spurton. Frank Spurton.

Ginelli reaches inside his coat pocket and
withdraws a wad of bills.

                    GINELLI
          Okay Mr Frank Spurton. How'd
          you like to earn some money?

Spurton, fully awake, gets out of the Nova.

                    SPURTON
          Okay, but I don't do nothin'
          that goes on videotape.

                    GINELLI
          Nothin' like that. There
          are some Gypsies camped out
          about a couple of miles down
          that way? They're gonna be
          leaving tomorrow morning.
          You find out where they go
          and you call me. That's all.

Ginelli counts out ten fifties from a wad he takes from his pocket.

On second thought, he hands Spurton another four of the bills.

MOMENTS LATER -

Ginelli, back in his Ford, leans out the window to Spurton.

                    GINELLI
          And what's the number you're
          gonna call?

Spurton peers at a scrap of paper with pencilled numbers on it.

                    SPURTON
          Four-Three-Three-Four-
          Thousand-Three. Room
          Nineteen. But what's your
          name in case somebody else
          answers?

                    GINELLI
          I'll answer.

Ginelli gives Spurton a curt nod then peels out.

                                        DISSOLVE TO:

INT. MOTEL ROOM - EARLY MORNING

Ginelli is lying on the twin bed, half asleep.

                    BILLY
          So what are we waiting for

now?

                    GINELLI
          A FedEx delivery.

The phone rings. Ginelli smiles and picks up
the receiver.

                    GINELLI (CONT'D)
          And a phone call.
                    (into phone)
          Yeah?

INTERCUT: "FILLING STATION - EARLY MORNING

Close up of Frank Spurton standing in a phone
booth, looking a little nervous.

                    SPURTON
          They're at a small farm off
          Route 92. Can't miss 'em.
          But I think they made me.

                    GINELLI
          If I were you, friend, I'd
          get the fuck away as quick
          as I could. And lose my
          number on the way.

                    SPURTON
          Yeah, you're probably right.

Spurton hangs up, and goes back to his car,
looking right and left. He's so nervous he
drops his keys. As he leans down to pick them
up...

A HAND -

comes into frame, takes the keys, and hands them to Spurton. Spurton looks up into the face of...

GABE -

the young Gypsy man. He's grinning at Spurton.

                              DISSOLVE TO:

INT. HOTEL ROOM - AFTERNOON

The sun pours into the room.

Billy is watching television, packing away chips and dip - now and then twingeing with some pain in his bandaged hand.

O.S. we hear the shower water running. It stops. Then a knock at the door.

                    GINELLI (O.S.)
            Sign for me, Billy!

Billy rises slowly, gets to the door and opens it.

A FEDERAL EXPRESS MAN with three packages stands on the other side, his truck parked laterally behind another car. The FedEx Man stares at Billy.

                    FEDEX MAN
            Didn't mean to stare,
            Mister.

                    BILLY
            I'm getting used to it.

                    FEDEX MAN
          I once seen a picture of a
          guy who was almost as thin
          as you are.

EXT. MOTEL - DAY - MOMENTS LATER

Billy stands in the doorway of his hotel room
as the Fed Ex van pulls away. Across the
parking lot, he sees Spurtons Chevy Nova. On
the side, in shaving cream, is the legend:

              WHITE MAN FROM TOWN

                                    CUT TO:

EXT. MOTEL PARKING LOT - DAY - MOMENTS LATER

Billy, who has been looking into the car,
turns as Ginelli approaches.

                    GINELLI
          Billy, what are you doing
          out here?

                    BILLY
          You said you left a message
          for Lempke last night - what
          was the message?

                    GINELLI
          I warned the bastard to take
          the curse off you.

Frank Spurton's corpse sits behind the wheel.
There are three precise round holes in his
face - one in each eye and a third where his
nose should be.

THE WORD "NEVER" -

has been carved into Spurton's forehead. In the young man's lap is the body of a strangled capon, and the bird's wide-eyed head pokes out of Spurton's mouth, like a cuckoo in rigor mortis.

                    BILLY
          I think it's time for us to
          move on.

                              DISSOLVE TO:

INT. BARN/GARAGE - NIGHT

A country farm building, half barn, half-garage. Ginelli's Ford is inside.

EXT. COUNTRY FARMHOUSE - NIGHT

19th Century, white clapboard, vertical lines. It looks uninhabited.

Maybe there's a hint of light behind one of the upstairs rooms.

INT. BEDROOM - COUNTRY FARMHOUSE - NIGHT

It's old-fashioned, cramped and dusty. Ginelli has unpacked his hardware store purchases and the contents of the Fed Ex boxes.

Arranged on the bed are a spring-loaded knife, a lady's draw-string leather evening bag, a box of leadshot, three dispensers of industrial strength strapping tape, a jar of lamp black, four carefully wrapped blue glass bottles with dark liquid inside, and a Kalashnikov AK-47 assault rifle with 400 rounds of ammunition.

Ginelli is wearing jungle assault clothes, and is blackening his face and hands.

Billy enters the room, shaking his head.

>   BILLY
> Where the hell are we?

>   GINELLI
> Rural Route 2, Box 21,
> Center Hovell Maine. Third
> floor attic.

>   BILLY
> Whose house is this?

>   GINELLI
> It belongs to Mr and Mrs
> Theodore Norcross.

Ginelli expertly pumps and tests the Kalashnikov. Billy looks sick.

>   BILLY
> Listen, you didn't -

>   GINELLI
>   (grinning)
> They're spending a free
> weekend at the Ritz-Carlton
> in Boston.

>   BILLY
> My wife gives me a blow-job
> and so far four people are
> dead.
>   (sincere)
> This thing can't escalate
> anymore.

                    GINELLI
          (with equal conviction)
     Billy, they killed that kid
     to show their contempt for
     me. Things like that - they
     make it personal.

By this time, Ginelli has blackened his face
and his hands. He shoulders the rifle, stuffs
the strapping tape into his pockets, and starts
for the door. Billy stops him.

                    BILLY
     The boy died because of me.
     You've got to let me help
     you.

                    GINELLI
     You can help me by staying
     here and lying low. And stay
     away from the windows.

                                        CUT TO:

EXT. GYPSY CAMP - NIGHT

The Gypsies have rented an empty field that's
situated in a vale nearby the old farmhouse
Ginelli and Billy occupy.

A Slow Car pulls up very quietly, parking on
the side of the road, its headlights off. As
the DRIVER stealthily gets out and starts to
open the trunk, a GYPSY SENTRY. leaps atop
him.

But just as quickly, the Sentry slips off
again, with a low laugh. The Driver gives the
Sentry a buddy-buddy punch in the arm. Then
both men lean into the trunk and take out a

caged and gagged Pit Bull Terrier. While the Sentry pokes at the Pit Bull with a stick, the Driver hefts the cage overhead and walks away...

GINELLI -

suddenly appears behind the Gypsy Sentry. The Gypsy closes the trunk and Ginelli clobbers him in the head with the butt end of the Kalashnikov.

Before the Sentry collapses onto the ground, Ginelli begins to bind him to a tree with the strapping tape.

IN THE GYPSY CAMP -

Everyone gathers around as the driver clips the ID collar off the stolen dog. Lempke watches from his open trailer door for a moment, then turns back inside.

GINELLI -

has crept round to another part of the dark vegetation encircling the camp. He lies down prone on a flat outcropping of rock. He looks down from the ledge to the Gypsy Camp.

                                        CUT TO:

INT. LEMPKE'S TRAILER - NIGHT - SAME TIME

The Old Man, seemingly distracted and pre-occupied, is counting out and rolling quarters with practiced speed and dexterity. He's being helped by a WIRY BOY, about 12, with big sad eyes. Suddenly O.S. there's a LOUD SHOT.

EXT. TRAILER

One of the Trailer's tires is hit and blown. A second shot. A second tire explodes.

RESUME INT. TRAILER

The entire trailer suddenly lists forward. Another SHOT, another PNEUMATIC EXPLOSION and one whole side of the trailer drops down against the earth.

The Wiry Boy throws himself bodily between Lempke and the direction the shots are coming from as Lempke's belongings are tossed from their shelving and smash and spill on the floor. the SHOUTING begins.

EXT. THE GYPSY CAMP

GYPSIES -

pour out of their vehicles and their tents, half dressed and a few of them armed. They're frantic and filled with fear.

GINELLI -

sights in on the remaining tire of Lempke's camper. He aims low, and hits the rear tire of the camper. It explodes. Not a single bullet hits the camper shell

LEMPKE -

calmly exits the flattened camper. The SHOTS CONTINUE - now high and harmless. Lempke's people rush to protect him, pushing him forwards. The gunfire drops and smashes all

the windows of the vehicle directly in front
of Lempke. The old man stops, impassive, and
does not duck as do everyone around him.

INT. ATTIC ROOM - NIGHT - SAME TIME

Billy hears the shots and becomes agitated.
Sitting on the couch, he begins to hyper-
ventilate. It looks as if this might be his
Waterloo as well.

RESUME EXT. GYPSY CAMP

The Gypsy Limousine is idling at the edge
of the circle. The tribe is hustling Lempke
towards it. Just as he seems safely inside the
back seat, another barrage of shots smashes
the back window first, and then the front. One
more single shot and -

The Engine Block bursts into flame.

GINELLI -

is coming to the end of his ammunition. He
puts in his last clip and starts firing, broad
and hard.

DOWN IN THE CAMP -

While the Gypsy Women huddle the Gypsy Children
together and bend over them protectively,
some of the GYPSY MEN point to the sniper's
location.

One of the Gypsy Men fires up into the darkness.
No return fire from the hill. The Gypsy Men
pause. Then grin at one another. But then...

A BARRAGE OF GUNFIRE -

smashes the windows in the few vehicles that remain intact. THE GYPSIES ....

all lie flat on the ground, covering their heads. Lempke stands erect, his appearance brave, unconcerned - and untroubled.

GINELLI -

continues to fire from his protected, invisible vantage. But then he falters when he sees...

LEMPKE -

looking directly at him. Slowly Lempke raises his arm and points in Ginelli's direction.

THE GYPSY MEN -

who realize no one's been hit by the Sniper. Emboldened, one of the Gypsy Men spots movement in the vegetation on the hillside, he squeezes off a sudden shot and there's a CURDLING SHRIEK...

The Gypsies - men, women, and children all cheer.

INT. ATTIC - NIGHT - SAME TIME

Billy tries to get up but collapses on the floor to his knees. He looks around the room in a panic. He's confused, and unfocussed.

> BILLY
> (uncertainly)
> Linda...?

He falls to his knees on the floor. barely
breathing.

RESUME EXT. GYPSY CAMP

Gina excitedly takes her grandfather's hands.

                    GINA
          He's dead, old-Papa! The
          eyelak is dead!

But Lempke only slowly shakes his head no.
Just then... THE GYPSY SENTRY -

staggers out of the darkness, still half
bound with Ginelli's tape. There's a big hole
in his lungs, and he wheezes blood. In his
outstretched hand is a blood-stained note.

The Sentry pitches forward onto the ground.
Someone wrests the note out of the dying man's
hand, and carries it to Lempke.

A LONG SHOT -

showing Ginelli creeping up the front. steps
of the house.

BACK TO SCENE - CU: THE NOTE

          The White Man from Town says
          take off the curse.

Lempke looks up. The Gypsy Sentry dies on the
ground before Lempke.

                              CUT TO:

INT. FARMHOUSE - NIGHT

Without turning on the lights, Ginelli creeps up the stairs. He goes down the hallway, and then opens a bedroom door.

Just inside the open doorway, Billy lies motionless on the floor.

                    GINELLI
          Billy ... ?

Ginelli presses two fingers to Billy's wrist to check for a pulse. Not finding one, he tries Billy's neck. It's feeble.

He scoops Billy up, carries him to a couch. He tears through the boxes he received, and finally finds what he wants; a tiny ampule of ammonia.

He pops it right beneath Billy's nose. Billy revives groggily.

                    GINELLI
          Relax, buddy.

                    BILLY
          Was I dead...?

                                        DISSOLVE TO:

EXT. GYPSY CAMP - MORNING

The destruction looks worse in the morning. The Gypsies appear nervous - as if eager to pack up and leave. But the camp is filled with local and state trooper cars. An ambulance is being loaded with the body of the dead sentry and several patrolmen prowl the bushes on the hillside, where the Sentry was shot. .

INT. KITCHEN - FARMHOUSE....: HORNING - SAME
TIME

In the b.g. out the dirty window can be seen
the Gypsy camp. Ginelli, dressed in sports coat
and tie, takes down two Mason jars of homemade
preserves, empties them into the trash, and
then washes them out. During this process we
see a shoulder holster with .38 - in fact,
Ginelli looks less like a Mobster than a field
operative with the FBI..

                    BILLY (O.S.)
          Richie...?!

INT. STAIRCASE - FARMHOUSE - MORNING - SAME
TIME

Billy, coughing, beating at his chest with his
fist, collapses on the stairs. He sits with
his head in his hand.

Ginelli calls from the kitchen.

                    GINELLI (O.S.)
          You okay?

Billy tries to respond but can't. Ginelli
comes out of the kitchen, carefully wiping off
the mason jar, now filled with a thick dark
liquid.

                    BILLY
                  (wheezing)
          Whatever you're gonna do,
          better do it in a hurry.

                    GIHELLI
          Stay down here. I'll be back
          in a while, and then we'll
          be leaving.

Billy tries to reply, but goes into a coughing
jag and can't. Slipping the Mason jars into
his pockets, Ginelli starts out the door.

                    GINELLI (CONT'D)
          Keep the curtains closed,
          and don't answer the door.

                                        CUT TO:

INT. FORTUNE TELLING VAN - MORNING

Gina sits with a board across her lap, working
on some papers. There's a knock at the back
doors of the van.

                    GINA
          Yes?

Ginelli opens the back doors and flashes a
laminated FBI I.D. card with his picture on
it.

                    GINELLI
          F.B.I. Special Agent Stoner.
          Could I ask you a few
          questions, Mrs Lempke?

Gina smiles a quiet, cultured smile. She sounds
like a graduate student:

                    GINA
          I'm not married, and if I
          don't get my correspondence-
          course lessons in the mail

by tomorrow morning I'm
going to lose points for
lateness. Can you talk to
somebody else?

He has to crouch, but Ginelli goes deeper into
the van.

He hands Gina a photograph of Halleck.

                    GINELLI
          Can you identify -

Gina interrupts, instantly returning to the
Gypsy Harpy:

                    GINA
          That pig?! He killed my
          tante-nyjad!

                    GINELLI
          Mister William Halleck -

                    GINA
          Arrest him! Throw him in
          jail! It was him last night,
          wasn't it?

                    GINELLI
          Not Halleck himself we
          think. We believe he hired
          someone to attack your camp:
          But we do have Mr Halleck in
          custody.

Gina draws her breath in sharply.

                    GINELLI (CONT'D)
          Would you be willing to
          identify him personally?

Gina throws down her board and papers.

She's stands, ready to go.

                                          CUT TO:

EXT. GYPSY CAMP - HORNING - MOMENTS LATER

Ginelli and Gina are heading through the camp towards the highway.

One of the STATE TROOPERS says something to Ginelli, but he flashes his badge, and the State Trooper steps aside.

Then, one of the Gypsy Women says something to Gina. Before she can answer...

                    GINELLI
          Don't tell 'em where you're
          going.

                    GINA
                   (wary)
          Why?

                    GINELLI
          Because I want an
          identification - not a
          lynching.

                                          CUT TO:

EXT. HIGHWAY - HORNING - MOMENTS LATER

Ginelli leads Gina past the line of Gypsy and official vehicles. They're heading uphill towards the Farmhouse where Billy is.

                  GINA
         Where's your car?

                  GINELLI
         Up there. And Halleck's in
         it.

There's a grim glee in Gina's expression.
Ginelli reacts to it.

              GINELLI (CONT'D)
         And that's all I want
         from you, too. Just an
         identification.

                                      CUT TO:

INT. KITCHEN - FARM HOUSE - MORNIN.6

Billy has set a chair directly in front of
the open refrigerator. He's weak, but he
steadfastly devours everything in there. He
washes down a jar of sweet pickles with a pint
of half-and-half.

As he lowers his arm, he catches sight of...

A SKIN LESION -

on his forearm.

                  BILLY
         Potassium. Where are the
         damned potassium tablets?

When he struggles to his feet, he sees, out
the window...

GINELLI AND GINA -

headed toward the garage. Startled and frightened, Billy drops back into his chair. He's weakening so rapidly that even small movement wracks him with pain.

He stifles his cry with his fist, so as not to be heard. Tears flow from his filmy eyes.

                                        CUT TO:

EXT. FARMHOUSE GARAGE - MORNING - SAME TIME

Gina is increasingly nervous. As Ginelli unlocks the garage door, she almost bolts. But he turns just in time to grab her arm. He hands her another photograph.

                    GINELLI
          Almost forgot. A photograph
          of the man we suspect of
          attacking your camp last
          night-

The photograph is a police mug shot of Ginelli, front view and profile. No name - just numbers at the bottom.

                    GINA
          You! It was you, you
          bastard!

Ginelli jerks open the garage door, and pushes Gina through It.

INT. GARAGE - MORNING - CONT ACTION

Gina has fallen against the hood of Ginelli's Ford. Ginelli comes in and locks the door behind him.

Gina starts to attack, but when Ginelli turns he's holding a Mason Jar filled with a dark liquid. Gina hesitates.

Ginelli opens the top of the Mason Jar.

                    GINELLI
          What this is really all
          about is making sure you
          don't put any more holes
          through people's hands.

He hurls the liquid in her face. Gina screams, claps her hands over her eyes and falls to the ground. Ginelli puts a foot on her neck.

                    GINELLI
          You scream and I'll kill
          you.
                    (Beat)
          You just got a faceful of
          Pepsi Cola.

He takes his foot off her.

                    GINELLI (CONT'D)
          And baking soda.

Gina gets to her knees and springs for Ginelli. He sidesteps and she bangs her head against an old support beam. Blood flows down her cheek. She slips to the cement floor, apparently unconscious.

Ginelli bends down to examine her. Suddenly, Gina's hand raises overhead with a large, rusty nail. She shears it across his forehead opening a long cut. Then she rips through his trousers' leg and draws more blood.

Ginelli slams her back to the concrete, and
pulls his .38. He pushes the barrel against
her eyelid, closes it, then applies a gentle
pressure to her eyeball beneath.

                    GINELLI
          Go for it, bitch!

He wipes the blood from his forehead.

                    GINELLI (CONT'D)
          Go ahead. You spoiled my
          face.

Gina's only movement is a snarling curl of her
lips.

                    GINELLI (CONT'D)
          I'd love for you to. I'd
          do it back to you, whore,
          and go out and order me a
          Porterhouse steak.

Gina's expression changes. Ginelli takes out
pre-cut lengths of rope and binds Gina's feet
and hands.

                    GINELLI (CONT'D)
          Halleck cursed you. And
          guess what little girl - I
          am the curse.

                    GINA
               (spits back)
          Fuck his curse, that pig!

                    GINELLI
          My friend Billy told me not
          to hurt anyone. That ends
          today when the sun goes

down. Tonight the old man
gets away with nothing. Tell
him to take off the curse.
His last chance. I'm not
going to ask again.

Ginelli pulls a piece of paper and a quarter
from his pocket and sticks them down the front
of her dress.

> GINELLI (CONT'D)
> At noon today you call this
> number. Give me the Old
> Man's answer. Is he gonna
> take off the curse?

> GINA
> Save your quarter. The
> answer is no.

> GINELLI
> Saves me some time. This
> evening I take out those
> twin boys - how old are
> they, eleven maybe? And in
> the morning I turn three
> women into widows. But this
> morning, even before the sun
> goes down... I start with
> you.

Ginelli pulls out a second jar of dark fluid,
opens it, and spills a few drops onto the
hem of Gina's skirt. It bubbles, burns, and
instantly dissolves the fabric.

Gina is silent; this time she believes him.
Ginelli places the open jar of acid between
her thighs.

He pushes open the garage doors, gets into the
car, and drives out.

                                    CUT TO:

EXT. HIGHWAY - MORNING - A FEW MINUTES LATER

Ginelli's Ford turns out of the driveway and
heads down the highway. A moment later Gina
hurtles out of the garage.

                    GINA
          Your friend is a pig and
          he'll die thin! But you'll
          die first, you bastard!

She hurls the bottle of acid at the retreating
car, already out of sight.

INT. FORD - MORNING - SAME TIME

Billy, weak and wretched, has a bed of pillows
and blankets on the back seat. He peers out the
back window at Gina's figure in the highway,
then collapses.

                    BILLY
          Where to now?

                    GINELLI
          International House of
          Pancakes.
                    (beat)
          The one in Bangor.

                                    CUT TO:

EXT. FILLING STATION- NOON

Lempke, head bowed and even grimmer than usual, sits in the passenger seat of the fortune-telling van. Outside, Gina enters the same telephone booth the unfortunate Spurton used a day or two before.

INSIDE THE TELEPHONE BOOTH -

Gina puts a quarter in the telephone, and dials the number on the scrap of paper Ginelli gave her.

> OPERATOR
> (filtered)
> Please deposit two dollars
> and twenty-five cents.

With disgust, Gina does so. The Call Rings through, and is answered immediately - by ANOTHER OPERATOR.

> ANOTHER OPERATOR
> (filtered)
> Ms Lempke? Please hold, and
> I'll patch you through.

> CUT TO:

INT. BEDROOM, GINELLI'S HOUSE - NOON - SAME TIME

It's Ginelli's Wife who's on the line with Gina. She's working two phones and some complex looking equipment. She puts one on hold, then picks up another receiver.

> GINELLI'S WIFE
> I've got her for you, baby.

As she punches more buttons...

                                        CUT TO:

INT. INTERNATIONAL HOUSE OF PANCAKES, BANGOR
- NOON

Ginelli talks on a pay phone.

IN A CORNER BOOTH -

Billy is trying to get the cap off the bottle
of potassium tablets.

He finally has to ask a WAITRESS for assistance.

When she gets the cap off, she pours the last
two tablets into Billy's bandaged palm. He
pops them, swills them down with coffee.

He tries to speak his thanks but can't.

The Waitress nods and goes off, meeting Ginelli
as he hangs up the phone.

                    WAITRESS
          Mister, take your friend to
          a doctor. Nobody oughta die
          -in a pancake house.

                    GINELLI
          I just made him an
          appointment with the man who
          can cure him.

Ginelli returns to the booth. He sees Billy's
weakening condition and reaches out and grabs
his forearm.

                    GINELLI (CONT'D)
          That old fucker gave in.
          Just a few hours, Billy, a
          few more hours and we got
          him.

                              DISSOLVE TO:

EXT. THE GREAT WHITE WATER TOWER OF BANGOR -
MORNING

This weird land-mark is of white-washed wood,
with lattice-work and a spiralling enclosed
stairway. Some kids are running under-manned
scrimmages. A WOULD-BE QUARTERBACK rears back
for a long pass, his WOULD-BE RECEIVER goes
out for a long pass, backing up, backing up,
until..-

HE SMASHES INTO BILLY -

knocking the pathetically weak, frail, thin
man backward and onto a bench.

                      RECEIVER
          Oh listen mister, I'm sor-

The Receiver breaks off, staring at Billy.
Billy's never looked worse: the collision
looks as if might have killed him. His eyes
are rolled up in his head, his breath is a
rattle, his bony hands clack like castanets.

The Receiver is just staring at Billy when the
Quarterback comes up and drags him away:

                      QUARTERBACK
          Come on Mickey, I got some
          Mac-Attack coupons from my
          idiot brother...

As the two boys back away - still staring at
Billy wheezing on the park bench...

GINELLI -

comes up from behind.

He puts his jacket around Billy's heaving
shoulders, and then sits down next to him.

                    GINELLI
          I'm right behind you. Parked
          right over there behind that
          hedge. Okay?

                    BILLY
          Richie... Thanks...

                    GINELLI
          You want to thank me? Get
          this old bastard.
                    (serious)
          I owed you...

Ginelli gets up and prepares to go.

                    GINELLI
          When you're dealing with the
          old bastard, Billy... keep
          it stiff.

When Ginelli leaves, Billy's head nods forward
onto his chest. His breathing is so light and
shallow it's difficult to tell whether he's
still on the earth.

                              DISSOLVE TO:

SOME TIME LATER

Billy looks dead. Somebody shakes him. Shakes him so hard he nearly tumbles off the end of the bench.

                    LEMPKE (O.S.)
          Wake up, White Man From
          Town.

Billy startles awake. Opening his eyes, he sees...

CU: LEMPKE'S FACE -

so close that the Old Man's breath blows Billy's hair.

                    LEMPKE
          Your dreams smell bad to me.
          They make you stink like a
          Greyhound toilet.

Billy tries to push Lempke away, but the old Gypsy grabs Billy's arm, pushes up the sleeve, and pinches the transparent skin between two fingers. He pulls and twists, until Billy is yelping and moaning.

                    BILLY
          I'm awake.

Lempke turns his head so that Billy finds himself staring at...

A GOLD HOOP -

dangling from the old man's earlobe. Lempke flicks the hoop. It glitters and glistens hypnotically.

                    LEMPKE
          Maybe you're still dreaming,
          White Man -

Suddenly Lempke whips his head back around so
that Billy is staring at...

LEMPKE'S DISEASED NOSE -

Here the rot has spread.

Dark lines now radiate out from the ruins of
his nose and across most of his left cheek.

                    LEMPKE (CONT'D)
             - maybe you dream I bring
             you something tastes so good
             it's gonna make you fat,
             White Man From Town!

Lempke's grin is evil.

He looks down, and Billy follows the old man's
gaze to....

A DOUBLE-CRUST PIE IN A DENTED TIN PLATE -

rested in the old Gypsy's narrow lap. Lempke
takes out a pocket knife.

                    LEMPKE (CONT'D)
             You kill my daughter,
             nothing happen to you till I
             make it happen.

With the pocket knife, Lempke makes a slit in
the upper crust of the pie.

When he withdraws the knife, red droplets fall
onto the crust.

                    LEMPKE (CONT'D)
          My daughter die, you deserve
          to die, fat or thin. So I
          curse you.

Lempke makes Billy take the knife.

Then he hooks his misshapen thumbs over opposing
sides of the pie plate and pulls gently.

                    LEMPKE (CONT'D)
          I give you this so your
          crazy friend don't hurt my
          children no more. You want
          your little girl hurt, White
          Man From Town?

                    BILLY
          Shut up, Lempke.

                    LEMPKE
               (quiet)
          Yes. You win, White Man From
          Town.

The slit in the pie gapes open, showing a
viscous red filling.

The lumps in it might be strawberries or they
might be blood clots.

                    LEMPKE (CONT'D)
          If you want to be rid of the
          curse first you give it to
          the pie -

Lempke takes the knife back and then suddenly

SLITS OPEN THE DRESSING OVER BILLYS PALM -

and then he rips off the gauze and tape.
Billy cries out between clenched teeth at the
unexpected pain.

                    LEMPKE (CONT'D)
               - and then you give the pie
               with the curse inside it to
               somebody else.

THE HOLE THROUGH BILLY'S HAND -

is a dark red, ragged circle in his white
frostlike palm. Lempke grabs Billy's fingers
and holds the wounded hand directly over the
pie. He holds out the pocket knife, still
stained red.

Billy hesitates, but understands what he must
do. He takes the knife and...

SAWS THROUGH THE HEALING FLESH OF HIS WOUND -

He yelps and twists with the pain, but Lempke
holds his hand tight over the pie.

BLOOD SPEWS. IN A THIN WATERY STREAM -

into the gaping slit in the crust of the pie.

Lempke -

begins a guttural incantation in Rom.

BILLY TWISTS THE KNIFE -

in the wound so that the blood flows thicker
and faster into the pie.

Finally...

                    LEMPKE (CONT'D)
          Enough.

Lempke takes the knife away.

Billy falls back against the bench, nearly
fainting.

He doesn't look strong enough to stand.

                    LEMPKE (CONT'D)
          You gain weight too, but
          somebody got to eat that pie
          and soon, or the curse come
          back on you double.

Lempke takes a bandana from his pocket and
wraps Billy's wounded hand.

The pie is on the bench between them.

                    LEMPKE (CONT'D)
          The pie is yours, White Man
          From Town. (Teasing) Why not
          eat it yourself? You die,
          but you die strong.

Billy seems suddenly to regain some strength.

Using his good hand, he angrily waves Lempke
away.

                    BILLY
          Get out of here, Old Man.
          What happens now is my
          business.

                                        CUT TO:

EXT. PARK AND FORD - AFTERNOON - MINUTES
LATER

The Ford was parked out of sight behind a
hedge across the street from the park.

Billy approaches with the pie. He still looks
bad but he's got some life in him now.

Ginelli is not inside the unlocked car.

Billy puts the pie on the back seat, covers
it with a road map, then looks all around the
area for Ginelli.

Billy senses something's wrong.

                    BILLY
                (to himself)
          Christ! Where the hell is
          he?

He gets in the passenger side of the car.

INT. FORD

Billy looks all around for some sort of clue
or message from Ginelli.

                    BILLY
          He must have left a message.
          And the keys.

Billy checks the ignition, then checks the
glove compartment but it's stuck.

He slams it with the side of his fist.

THE GLOVE COMPARTMENT SPRINGS OPEN -

and a handful of ball bearings spill out into
Billy's lap. And after the ball bearings comes
Ginelli's severed hand, with one of his fingers
punching through the steel ring holding the
car keys.

Billy presses his head back against the seat,
his eyes shut tight in grief.

                                        CUT TO:

EXT. INTERSTATE 95, MAINE - DAY

The sign reads: SOUTH - BOSTON/ PROVIDENCE/
NEW YORK

EXT. REST STOP, INTERSTATE 95 - MAINE - DAY

Billy has pulled the Ford to an unoccupied end
of the parking area.

INSIDE THE FORD -

Ginelli's bag is open on the back seat. Billy
gingerly slips Ginelli's hand into the pocket
of a jacket, rolls the jacket up, and sticks
it into a rumpled grocery sack.

RESUME EXT. REST STOP

Billy gets out, and dunks the sack into a
trash barrel with a sign reading <u>Put Trash In
Its Place</u>.

Then he heads for a bank of pay phones.

INT. KITCHEN, HALLECK HOUSE - DAY

Linda, all but jumping up and down, is on the
phone with her father.

                    LINDA
                (into phone)
            Daddy? Are you okay?

INTERCUT: I-95 SERVICE AREA - DAY

Billy is on a pay phone.

Linda hesitates.

                    BILLY
                (into phone)
            I'm still pretty thin - but
            I feel much better. I'm
            gonna be fine. Honey, I need
            you to do something for me.

                    LINDA
                (into phone)
            Anything, Daddy. You know
            that.

                    BILLY
                (into phone)
            I want you to stay at
            Georgia's tonight. I'm
            coming home but I want to
            surprise your mother so
            don't tell her.

                    LINDA
            Ah, Dad. Mom has company.
            Maybe you should-

                    BILLY
          That's all right, honey,
          I'll need to talk to Dr
          Houston, too.

INT. POWDER ROOM, HALLECK HOUSE - DAY

Mike Houston is swallowing two pills with a
palmful of water.

He dries his hands,- flushes the toilet, and
exits into...

INT. DEN, HALLECK HOUSE - DAY - SAME TIME

Heidi, with a radically new hair-style, sits
on the edge of the couch, talking on the phone.

                    HEIDI
                 (into phone)
          Billy, is that you?
                 (listens)
          Oh my God really?! Billy,
          You're not -

She puts her hand over the receiver and hisses
to Houston:

                    HEIDI
          He's coming back!

                    HOUSTON
          When?!

                    HEIDI
                 (into phone)
          Billy when are you -

RESUME BILLY AT THE PAY PHONE

He interrupts Heidi impatiently.

                    BILLY
               (into phone)
          In a couple of days. Heidi,
          there's one thing you have
          to do. Get in touch with
          Michael Houston - you can
          do that tonight, can't you?
          And tell him that you've
          changed your mind about the
          committal order.

                    HEIDI
          I'll try to find him.

                    BILLY
          I imagine he's around
          somewhere. Tell him he
          needs to have the <u>Res Geste</u>
          declared null and void. I
          don't want to get arrested
          as soon as I cross the state
          line.

Billy hangs up, and heads back to his car.

RESUME INT. DEN

Houston is fixing a drink for Heidi.

He brings it to her.

                    HEIDI
          Sometime tomorrow. The next
          day. God, I dread this.

                    HOUSTON
          We'll be ready for him. I've
          found a nice, quiet place
          up in Farmington. I'll give
          'em a call in the morning so
          they'll expect him.

Houston makes a quick signal for silence.
Linda enters.

                    LINDA
                   (COLD)
          Hi. Is my notebook out here?

Houston hands her a binder notebook with LINDA
in huge diagonal letters.

                    HOUSTON
          I almost sat on it.

                    LINDA
          Thanks. Mom, I'm going
          to spend the night with
          Georgia again. I'll be back
          tomorrow.
                   (beat)
          You two have a nice evening.

She exits.

                                        CUT TO:

EXT. DRIVEWAY, HALLECK HOUSE - NIGHT

Ginelli's Ford ticks away the heat. In the
back seat, the pie crust picks up the orange
light of the street lamp. It's pulsing again.

The house is unlighted. Sound of a key in the
lock.

CUT TO:

INT. FIRST FLOOR, HALLECK HOUSE - NIGHT

Everything's as black as pitch. Billy calls out tentatively:

              BILLY
    Heidi...?!

He bangs sharply against something in the darkness.

            BILLY (CONT'D)
    Damn! Damn!

Heidi's voice sounds from the stairway, low and tense:

             HEIDI
    Billy? Didn't expect you
    back so soon.

She turns on the light. Billy and Heidi look at one another.

             BILLY
    I like your hair that way.

There's a pause. They should hug and kiss at this point. They don't.

             HEIDI
    Billy you're so thin...

             BILLY
    And totally exhausted. You
    mind if I turn in?

Billy starts up the stairs.

> HEIDI
> Linda went to Georgia's for
> the night. I'll sleep in her
> room. So I won't disturb
> you.

Heidi is coming downstairs and Billy goes up.

He blocks her way.

> BILLY
> Did you see Mike Houston
> today?

> HEIDI
> (startled)
> Ah -

> BILLY
> About lifting "the
> commitment order.

> HEIDI
> (relieved)
> He said he'd take care of it
> first thing tomorrow morning.

> BILLY
> Fine - and you don't have to
> explain, I know you did it
> for my own good.

Billy continues upstairs; Heidi comes down.

> CUT TO:

INT. MASTER BEDROOM, HALLECK HOUSE - NIGHT

Billy has undressed, and put on the same
bathrobe we first saw him in.

It nearly wraps around him twice, but he feels
comfortable in it.

He glances at his wrist watch, and then
notices...

THE WHITE BAND OF SKIN AROUND HIS RING FINGER
-

but there's no ring.

Billy laughs bitterly to himself:

                    BILLY
          When did that fall off...?

O.S. he hears Heidi's hushed voice. He goes
out into...

INT. SECOND FLOOR HALLWAY - NIGHT - CONT
ACTION

He heads towards the stairs. He can hear
Heidi's anxious voice from below.

                    HEIDI (O.S.)
          No, I tried at the hospital.
          So would you please beep
          him?
                    (Listens)
          Michael always has his
          beeper. It's an emergency-

Grimly, Billy goes towards the stairwell.

INT. DEN - HALLECK HOUSE - NIGHT - SAME TIME

Heidi's on the phone in here.

                    HEIDI
                 (into phone)
          All right - just tell him
          - ah - tell him that Billy
          is -

Billy's voice sounds from above:

                    BILLY (O.S.)
          Heidi? You on the phone?

Realizing with frustration she can't continue
the phone call message, she reluctantly hangs
up the phone.

                    HEIDI
          No... You need something
          Billy?

She stands at the bottom of the stairwell,.

She looks up at him uncertainly - wondering if
he'd heard anything.

But Billy has only a sweet smile for her.

                    BILLY
          There's a present for you on
          the back seat of the car.
          I'm not dressed so would you
          mind -

                    HEIDI
          Don't worry, I'll get it.
          You stay up there and take
          it easy.

EXT. HALLECK DRIVEWAY - NIGHT

Heidi takes the pie out of Ginelli's Ford. She raises the pie close to her face and peers at it curiously in the illumination of the security light over the garage.

INT. DOWNSTAIRS - HALLECK HOUSE - NIGHT

Billy stands halfway up the stairs, his face in shadow. Heidi enters with the pie. She smiles half-heartedly.

> HEIDI
> Looks scrumptious. What kind
> is it?

> BILLY
> Try it and see.

Billy turns and climbs the stairs. He enters the bedroom, drops the robe from his shoulders, and slips into bed. He smiles peacefully, then turns his head aside on the pillow and closes his eyes.

THE CAMERA pans back to the open bedroom door, out into the second floor hallway, down the stairs, and through the den.

O.S we hear a cabinet opened and a plate taken out, a utensil drawer opened and rummaged through, a piece of silverware washed in the drain, the scraping of a chair across the floor.

The Camera reaches the open kitchen doorway. Heidi sits at the table, cutting a narrow slice of the pie, and putting it on her plate. She pokes at it with her fork, peers at whatever

molten fruit is inside. Hesitates. Then takes
a bite. Judges it tasty. She takes a bigger
bite.

INT. MASTER BEDROOM - NIGHT - SAME TIME

Billy rolls his head over in the down pillow.
He beats it with his fist to get the shape
right, then opens his eyes. He listens to the
familiar sounds of Heidi in the kitchen below.

                    BILLY
                 (reflective)
          Sorry, Heidi. But now you'll
          see what it's like.

                              DISSOLVE TO:

INT. KITCHEN - HALLECK HOUSE - EARLY MORNING

The house is quiet and still.

Billy comes down the stairs, and smiles with
grim satisfaction when he sees...

THE PIE PLATE - A DESSERT PLATE, FORK, AND
NAPKIN -

on the kitchen table. Nearly a third of it is
gone. Billy smiles a smile of grim satisfaction
as he tosses the crumbled napkin, and carries
the dessert plate and dessert fork towards the
sink. But then...

THE PLATE DROPS FROM HIS HAND AND SHATTERS-

on the floor. Billy stares at another dessert
plate and fork, also with crumbs and bits of
filling, on top of the counter. Right next to

the plate is Linda's notebook binder.

As Billy whirls round, Linda enters, dressed
in a jogging outfit.

                    LINDA
          Surprise! Oh, Daddy you look
          terrible, but I'm so glad to
          see you!

                    BILLY
          Linda - did you eat any of
          that pie?

Linda starts picking up the broken plate.

                    LINDA
          It was delicious I'm gonna
          go for my run now.
                    (beat)
          Daddy, I want you to promise
          me something...

Billy doesn't reply. He's in shock.

                    LINDA (CONT'D)
          Promise me that if something
          bad happens, you won't run
          away again.

Linda throws away the broken plate, then kisses
her father.

                    LINDA (CONT'D)
          You promise...?

Billy kisses Linda. He whispers something to
her. Linda smiles and exits the back door.

CUT TO:

INT. KITCHEN - DAY - MINUTES LATER

In the center of the table is the pie plate, the half of the pie remaining just starting to pulsate. Next to the pie plate is a...

DESSERT PLATE WITH A SINGLE SLICE OF PIE...

This piece is also pulsating. Then it stops as...

A FORK -

enters frame, and cuts out a large, dripping bite of crust and filling.

CAMERA follows fork and pie as it rises slowly to...

BILLY'S FACE -

He slowly opens his mouth, but he does not look down.

With the fork so close to his mouth, that the crust crumbs spill onto his lips...

Billy hesitates.

                              FADE TO BLACK